TAINTED BLOOD

Arnaldur In...   f

newspaper, he began writing novels. He won the
Nordic Crime Novel Award for *Tainted Blood*
(originally published in the UK under the title *Jar
City*) and, in the following year, for its sequel,
Silence of the Grave. *Tainted Blood* is his first novel
to be translated into English.

ALSO BY ARNALDUR INDRIÐASON

Silence of the Grave

ARNALDUR INDRIÐASON

Tainted Blood

TRANSLATED FROM THE ICELANDIC BY
Bernard Scudder

VINTAGE BOOKS
London

Published by Vintage 2006

2 4 6 8 10 9 7 5 3 1

Copyright © Arnaldur Indriðason 2000, 2004
English translation copyright © Bernard Scudder 2004

First published in Great Britain in 2004 with the title *Jar City* by
The Harvill Press
Random House, 20 Vauxhall Bridge Road,
London SW1V 2SA

First published with the title *Mýrin* by Edda Publishing, Reykjavík, 2000
www.edda.is

www.randomhouse.co.uk/vintage

Addresses for companies within The Random House Group Limited
can be found at:
www.randomhouse.co.uk/offices.htm

The Random House Group Limited Reg. No. 954009

A CIP catalogue record for this book
is available from the British Library

ISBN 9780099513124

The Random House Group Limited makes every effort to ensure that
the papers used in its books are made from trees that have been legally
sourced from well-managed and credibly certified forests. Our paper
procurement policy can be found at: www.randomhouse.co.uk/paper.htm

Printed and bound in Great Britain by
Cox & Wyman Ltd, Reading, Berkshire

It's all one great big bloody mire
– INSPECTOR ERLENDUR SVEINSSON

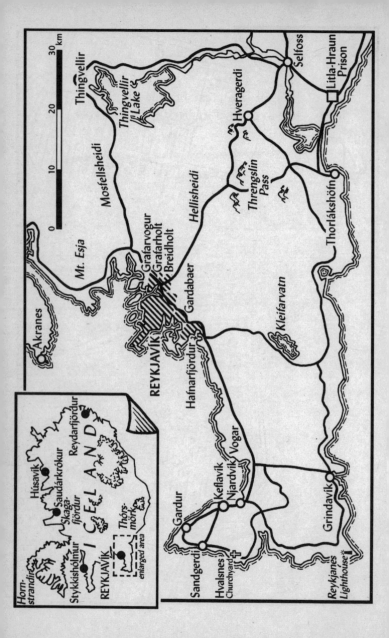

A NOTE ON ICELANDIC NAMES

Icelanders always address each other using first names, since most people have a patronymic rather than a "proper surname", ending in *-son* for a son and *-dóttir* for a daughter. People are listed by first names even in the telephone directory. Strange as it may sound to the English ear, first names are therefore used throughout the police hierarchy and when police and criminals address one another. Erlendur's full name is *Erlendur Sveinsson*, and his daughter is *Eva Lind Erlendsdóttir*. Matronymics are rare, although Audur is specifically said to be *Kolbrúnardóttir*, "Kolbrún's daughter". Some families do have traditional surnames, however, either derived directly from or else modelled on Danish, as a result of the colonial rule which lasted until early in the twentieth century. *Briem* is one of these traditional surnames, and as such it does not reveal the gender of the bearer – in the case of *Marion Briem* the ambiguous first name compounds this secondary mystery.

REYKJAVÍK

2001

I

The words were written in pencil on a piece of paper placed on top of the body. Three words, incomprehensible to Erlendur.

It was the body of a man of about 70. He was lying on the floor on his right side, against the sofa in a small sitting room, wearing a blue shirt and fawn corduroy trousers. He wore slippers on his feet. His hair was starting to thin, almost completely grey. It was stained with blood from a large wound on his head. On the floor not far from the body was a big glass ashtray with sharp corners. It too was covered in blood. The coffee table had been overturned.

This was a basement flat in a two-storey house in Nordurmýri. It stood in a small garden enclosed on three sides by a stone wall. The trees had shed their leaves, which carpeted the garden and covered the ground, and the knotty branches stretched up towards the darkness of the sky. Along a gravel drive which led to the garage, Reykjavík CID were arriving at the scene. The District Medical Officer was expected, he would sign the death certificate. The body had been reported found about 15 minutes earlier. Erlendur, Detective Inspector with the Reykjavík police, was one of the first on the scene. He expected his colleague Sigurdur Óli any minute.

The October dusk spread over the city and the rain slapped around in the autumn wind. Someone had switched on a lamp which stood on a table in the sitting room and cast a gloomy light on the surroundings. In other respects nothing at the scene had been touched. The forensics team were setting up powerful fluorescent lights on a tripod to illuminate the flat. Erlendur noticed a bookcase and a worn suite of furniture, the overturned coffee table, an old desk in one corner, a carpet on the floor, blood on the carpet. The sitting room opened into the kitchen and another door led from it to the den and on to a small corridor where there were two rooms and a toilet.

The police had been notified by the upstairs neighbour. He had come home that afternoon after collecting his two boys from school and it struck him as strange to see the basement door wide open. He could see inside his neighbour's flat and called out to discover whether he was in. There was no answer. He peered inside the flat and called his name again, but there was no response. They'd been living on the upper floor for several years but did not know the old man in the basement well. The elder son, 9 years old, was not as cautious as his father and quick as a flash he was in the neighbour's sitting room. A moment later the child came back and said there was a dead man in the flat, and he really didn't seem too perturbed by it.

"You watch too many movies," the boy's father said and cautiously made his way into the flat where he saw his neighbour lying dead on the sitting-room floor.

Erlendur knew the dead man's name. It was on the doorbell. But to avoid the risk of making an idiot of himself he put on some thin rubber gloves and fished the man's wallet out of a jacket hanging on a peg by the front doorway and found a payment card with a photograph on it. The man's name was Holberg, 69 years old. Dead in his home. Presumed murdered.

Erlendur walked around the flat and pondered the simplest questions. That was his job: investigating the obvious. Forensics handled the mysterious. He could see no signs of a break-in, neither on the windows nor the doors. On first impression the man seemed to have let his assailant into the flat himself. The upstairs neighbours had left footprints all over the front hallway and sitting-room carpet when they came in out of the rain and the attacker must have done the same. Unless he took off his shoes by the front door. It looked to Erlendur as if he had been in too much of a rush to have had the chance to take off his shoes.

The forensic team had brought along a vacuum cleaner to collect the tiniest particles and granules from which to produce clues. They searched for fingerprints and mud that did not belong in the house. They looked for something extraneous. Something that had left destruction in its wake.

For all Erlendur could see, the man had shown his visitor no particular hospitality. He hadn't made coffee. The percolator in the kitchen had apparently not been used in the past few hours. There were no signs of tea having been drunk, no cups taken out of the cupboards. Glasses stood untouched where they belonged. The murdered man had been the orderly type. Everything neat and tidy. Perhaps he did not know his assailant well. Perhaps the visitor had attacked him without any preamble, the moment the door opened. Without taking off his shoes.

Can you murder someone in your socks?

Erlendur looked all around and told himself that he really must organise his thoughts better.

In any case, the visitor had been in a hurry. He hadn't bothered to close the door behind him. The attack itself showed signs of haste, as if it had come out of the blue and without warning. There were no signs of a scuffle in the flat. The man had apparently fallen straight to the floor, struck the coffee table and overturned it. On first impression everything else seemed untouched. Erlendur could see no sign that the flat had been robbed. All the cupboards were firmly closed, the drawers too, a fairly new computer and an old stereo where they belonged, the man's jacket on a peg by the front doorway still contained his wallet, in it one 2,000-crown note and two payment cards, one debit and the other credit.

It was as if the attacker had grabbed the first thing

at hand and hit the man on the head. The ashtray was made of thick, green glass and weighed at least a kilo and a half, Erlendur thought. A murder weapon there for the taking. The assailant would hardly have brought it with him and left it behind on the sitting-room floor, covered in blood.

These were the obvious clues: The man had opened the door and invited his visitor in or at least walked with him into the sitting room. Probably he knew his visitor, but not necessarily. He was attacked with an ashtray, one hard blow and the assailant quickly made his getaway, leaving the front door open. As simple as that.

Apart from the message.

It was written on a sheet of ruled A4 paper that looked as if it had been torn from a spiral-bound exercise book and was the only clue that a premeditated murder had been committed here; it suggested that the visitor had entered the house with the express purpose of killing. The visitor hadn't been seized suddenly by a mad urge to murder as he stood there on the sitting-room floor. He had entered the flat with the intention of committing a murder. He had written a message. Three words Erlendur could make neither head nor tail of. Had he written the message before going to the house? Another obvious question that needed answering. Erlendur went over to the desk in the corner of the sitting room. It was a sprawl of documents, bills, envelopes and papers. On top of them all lay a spiral-bound exercise book, the corner ripped from one page. He looked for a pencil that could have been used to write the message but couldn't see one. Looking around the desk, he found one underneath. He did not touch anything. Looked and thought.

"Isn't this your typical Icelandic murder?" asked Detective Sigurdur Óli who had entered the basement without Erlendur noticing him and was now standing beside the body.

"What?" said Erlendur, engrossed in his thoughts.

"Squalid, pointless and committed without any attempt to hide it, change the clues or conceal the evidence."

"Yes," said Erlendur. "A pathetic Icelandic murder."

"Unless he fell onto the table and hit his head on the ashtray," Sigurdur Óli said. Their colleague Elínborg was with him. Erlendur had tried to limit the movements of the police, forensics team and paramedics while he strode around the house, his head bowed beneath his hat.

"And wrote an incomprehensible message as he fell?" Erlendur said.

"He could have been holding it in his hands."

"Can you make anything of the message?"

"Maybe it's God," Sigurdur Óli said. "Maybe the murderer, I don't know. The emphasis on the last word is intriguing. Capital letters for HIM."

"It doesn't look hurriedly written to me. The last word's in block capitals but the first two are cursive. The visitor wasn't hurried when he was writing this. But he didn't close the door behind him. What does that mean? Attacks the man and runs out, but writes a cryptic note on a piece of paper and takes pains to emphasise the final word."

"It must refer to him," Sigurdur Óli said. "The body, I mean. It can't refer to anyone else."

"I don't know," Erlendur said. "What's the point in leaving that sort of message behind and putting it on top of the body? What's he trying to say by doing that? Is he telling us something? Is the murderer talking to himself? Is he talking to the victim?"

"A bloody nutter," Elínborg said, reaching down to pick up the message. Erlendur stopped her.

"There may have been more than one of them," Sigurdur Óli said. "Attackers, I mean."

"Remember your gloves, Elínborg," Erlendur said, as if talking to a child. "Don't ruin the evidence."

"The message was written out on the desk over there," he added, pointing at the corner. "The paper was torn out of an exercise book owned by the victim."

"There may have been more than one of them," Sigurdur Óli repeated. He thought he had hit on an interesting point.

"Yes, yes," Erlendur said. "Maybe."

"A bit cold-hearted," Sigurdur Óli said. "First you kill an old man and then you sit down to write a note. Doesn't that take nerves of steel? Isn't it a total bastard who does that sort of thing?"

"Or a fearless one," Elínborg said.

"Or one with a Messiah complex," Erlendur said.

He stooped to pick up the message and studied it in silence.

One huge Messiah complex, he thought to himself.

2

Erlendur got back to the block of flats where he lived at around 10 p.m. and put a ready meal in the microwave to heat through. He stood and watched the meal revolving behind the glass. Better than television, he thought. Outside, the autumn winds howled, nothing but rain and darkness.

He thought about people who left messages and vanished. In such a situation, what would he possibly write? Who would he leave a message for? His daughter, Eva Lind, entered his mind. She had a drug addiction and would probably want to know if he had any money. She had become increasingly pushy in that respect. His son, Sindri Snaer, had recently completed a third period in rehab. The message to him would be simple: No more Hiroshima.

Erlendur smiled to himself as the microwave made three beeps. Not that he had ever thought of vanishing at all.

Erlendur and Sigurdur Óli had talked to the neighbour who found the body. His wife was home by then and talked about taking the boys away from the house and to her mother's. The neighbour, whose name was Ólafur, had said that he and all his family, his wife and two sons, went to school and work every day at 8 a.m. and no-one came home until, at the earliest, 4 p.m. It was his job to fetch the boys from school. They hadn't noticed anything unusual when they had left home that morning. The door to the man's flat had been closed. They'd slept soundly the previous night. Heard nothing. They didn't have much to do with their neighbour. To all intents and purposes he was a stranger, even though they had lived on the floor above him for several years.

The pathologist had yet to ascertain a precise time of death, but Erlendur imagined the murder had been committed around noon. In the busiest time of day as it was called. How could anyone even have the time for that these days? he thought to himself. A statement had been issued to the media that a man named Holberg aged about 70 had been found dead in his flat in Nordurmýri, probably murdered. Anyone who had noticed suspicious movements over the previous 24 hours in the area where Holberg lived was requested to contact the Reykjavík police.

Erlendur was roughly 50, divorced many years earlier, a father of two. He never let anyone sense that he couldn't stand his children's names. His ex-wife, with whom he had hardly spoken for more than two decades, thought they sounded sweet at the time. The divorce was a messy one and Erlendur had more or less lost touch with his children when they were young. They sought him out when they were older and he welcomed them, but regretted how they had turned out. He was particularly grieved by Eva Lind's fate. Sindri Snaer had fared better. But only just.

He took his meal out of the microwave and sat at the kitchen table. It was a one-bedroom flat filled with books wherever there was any room to arrange them. Old family photographs hung on the walls showing his relatives in the East Fjords, where he was born. He had no photographs of himself or of his children. A battered old Nordmende television stood against one wall with an even more battered armchair in front of it. Erlendur kept the flat reasonably tidy with a minimum of cleaning.

He didn't know exactly what it was that he ate. The ornate packaging promised something about oriental delights but the meal itself, concealed within some kind of pastry roll, tasted like hair oil. Erlendur pushed it away. He wondered whether he still had the rye bread he'd bought several days before. And the lamb pâté. Then the doorbell rang. Eva Lind had decided to drop in.

"How's it hanging?" she asked as she darted in through the door and flopped onto the sofa in the sitting room. The way she talked irritated him.

"Aiyee," Erlendur said, and closed the door. "Don't talk that nonsense to me."

"I thought you wanted me to choose my words carefully," said Eva Lind, who had repeatedly been lectured about language by her father.

"Say something sensible then."

It was difficult to tell which personality she was sporting this evening. Eva Lind was the best actress he'd ever known, although this didn't say much as he never went to the theatre or cinema and mostly watched educational programmes on television. Eva Lind's play was generally a family drama in one to three acts and dealt with the best way to get money out of her father. This didn't happen very often because Eva Lind had her own ways of getting hold of money, which Erlendur preferred to know as little about as possible. But occasionally, when she didn't have "a goddamn cent", as she put it, she would turn to him.

Sometimes she was his little girl, snuggling up to him and purring like a cat. Sometimes she was on the brink of despair, stomping around the flat completely out of her mind, laying into him with accusations that he was a bad father for leaving her and Sindri Snaer when they were so young. She could also be coarse, and malicious and evil. But sometimes he thought she was her true self, almost normal, if indeed there is such a thing, and Erlendur felt he could talk to her like a human being.

She wore tattered jeans and a black leather bomber jacket. Her hair was short and jet black, she had two silver rings in her right eyebrow and a silver cross hanging from one ear. She'd had beautiful white teeth once but they were starting to show the signs: when she gave a wide smile it transpired that two upper ones were missing. She was very thin, and her face was drawn, with dark rings under the eyes. Erlendur sometimes felt he could see his own mother's likeness in her. He cursed Eva Lind's fate and blamed his own neglect for the way she had turned out.

"I talked to Mum today. Or rather, she talked to me and asked if I would talk to you. Great having divorced parents."

"Does your mother want something from me?" Erlendur asked in surprise. After 20 years she still hated him. He'd caught just one glimpse of her in all that time and there had been no mistaking the loathing on her face. She'd spoken to him once about Sindri Snaer, but that was a conversation he preferred to forget.

"She's such a snobby bitch."

"Don't talk about your mother like that."

"It's about some filthy rich friends of hers from Gardabaer. Married their daughter off at the weekend and she just did a runner from the wedding. Really embarrassing. That was on Saturday and she hasn't been in touch since. Mum was at the wedding and she's knocked out by the scandal of it. I'm supposed to ask if you'll talk to the parents. They don't want to put an announcement in the papers, bloody snobs, but they know you're in the CID and reckon they can do it all really hush-hush. I'm the one who's supposed to ask you to talk to that crowd. Not Mum. You get it? Never!"

"Do you know these people?"

"Well, I wasn't invited to the wedding party the little bimbo fucked up."

"Did you know the girl then?"

"Hardly."

"And where could she have run off to?"

"How should I know?"

Erlendur shrugged.

"I was thinking about you just a minute ago," he said.

"Nice," Eva Lind said. "I just happened to be wondering if . . ."

"I haven't got any money," Erlendur said, sitting down in his armchair to face her. "Are you hungry?"

Eva Lind arched her back.

"Why can't I ever talk to you without you going on about money?" she said and Erlendur felt as though she'd stolen his line.

"And why can't I ever talk to you, period?"

"Oh, fuck you."

"What are you speaking like that for? What's wrong? 'Fuck you!' 'How's it hanging?' What kind of language is that?"

"Jesus," Eva Lind groaned.

"Who are you this time? Which one am I talking to now? Where's the real you in all this pile of dope?"

"Don't start that crap again. 'Who are you?' " she mimicked him. "Where's the real you? I'm here. I'm sitting in front of you. I'm me!"

"Eva."

"Ten thousand crowns!" she said. "What's that to you? Can't you come up with ten thousand? You're rolling in cash."

Erlendur looked at his daughter. There was something about her that he'd noticed the moment she'd arrived. She was short of breath, there were beads of sweat on her forehead and she constantly wriggled in her seat. As if she were ill.

"Are you ill?" he asked.

"I'm fine. I just need a bit of money. Please, don't be difficult."

"Are you ill?"

"Please."

Erlendur went on looking at his daughter.

"Are you trying to quit?" he said.

"Please, ten thousand. That's nothing. Nothing for you. I'll never come back and ask you for money again."

"Yes, quite. How long is it since you ..." Erlendur hesitated, unsure how to phrase it, "... used that stuff?"

"Doesn't matter. I've given up. Given up giving up giving up giving up giving up giving up giving up!" Eva Lind was on her feet. "Let me have ten thousand. Please. Five. Let me have five thousand. Haven't you got that in your pocket? Five! That's peanuts."

"Why are you trying to stop now?"

Eva Lind looked at her father. "No stupid questions. I'm not giving up. Giving up what? What should I give up? You give up talking such crap!"

"What's going on? What are you so worked up about? Are you ill?"

"Yeah, I'm sick as a pig. Can you lend me ten thousand? It's a loan, I'll pay you back, eh? Avaricious bastard."

"Avaricious is a good word. Are you ill, Eva?"

"What do you keep asking that for?" she said and grew still more agitated.

"Are you running a temperature?"

"Let me have the money. Two thousand! That's nothing! You don't understand. Stupid old git!"

Erlendur was now on his feet too and she went up to him as if she was going to attack.

He couldn't fathom this sudden aggressiveness. He looked her up and down.

"What are you looking at?" she shouted in his face. "Fancy a bit? Eh? Does dirty old Daddy fancy a bit?"

Erlendur slapped her face, but not very hard.

"Did you enjoy that?" she said.

He slapped her again, harder this time.

"Getting a hard-on?" she said, and Erlendur leapt back from her. She'd never talked to him like this. In an instant she'd become a monster. He'd never seen her in this mood before. He felt helpless towards her and his anger gradually gave way to pity.

"Why are you trying to give up now?" he repeated.

"I'm not trying to give up now!" she shouted. "What's wrong with you? Can't you understand what I'm saying? Who's talking about giving up?"

"What's wrong, Eva?"

"You stop that 'what's wrong, Eva'! Can't you let me have five thousand? Can you answer me?" She appeared to be calming down. Maybe she realised she'd gone too far, she couldn't talk to her father that way.

"Why now?" Erlendur asked.

"Will you let me have ten thousand if I tell you?"

"What's happened?"

"Five thousand."

Erlendur stared at his daughter.

"Are you pregnant?" he asked.

Eva Lind looked at her father with a submissive smile.

"Bingo," she said.

"But how?" Erlendur groaned.

"What do you mean, how? Do you want me to go into details?"

"None of that clever talk. You use protection, surely? Condoms? The pill?"

"I don't know what happened. It just happened."

"And you want to give up dope?"

"Not any more. I can't. Now I've told you everything. Everything! You owe me ten thousand."

"To get your baby stoned."

"It's not a baby, you jerk. It's not anything. It's a grain of sand. I can't give up right away. I'll give up tomorrow. I promise. Just not now. Two thousand. What's that to you?"

Erlendur walked back to her. "But you tried. You want to give up. I'll help you."

"I can't!" Eva Lind shouted. The sweat poured from her face and she tried to conceal the trembling that ran through her whole body.

"That's why you came to see me," Erlendur said. "You could have gone somewhere else to get money. You've done that until now. But you came to me because you want . . ."

"Cut that bullshit. I came because Mum asked me to and because you've got money, no other reason. If you don't let me have it I'll get it anyway. That's no problem. There are plenty of old guys like you who are prepared to pay me."

Erlendur refused to let her throw him off balance.

"Have you been pregnant before?"

"No," answered Eva Lind, looking the other way.

"Who's the father?"

Eva Lind was dumbstruck and looked up at her father with wide eyes.

"HELLO!" she shouted. "Do I look as if I've just come from the bridal suite at Hotel fucking Saga?"

And before Erlendur had the chance to do anything she'd pushed him away and run out of the flat, down the stairs and into the street where she vanished into the cold autumn rain.

He closed the door slowly behind her, wondering whether he'd used the right approach. It was as if they could never talk to each other without arguing and shouting, and he was tired of that.

With no appetite for his food any more, he sat back down in his armchair, staring pensively into space and worrying about what Eva Lind might resort to. Eventually he picked up the book he was reading, which lay open on a table beside the chair. It was from one of his favourite series, describing ordeals and fatalities in the wilderness.

He continued reading where he'd left off in the story called "Lives Lost on Mosfellsheidi" and he was soon in a relentless blizzard that froze young men to death.

3

The rain poured down on Erlendur and Sigurdur Óli as they hurried out of their car, ran up the steps to the apartment block on Stigahlíd and rang the bell. They had contemplated waiting until the shower ended, but Erlendur got bored and leapt out of the car. Not wanting to be left behind, Sigurdur Óli followed. They were drenched in an instant. Rain dripped off Sigurdur Óli's hair and down his back and he glared at Erlendur while they waited for the door to open.

At a meeting that morning the policemen who were engaged on the investigation had considered the possibilities. One theory was that Holberg's murder was completely without motive and the attacker had been prowling around the quarter for some time, possibly even for days: a burglar looking for somewhere to break in. He had knocked on Holberg's door to find out if anyone was at home, then panicked when the owner answered it. The message he had left behind was merely intended to lead the police astray. It had no other immediately obvious meaning.

On the same day that Holberg was murdered, the

residents of a block of flats on Stigahlíd had reported that two elderly women, twin sisters, had been attacked by a young man in a green army jacket. Someone had let him in the front entrance and he had knocked on the door to their flat. When they answered he burst in, slammed the door behind him and demanded money. When they refused he punched one of them in the face with his bare fist and pushed the other to the floor, kicking her before he finally fled.

A voice answered the intercom and Sigurdur Óli said his name. The door buzzed and they went inside. The stairway was badly lit and smelled unhygienic. When they reached the upper floor one of the women was standing in the doorway waiting for them.

"Have you caught him?" she asked.

"Unfortunately not," Sigurdur Óli said, shaking his head, "but we'd like to talk to you about . . ."

"Have they caught him?" said a voice inside the flat and an exact replica of the first woman appeared before them in the doorway. They were aged about 70 and both wore black skirts and red sweaters. They were of stout build with grey, bouffant hair atop round faces with an obvious look of expectation.

"Not yet," Erlendur said.

"He was a poor wretch," said woman number one, whose name was Fjóla. She invited them in.

"Don't you go taking pity on him," said woman number two, whose name was Birna, and she closed the door behind them. "He was an ugly brute who hit you over the head. That's some wretch for you, eh."

The detectives sat down in the sitting room, looking first at the women in turn and then at each other. It was a small flat. Sigurdur Óli noticed two adjoining bedrooms. From the sitting room he could see into the small kitchen.

"We read your statement," said Sigurdur Óli, who had flicked through it in the car on the way to the sisters. "Can you give us any more details about the man who attacked you?"

"Man?" Fjóla said. "He was more like a boy."

"Old enough to attack us though," Birna said. "He was old enough for that. Pushed me to the floor and kicked me."

"We haven't got any money," Fjóla said.

"We don't keep money here," Birna said. "And we told him so."

"But he didn't believe us."

"And he attacked us."

"He was wild."

"And swore. The things he called us."

"In that horrible green jacket. Like a soldier."

"And wearing these sort of boots, heavy, black ones laced up his legs."

"But he didn't break anything."

"No, just ran away."

"Did he take anything?" Erlendur said.

"It was like he wasn't in his right mind," said Fjóla, who was trying as hard as she could to find

24

some saving grace for her attacker. "He didn't break anything and he didn't take anything. Just attacked us when he realised he wouldn't get any money from us. Poor wretch."

"Stoned out of his mind more like," Birna spat out. "Poor wretch?" She turned to her sister. "Sometimes you can be a real dimwit. He was stoned out of his mind. You could tell from his eyes. Harsh, glazed eyes. And he was sweating."

"Sweating?" Erlendur said.

"It was running down his face. The sweat."

"That was the rain," Fjóla said.

"No. And he was shaking all over."

"The rain," Fjóla repeated and Birna gave her the evil eye.

"He hit you over the head, Fjóla. That's the last thing you needed."

"Does it still hurt where he kicked you?" Fjóla asked, and she looked at Erlendur. He could have sworn her eyes were dancing with glee.

It was still early morning when Erlendur and Sigurdur Óli arrived in Nordurmýri. Holberg's neighbours on the ground and first floor were waiting for them. The police had already taken a statement from the family who had found Holberg but Erlendur wanted to talk to them further. A pilot lived on the top floor. He'd arrived home from Boston at midday on the day Holberg was murdered, gone to bed in the afternoon and not stirred until the police knocked on his door.

They started with the pilot, who answered the door unshaven and wearing a vest and shorts. He was in his thirties, he lived alone and his flat was like a rubbish heap; clothes strewn everywhere, two suitcases open on a newish leather sofa, plastic bags from the duty-free shop on the floor, wine bottles on the tables and open beer cans wherever there was space for them. He looked at the two of them then walked back inside the flat without saying a word and slumped into a chair. They stood in front of him. Couldn't find anywhere to sit. Erlendur looked around the room and thought to himself that he wouldn't even board a flight simulator with this man.

For some reason the pilot started talking about the divorce he was going through and wondered whether it could become a police matter. The bitch had started playing around. He was away, flying. Came home from Oslo one day to find his wife with his old school-friend. Godawful, he added, and they didn't know which he found more godawful, his wife being unfaithful to him or his having to stay in Oslo.

"Concerning the murder that was committed in the basement flat," Erlendur said, interrupting the pilot's slurred monologue.

"Have you ever been to Oslo?" the pilot asked.

"No," Erlendur said. "We're not going to talk about Oslo."

The pilot looked first at Erlendur and then at Sigurdur Óli, and finally he seemed to cotton on.

"I didn't know the man at all," he said. "I bought this flat four months ago, as far as I understand it had been empty for a long while before that. Met him a few times, just outside. He seemed all right."

"All right?" Erlendur said.

"Okay to talk to, I mean."

"What did you talk about?"

"Flying. Mostly. He was interested in flying."

"What do you mean, interested in flying?"

"The aircraft," the pilot said, opening a can of beer that he fished from one of the plastic bags. "The cities," he said, and gulped down some beer. "The hostesses," he said and belched. "He asked a lot about the hostesses. You know."

"No," Erlendur said.

"You know. On the stopovers. Abroad."

"Yes."

"What happened, were they hot. Stuff like that. He'd heard things get pretty wild ... on international flights."

"When was the last time you saw him?" Sigurdur Óli asked.

The pilot thought. He couldn't remember.

"It was a few days ago," he said eventually.

"Did you notice whether anyone had visited him recently?" Erlendur asked.

"No, I'm not home much."

"Did you notice any people snooping around in the neighbourhood, acting suspiciously, or just loitering around the houses?"

"No."

"Anyone wearing a green army jacket?"

"No."

"A young man wearing army boots?"

"No. Was it him? Do you know who did it?"

"No," Erlendur said, and knocked over a half-full can of beer as he turned to leave the flat.

The woman had decided to take her children to her mother's for a few days and was ready to leave. She didn't want the children to be in the house after what had happened. Her husband nodded. It was the best thing for them. The parents were visibly shocked. They'd bought the flat four years before and liked living in Nordurmýri. A good place to live. For people with children too. The boys were standing by their mother's side.

"It was terrible finding him like that," the husband said, in a voice like a whisper. He looked at the boys. "We told them he was asleep," he added. "But . . ."

"We know he was dead," the elder boy said.

"Murdered," the younger one said.

The couple gave embarrassed smiles.

"They're taking it well," the mother said and stroked the elder boy on the cheek.

"I didn't dislike Holberg," the husband said. "We sometimes talked together outside. He'd lived in the house for a long time, we talked about the garden and maintenance, that sort of thing. As you do with your neighbours."

"But it wasn't close," the mother said. "Our

contact with him, I mean. I think that's as it should be. I don't think it should be too close. Privacy, you know."

They hadn't noticed any unusual people in the vicinity of the house and hadn't seen anyone in a green army jacket roaming the neighbourhood. The wife was impatient to take the boys away.

"Did Holberg have many visitors?" Sigurdur Óli asked.

"I never noticed any," the wife said.

"He gave the impression of being lonely," her husband said.

"His flat stank," the elder son said.

"Stank," his brother chorused.

"There's rising damp in the basement," the husband said apologetically.

"Spreads up here sometimes," the wife said. "The damp."

"We talked to him about it."

"He was going to look into it."

"That was two years ago."

4

The couple from Gardabaer looked at Erlendur with anguish in their eyes. Their little daughter had gone missing. They hadn't heard from her for three days. Not since the wedding she'd run out from. Their little girl. Erlendur was imagining a child with curly golden locks until he was told she was a 23-year-old psychology student at the University of Iceland.

"The wedding?" Erlendur said, looking around the spacious lounge; it was like a whole storey of the block of flats where he lived.

"Her own wedding!" the father said as if he still couldn't understand it. "The girl ran away from her own wedding!"

The mother put a crumpled handkerchief to her nose.

It was midday. Due to road works on the way from Reykjavík it had taken Erlendur half an hour to reach Gardabaer and he found the large detached house only after a considerable search. It was almost invisible from the street, enclosed by a large garden with all kinds of trees growing in it, up to six metres high. The couple met him in a clear state of shock.

Erlendur thought this was a waste of time. Other

more important matters were waiting for him, but even though he'd hardly spoken to his ex-wife for two decades he still felt inclined to do her a favour.

The mother wore a smart, pale green dress suit, the father a black suit. He said he was growing increasingly worried about his daughter. He knew she would come home eventually and that she was safe and sound – he refused to believe otherwise – but he wanted to consult the police, although he didn't see any reason to call out the search parties and rescue teams immediately or to send announcements to the radio, newspapers and television.

"She just disappeared," the mother said. The couple looked a little older than Erlendur, probably about 60. They ran a business importing children's wear and that provided for them amply to enjoy a prosperous lifestyle. The nouveaux riches. Age had treated them kindly. Erlendur noticed two new cars in front of their double garage, polished to a shine.

She braced herself and started to tell Erlendur the story. "It happened on Saturday – three days ago, my God how time flies – and it was such a wonderful day. They had just been married by that vicar who's so popular."

"Hopeless," her husband said. "Came rushing in, delivered a few clichés and then he was off again with his briefcase. I can't understand why he's so popular."

His wife wouldn't let anything mar the beauty of the wedding.

"A marvellous day! Sunshine and lovely autumn

weather. Definitely a hundred people at the church alone. She has so many friends. Such a popular girl. We held the reception at a hall here in Gardabaer. What's that place called? I always forget."

"Gardaholt," the father said.

"Such a wonderful cosy place," she went on. "We filled it. The hall, I mean. So many presents. And then when . . . then when . . ."

"They were supposed to dance the first dance," the father continued when his wife burst into tears, "and that idiot of a boy was standing on the dance floor. We called out to Dísa Rós, but she didn't show up. We started looking for her, but it was as if the ground had opened up and swallowed her."

"Dísa Rós?" Erlendur said.

"It turned out that she'd taken the wedding car."

"The wedding car?"

"The limousine. With the flowers and ribbons, that brought them from the church. She just ran away from the wedding. No warning! No explanation!"

"From her own wedding!" the mother shouted.

"And you don't know what made her do that?"

"She obviously changed her mind," the mother said. "Must have regretted the whole thing."

"But why?" Erlendur said.

"Please, can you find her for us?" the father asked. "She hasn't been in touch and you can see how terribly worried we are. The party was a total flop. The wedding was ruined. We're completely stumped. And our little girl is missing."

"The wedding car. Was it found?"

"Yes. In Gardastraeti."

"Why there?"

"I don't know. She doesn't know anyone there. Her clothes were in the car. Her proper clothes."

Erlendur hesitated.

"Her proper clothes were in the wedding car?" he said eventually, briefly pondering the plane this conversation had dropped to and whether he was in some way responsible.

"She took off her wedding gown and put on the clothes she'd apparently kept in the car," the wife said.

"Do you think you can find her?" the father asked. "We've contacted everyone she knows and no-one knows a thing. We just don't know where to turn. I have a photo of her here."

He handed Erlendur a school photograph of the young, beautiful blonde who was now in hiding. She smiled at him from the photograph.

"You have no idea what happened?"

"Not a clue," the girl's mother replied.

"None," the father said.

"And these are the presents?" Erlendur looked at the gigantic dining table, piled high with colourful parcels, pretty bows, cellophane and flowers. He walked towards it as the couple watched. He'd never seen so many presents in his life and he wondered what was inside the parcels. Crockery and more crockery, he imagined.

What a life.

"And what's this here?" he said, pointing to some offcuts from a tree that stood in a large vase at one end of the table. Heart-shaped red cards hung from the branches by ribbons.

"It's a message tree."

"A what?" Erlendur said. He'd only been to one wedding in his life and that was a long time ago. No message trees there.

"The guests write greetings to the bride and groom on cards and then hang them on the tree. A lot of cards had been hung up before Dísa Rós went missing," the mother said, still holding her handkerchief to her nose.

Erlendur's mobile phone rang in his overcoat pocket. As he fumbled to get it, the phone got stuck in the opening and, instead of patiently working it loose, which would have been so easy, Erlendur tugged at it vigorously until the pocket gave way. The hand holding the phone flew back and sent the message tree flying to the floor. Erlendur looked at the couple apologetically and answered his phone.

"Are you coming with us to Nordurmýri?" Sigurdur Óli said without any preamble. "To take a better look at the flat."

"Are you down there already?" Erlendur asked. He had withdrawn to one side.

"No. I'll wait for you," Sigurdur Óli said. "Where the hell are you?"

Erlendur hung up.

"I'll see what I can do," he said to the couple. "I don't think there's any danger involved. Your daughter probably just lost her nerve and she's staying with some friends. You shouldn't worry too much. I'm sure she'll ring before long."

The couple bent down over the little cards that had fallen to the floor. He noticed that they had overlooked several cards that had slid under a chair and he bent down to pick them up. Erlendur read the greetings and looked at the couple.

"Had you seen this?" he asked and handed them the card.

The father read the message and a look of astonishment crossed his face. He handed the card to his wife. She read it over and again but didn't seem to understand. Erlendur held out his hand for the card and read it again. The message was unsigned.

"Is this your daughter's handwriting?" he asked.

"I think so," the mother replied.

Erlendur turned the card over in his hands and reread the message:

HE'S A MONSTER WHAT HAVE I DONE?

5

"Where have you been?" Sigurdur Óli asked Erlendur when he came back to work, but he received no answer.

"Has Eva Lind tried to contact me?" he asked.

Sigurdur Óli said he didn't think so. He knew about Erlendur's daughter and her problems, but neither of them ever mentioned it. Personal matters seldom entered into their conversations.

"Anything new on Holberg?" Erlendur asked and walked straight into his office. Sigurdur Óli followed him and closed the door. Murders were rare in Reykjavík and generated enormous publicity on the few occasions they were committed. The CID made it a rule not to inform the media of details of their investigations unless absolutely necessary. That did not apply in this case.

"We know a little more about him," Sigurdur Óli said, opening a file he was holding. "He was born in Saudárkrókur, 69 years old. Spent his last years working as a lorry driver for Iceland Transport. Still worked there on and off."

Sigurdur Óli paused.

"Shouldn't we talk to his workmates?" he said,

straightening his tie. Sigurdur Óli was wearing a new suit, tall and handsome, a graduate in criminology from an American university. He was everything that Erlendur was not: modern and organised.

"What do people in the office think?" Erlendur asked, twiddling with a loose button on his cardigan which eventually dropped into his palm. He was stout and well-built with bushy ginger hair, one of the most experienced detectives on the team. He generally got his way. His superiors and colleagues had long since given up doing battle with him. Things had turned out that way over the years. Erlendur didn't dislike it.

"Probably some nutcase," Sigurdur Óli said. "At the minute we're looking for that green army jacket. Some kid who wanted money but panicked when Holberg refused."

"What about Holberg's family? Did he have any?"

"No family, but we haven't got all the information yet. We're still gathering it together; family, friends, workmates."

"From the look of his flat I'd say he was single and had been for a long time."

"You would know, of course," Sigurdur Óli blurted out, but Erlendur pretended not to hear.

"Anything from the pathologist? Forensics?"

"The provisional report's in. Nothing in it we didn't know. Holberg died from a blow to the head. It was a heavy blow, but basically it was the shape of the ashtray, the sharp edges, that were decisive.

His skull caved in and he died instantly ... or almost. He seems to have struck the corner of the coffee table as he fell. He had a nasty wound on his forehead that fitted the corner of the table. The fingerprints on the ashtray were Holberg's but then there are at least two other sets, one of which is also on the pencil."

"Are they the murderer's then?"

"There's every probability that they are the murderer's, yes."

"Right, a typical clumsy Icelandic murder."

"Typical. And that's the assumption we're working on."

It was still raining. The low-pressure fronts that moved in from deep in the Atlantic at that time of year headed east across Iceland in succession, bringing wind, wet and dark winter gloom. The CID was still at work in the building in Nordurmýri. The yellow police tape that had been set up around the building reminded Erlendur of the electricity board; a hole in the road, a filthy tent over it, a flicker of light inside the tent, all neatly gift-wrapped with yellow tape. In the same way, the police had wrapped the murder scene up with neat yellow plastic tape with the name of the authority printed on it. Erlendur and Sigurdur Óli met Elínborg and the other detectives who had been combing the building through the autumn night and into the morning and were just finishing their job.

People from neighbouring buildings were questioned but none of them had noticed any suspicious movements at the murder scene between the Monday morning and the time the body was found.

Soon there was no-one left in the building but Erlendur and Sigurdur Óli. The blood on the carpet had turned black. The ashtray had been removed as evidence. The pencil and pad too. In other respects it was as though nothing had happened. Sigurdur Óli went to look in the den and the passage to the bedroom, while Erlendur walked around the sitting room. They put on white rubber gloves. Prints were mounted and framed on the walls and looked as if they'd been bought at the front door from travelling salesmen. In the bookcase were thrillers in translation, paperbacks from a book club, some of them read, others apparently untouched. No interesting hard-bound volumes. Erlendur bent down almost to the floor to read the titles on the bottom shelf and recognised only one: *Lolita* by Nabokov; paperback. He took it from the bookshelf. It was an English edition and had clearly been read.

He replaced the book and inched his way towards the desk. It was L-shaped and took up one corner of the sitting room. A new, comfortable office chair was by the desk, with a plastic mat underneath it to protect the carpet. The desk looked much older than the chair. There were drawers on both sides underneath the broader desktop and a long one in the middle, nine in all. On the shorter desktop stood a 17-inch computer monitor with a sliding tray for a keyboard fitted beneath it. The tower was kept on the floor. All the drawers were locked.

Sigurdur Óli went through the wardrobe in the bedroom. It was reasonably organised, with socks in one drawer, underwear in another, trousers, sweaters. Some shirts and three suits were hanging on a rail, the oldest suit from the disco era, Sigurdur Óli thought, brown striped. Several pairs of shoes on the wardrobe floor. Bedclothes in the top drawer. The man had made his bed before his visitor arrived. A white blanket covered the duvet and pillow. It was a single bed.

On the bedside table were an alarm clock and two books, one a series of interviews with a well-known politician and the other a book of photographs of Scania-Vabis trucks. The bedside table had a cupboard in it too, containing medicine, surgical spirit, sleeping pills, Panadol and a small jar of Vaseline.

"Can you see any keys anywhere?" asked Erlendur, who was now by the door.

"No keys. Door keys, you mean?"

"No, to the desk."

"None of those either."

Erlendur went into the den and from there into the kitchen. He opened drawers and cupboards but could see only cutlery and glasses, ladles and plates. No keys. He went over to the hangers by the door, frisked the coats but found nothing except a little black pouch with a ring of keys and some coins in it. Two small keys were hanging from the ring with others to the front door, to the flat and to the rooms.

Erlendur tried them on the desk. The same one fitted all nine drawers.

He opened the large drawer in the centre of the desk first. It contained mainly bills – telephone, electricity, heating and credit-card bills – and also a newspaper subscription. The bottom two drawers to the left were empty and in the next one up were tax forms and wage slips. In the top drawer was a photograph album. All black-and-white, old photographs of people from various times, sometimes dressed up in what appeared to be the sitting room in Nordurmýri, sometimes on picnics: dwarf birch, Gullfoss waterfall and Geysir. He saw two photographs that he thought might be of the murdered man when he was young, but nothing taken recently.

He opened the drawers on the right-hand side. The top two were empty. In the third he found a pack of cards, a folding chess set, an old inkwell.

He found the photograph underneath the bottom drawer.

Erlendur was closing the bottom drawer again when he heard what sounded like a slight rustling from inside it. When he opened and closed it again he heard the same rustling. It rubbed against something on its way in. He sighed and squatted down, looked inside but could see nothing. He pulled it back out but heard nothing, then closed it and the noise came again. He knelt on the floor, pulled the drawer right out, saw something stuck and stretched out to get it.

It was a small black-and-white photograph, showing a grave in a cemetery in wintertime. He didn't recognise the cemetery. There was a headstone on the grave and most of the inscription on it was fairly clear. A woman's name was carved there. AUDUR. No second name. Erlendur couldn't see the dates very clearly. He fumbled in his jacket pocket for his glasses, put them on and held the photograph up to his nose. 1964–1968. He could vaguely make out an epitaph, but the letters were small and he could not read it. Carefully he blew the dust off the photo.

The girl was only four when she died.

Erlendur looked up as the autumn rain thrashed against the windows. It was the middle of the day but the sky was a gloomy black.

6

The big lorry rocked in the storm like a prehistoric beast and the rain pounded against it. It had taken the police some time to locate as it wasn't parked where Holberg lived in Nordurmýri, but in a car park west of Snorrabraut, by the Domus Medica health centre, several minutes' walk from Holberg's home. In the end they had made a radio announcement asking for information about the lorry's whereabouts. A police patrol had found it at about the same time that Erlendur and Sigurdur Óli left Holberg's flat with the photograph. A forensic team was called out to comb the vehicle for clues. It was an MAN model with a red cab. All that a quick search revealed was a collection of hardcore pornographic magazines. It was decided to move the lorry to CID headquarters for further investigation.

While this was going on, forensics got to work on the photograph. It transpired that it was printed on Ilford photographic paper, which was used a lot in the 1960s but had long since been discontinued. Probably the photograph had been developed by the photographer himself or by an amateur; it had begun to fade as if the job had not been done very carefully. There was nothing written on the back and there were no landmarks by which to determine the cemetery in which it had been taken. It could be anywhere in the country.

The photographer had stood about three metres from the headstone. The shot was taken more or less directly in front of it; the photographer must have had to bend his knees unless he was very short. Even from that distance the angle was quite narrow. There was nothing growing near the grave. A powdery snow lay on the ground. No other grave could be seen. Behind the headstone, all that was visible was a white haze.

Forensics concentrated on the epitaph which was largely indistinguishable because the photographer had stood so far away. Numerous reproductions were made of the photograph and the epitaph was enlarged until every single letter had been printed out on A5 paper, numbered and arranged in the same sequence as on the headstone. They were coarse-grained pictures, hardly more than alternating black-and-white dots that created nuances of light and shade, but once scanned into a computer the shadowing and resolution could be processed. Some letters were clearer than others, which left the forensic team to fill in the gaps. The letters M, F and O were clearly discernible. Others were more difficult.

Erlendur phoned the home of a department manager from the National Statistics Office who agreed, cursing and swearing, to meet him at the offices on Skuggasund. Erlendur knew all the death certificates issued since 1916 were housed there. No-one was in the building, all the staff having left work some time before. The department manager pulled up in his car outside the Statistics Office half an hour later and shook Erlendur's hand curtly. He entered a PIN in the security system and let them into the building with a card. Erlendur outlined the matter to him, telling him only the bare essentials.

They looked at all death certificates issued in 1968 and found two in the name of Audur. One was in her fourth year. She had died in the February. A doctor had signed the death certificate and they soon found his name in the national registry. He lived in Reykjavík. The girl's mother was named on the certificate. They found her without any problems. Her name was Kolbrún. She had last been domiciled in Keflavík in the early 1970s. They then checked again among the death certificates. Kolbrún had died in 1971, three years after her daughter.

The girl had died from a malignant tumour on the brain.

The mother had committed suicide.

7

The bridegroom welcomed Erlendur into his office. He was a quality and marketing manager for a wholesaling company that imported breakfast cereal from America and Erlendur, who had never tasted American breakfast cereal in his life, pondered as he sat down in the office what a quality and marketing manager at a wholesaling company actually did. He couldn't be bothered to ask. The bridegroom was wearing a well-ironed white shirt and thick braces and he had rolled up his sleeves as if managing quality issues required every ounce of his strength. Average height, a little chubby and with a ring of beard around his thick-lipped mouth. Viggó was his name.

"I haven't heard from Dísa," Viggó said quickly and sat down facing Erlendur.

"Was it something you said to her that . . ."

"That's what everyone thinks," Viggó said. "Everyone assumes it's my fault. That's the worst thing. The worst part of the whole business. I can't stand it."

"Did you notice anything unusual about her

before she ran away? Anything that might have upset her?"

"Everyone was just having fun. You know, a wedding, you know what I mean."

"No."

"Surely you've been to a wedding?"

"Once. A long time ago."

"It was time for the first dance. The speeches were over and Dísa's girlfriends had organised some entertainment, the accordionist had arrived and we were supposed to dance. I was sitting at our table and everyone started looking for Dísa, but she was gone."

"Where did you last see her?"

"She was sitting with me and said she needed to go to the toilet."

"And did you say anything that could have made her sulk?"

"Not at all! I gave her a kiss and told her to be quick."

"How much time passed from when she left until you started looking for her?"

"I don't know. I sat down with my friends and then went outside for a smoke – all the smokers had to go outside – I talked to some people there and on the way out and back, sat down again and the accordionist came over and talked to me about the dance and music. I talked to some other people, I guess it must have been half an hour, I don't know."

"And you never saw her during that time?"

"No. When we realised she was gone it was a

total disaster. Everyone stared at me as though it was my fault."

"What do you think has happened to her?"

"I've looked everywhere. Spoken to all her friends and relatives but no-one knows a thing, or that's what they say anyway."

"Do you think someone's lying?"

"Well, she must be somewhere."

"Did you know she left a message?"

"No. What message? What do you mean?"

"She hung a card on the message tree thing. 'He's a monster, what have I done?' it said. Do you know what she means by that?"

"He's a monster," Viggó repeated. "Who was she talking about?"

"I had thought it might be you."

"Me?" said Viggó, becoming agitated. "I haven't done a thing to her, not a thing. Never. It's not me. It can't be me."

"The car she took was found on Gardastraeti. Does that tell you anything?"

"She doesn't know anyone there. Are you going to report her missing?"

"I think her parents want to give her time to come back."

"And if she doesn't?"

"Then we'll see." Erlendur hesitated. "I would have thought she'd have contacted you. To tell you everything's all right."

"Wait a minute, are you suggesting it was my fault and she won't talk to me because I did something to her? Jesus, what a bloody horror story. Do you know what it was like coming to work on Monday? All my colleagues were at the party. My boss was at the party! Do you think it's my fault? Fuck it! Everyone thinks it's my fault."

"Women," Erlendur said as he stood up. "They're difficult to quality control."

Erlendur had just arrived at his office when the phone rang. He recognised the voice immediately although he had not heard it for a long time. It was still clear and strong and firm despite its advanced age. Erlendur had known Marion Briem for almost 30 years and it hadn't always been plain sailing.

"I've just come from the chalet", the voice said, "and I didn't hear the news until I reached town just now."

"Are you talking about Holberg?" Erlendur asked.

"Have you looked at the reports on him?"

"I know Sigurdur Óli was checking the computer records but I haven't heard from him. What reports?"

"The question is whether they're actually on file in the computers. Maybe they've been thrown out. Is there any law about when reports become obsolete? Are they destroyed?"

"What are you driving at?"

"Turns out Holberg was no model citizen," Marion Briem said.

"In what way?"

"The chances are that he was a rapist."

"Chances are?"

"He was charged with rape, but never convicted. It was in 1963. You ought to take a look at your reports."

"Who accused him?"

"A woman by the name of Kolbrún. She lived in . . ."

"Keflavík?"

"Yes, how did you know that?"

"We found a photograph in Holberg's desk. It was as if it had been hidden there. It was a photograph of the gravestone of a girl called Audur, in a cemetery we still haven't identified. I woke up one of the living dead from the National Statistics Office and found Kolbrún's name on the death certificate. She was the little girl's mother. Audur's mother. She's dead too."

Marion said nothing.

"Marion?" Erlendur said.

"And what does that tell you?" the voice replied.

Erlendur thought.

"Well, if Holberg raped the mother he may well be the father of the girl and that's why the photo was in his desk. The girl was only 4 years old when she died, born in 1964."

"Holberg was never convicted," Marion Briem said. "The case was dropped due to insufficient evidence."

"Do you think she made it up?"

"It would be unlikely in those days, but nothing

50

could be proved. Of course it's never easy for women to press charges for that kind of violence. You can't imagine what she would have gone through almost 40 years ago. It's difficult enough for women to come forward these days, but it was much more difficult then. She could hardly have done it for fun. Maybe the photo's some kind of proof of paternity. Why should Holberg have kept it in his desk? The rape took place in 1963. You say Kolbrún had her daughter the following year. Four years later the daughter dies. Kolbrún has her buried. Holberg is implicated somehow. Maybe he took the photo himself. Why, I don't know. Maybe that's irrelevant."

"He certainly wouldn't have been at the funeral, but he could have gone to the grave later and taken a photograph. Do you mean something like that?"

"There's another possibility too."

"Yes?"

"Maybe Kolbrún took the photo herself and sent it to Holberg."

Erlendur thought for a moment.

"But why? If he raped her, why send him a photograph of the little girl's grave?"

"Good question."

"Did the death certificate say what Audur died of?" Marion Briem asked "Was it an accident?"

"She died of a brain tumour. Do you think that could be important?"

"Did they perform an autopsy?"

"Definitely. The doctor's name is on the death certificate."

"And the mother?"

"Died suddenly at her home."

"Suicide?"

"Yes."

"You've stopped calling in to see me," Marion Briem said after a short silence.

"Too busy," Erlendur said. "Too damned busy."

8

Next morning it was still raining and on the road to Keflavík the water collected in deep tyre tracks that the cars tried to avoid. The rain was so torrential Erlendur could hardly see out of the car windows, which were veiled in spray and rattled in the unrelenting south-easterly storm. The wipers couldn't clear the water from the windscreen fast enough and Erlendur gripped the steering wheel so tightly that his knuckles turned white. He could vaguely make out the red rear lights of the car in front and tried to follow them as best he could.

He was travelling alone. Thought this was best after a difficult telephone conversation with Kolbrún's sister earlier that morning. She was listed as next of kin on the death certificate. The sister was not cooperative. She refused to meet him. The papers had printed a photograph of the dead man, along with his name. Erlendur asked whether she'd seen it and was about to ask whether she remembered him when she hung up. He decided to test what she would do if he appeared on her doorstep. He preferred not to have the police bring her in to him.

Erlendur had slept badly that night. He was worried about Eva Lind and feared she would do something stupid. She had a mobile phone, but every time he called a mechanical voice answered saying that the number could not be reached. Erlendur rarely remembered his dreams. It made him uncomfortable when he awoke to snatches of a bad dream passing through his mind before finally vanishing from him completely.

The police had precious little information about Kolbrún. She was born in 1934 and brought charges of rape against Holberg on November 23, 1963. Before Erlendur set off to Keflavík, Sigurdur Óli had outlined the rape charge to him, including a description of the incident taken from a police file he'd found in the archives – after a tip-off from Marion Briem.

Kolbrún was 30 when she gave birth to her daughter, Audur. Nine months after the rape. According to Kolbrún's witnesses, she'd met Holberg at the Cross dancehall between Keflavík and Njardvík. It was a Saturday night. Kolbrún didn't know him and had never seen him before. She was with two girlfriends and Holberg and two other men had been with them at the dance that evening. When it finished they all went to a party at the house of one of Kolbrún's girlfriends. Quite late into the night Kolbrún had got ready to go home. Holberg offered to accompany her, for safety's sake. She didn't object. Neither of them was under the influence of alcohol. Kolbrún stated that she'd had two single vodka and Cokes at the dance and nothing after she left. Holberg drank nothing that evening. He said, in Kolbrún's hearing, that he was taking penicillin for an ear infection. A doctor's certificate, included with the charge sheet, confirmed this.

Holberg asked if he could phone a taxi to take him to Reykjavík. She hesitated for a moment then told him where the phone was. He went into the sitting room to make this call while she took off her coat in the hallway and then went to the kitchen for a glass of water. She did not hear him finish his telephone conversation, if indeed there was one. She sensed that he was suddenly behind her as she stood at the kitchen sink.

She was so startled that she dropped her glass, spilling water over the kitchen table. She shouted out when his hands grabbed her breasts, and backed away from him into a corner.

"What are you doing?" she asked.

"Shouldn't we have a bit of fun?" he said and stood in front of her, muscularly built with strong hands and thick fingers.

"I want you to leave," she said firmly. "Now! Will you please get out of here."

"Shouldn't we have a bit of fun?" he repeated. He took a step closer to her and she held out her arms as if in self-defence.

"Keep off!" she shouted. "I'll phone the police!" Suddenly she could feel how alone and defenceless she was facing this stranger whom she had let into her home and who by now had moved up close to her, had twisted her arms behind her back and was trying to kiss her.

She fought back, but it was useless. She tried to talk to him, talk him out of it, but all she could feel was her own vulnerability.

Erlendur snapped out of his thoughts when a gigantic lorry sounded its horn and overtook him with a mighty rumbling that sent waves of rainwater washing over his car. He tugged at the steering wheel and the car danced on the water for a moment. The rear of the car slid around and, for a second, Erlendur thought he was going to lose control and be thrown out into the lava field. He ground almost to a halt and managed to keep himself on the road, then hurled abuse at the lorry driver who by now had vanished from his sight in the spray of rain.

Twenty minutes later he pulled up outside a small corrugated-iron-clad house in the oldest part of Keflavík. It was painted white with a little white fence around it and a garden that was kept almost too fastidiously. The sister's name was Elín. She was several years older than Kolbrún and now retired. She was standing in the hallway, wearing her coat and on her way out, when Erlendur rang the doorbell. She looked at him in astonishment, a short, slim woman with a tough expression on her face, piercing eyes, high cheekbones and wrinkles around her mouth.

"I thought I told you on the phone I didn't want anything to do with you or the police," she said angrily when Erlendur had introduced himself.

"I know," Erlendur said, "but . . ."

"I'm asking you to leave me alone," she said. "You shouldn't have wasted your time coming all the way out here."

She stepped out onto the doorstep, closed the door behind her, went down the three steps leading to the garden and opened the little gate in the fence, leaving it open as a sign that she wanted Erlendur to leave. She didn't look at him. Erlendur stood on the steps, watching her walk away.

"You know Holberg's dead," he called out.

She didn't answer.

"He was murdered in his home. You know that."

Erlendur was at the bottom of the steps, hurrying after her. She held a black umbrella onto which the rain poured above her head. He had nothing more than a hat to keep the rain off. She quickened her pace. He ran to catch up with her. He didn't know what to say to make her listen to him. Didn't know why she reacted to him as she did.

"I wanted to ask you about Audur," he said.

Elín suddenly stopped and turned round and marched up to him with a contemptuous look on her face.

"You bloody cop," she hissed between her clenched teeth. "Don't you dare mention her name.

57

How dare you? After what you did to her mother. Get lost! Get lost this minute! Bloody cop!"

She looked at Erlendur with hatred in her eyes and he stared back at her.

"After all we did to her?" he said. "To whom?"

"Go away," she shouted, and turned and walked away, leaving Erlendur where he was. He gave up the chase and watched her disappearing in the rain, stooping slightly, in her green raincoat and black ankle boots. He turned around and walked back to her house and his car, deep in thought. He got inside and lit a cigarette, opened the window a crack, started the engine and slowly drove away from the house.

As he inhaled he felt a slight pain in the middle of his chest again. It wasn't new. It had been causing Erlendur some concern for almost a year now. A vague pain that greeted him in the mornings but generally disappeared soon after he got out of bed. He didn't have a good mattress to sleep on. Sometimes his whole body ached if he lay in bed for too long.

He inhaled the smoke. Hopefully it was the mattress.

As Erlendur was putting out his cigarette his mobile phone rang in his coat pocket. It was the head of forensics with the news that they had managed to decipher the inscription on the grave and had located it in the Bible.

"It's taken from Psalm 64," the head of forensics said.

"Yes," said Erlendur.

" 'Preserve my life from fear of the enemy.' "

"Pardon?"

"It's what it says on the gravestone: Preserve my life from fear of the enemy. From Psalm 64."

"'Preserve my life from fear of the enemy'."

"Does that help you at all?"

"I've no idea."

"There were two sets on fingerprints on the photograph."

"Yes, Sigurdur Óli told me."

"One set is Holberg's but we don't have the others on our files. They're quite blurred. Very old fingerprints."

"Can you tell what kind of camera the photo was taken with?" Erlendur asked.

"Impossible to tell. But I doubt it was a high-quality one."

9

Sigurdur Óli parked his car in the Iceland Transport yard where he hoped it would be out of the way. Lorries were standing in rows in the yard. Some were being loaded, some driven away, others reversed up to the cargo warehouse. A stench of diesel and oil filled the air and the noise from the engines of the trucks was deafening. Staff and customers were rushing around the yard and the warehouse.

The Met Office had forecast yet more wet weather. Sigurdur Óli tried to protect himself from the rain by pulling his coat over his head as he ran to the warehouse. He was directed to the foreman who was sitting in a glass cubicle checking papers and appeared to be extremely busy.

A plump man wearing a blue anorak done up with a single button across his paunch and holding a cigar stub between his fingers, the foreman had heard about Holberg's death and said he'd known him quite well. Described him as a reliable man, a hard worker who'd been driving from one end of the country to the other for decades and knew Iceland's road network like the back of his hand.

Said he was a secretive type, never talked about himself or in personal terms, never made any friends at the company or talked about what he'd done before, thought he'd always been a lorry driver. Talked as if he had been. Unmarried with no children, as far as he knew. Never talked about his nearest and dearest.

"That's the long and the short of it," the foreman said as if to put an end to the conversation, took a lighter from his anorak pocket and lit the cigar stub. "Damn shame," puff, puff, "to go like that," puff.

"Who did he associate with here mainly?" Sigurdur Óli asked, trying not to inhale the foul-smelling cigar smoke.

"You can talk to Hilmar, I reckon he knew him best. Hilmar's out the front. He's from Reydarfjördur so sometimes he used to stay at Holberg's place in Nordurmýri when he needed to rest in town. There are rest rules that drivers have to comply with, so they have to have somewhere to stay in the city."

"Did he stay there last weekend, do you know?"

"No, he was working in the east. But he might have been there the weekend before."

"Can you imagine who would have wanted to do Holberg any harm? Some friction here at work or . . ."

"No, no, nothing", puff, "like", puff, "that," puff. The man was having trouble keeping his cigar alight. "Talk to", puff, "Hilmar," puff, "mate. He might be able to help you."

Sigurdur Óli found Hilmar after following the foreman's directions. He was standing by one of the warehouse bays supervising a lorry being unloaded. Hilmar was a hulk, two metres tall, muscular, ruddy, bearded and with hairy arms protruding from his T-shirt. Looked about 50. Old-fashioned blue braces held up his tatty jeans. A small forklift was unloading the lorry. Another lorry was backing up to the next bay along; at the same time two drivers beeped their horns and hurled abuse at each other in the yard.

Sigurdur Óli went up to Hilmar and tapped him lightly on the shoulder, but the man didn't notice him. He tapped harder and eventually Hilmar turned round. He could see Sigurdur Óli talking to him but couldn't hear what he was saying and looked down at him with bovine eyes. Sigurdur Óli raised his voice, but to no avail. He raised his voice further and thought he detected a glimmer of comprehension in Hilmar's eyes, but he was mistaken. Hilmar just shook his head and pointed at his ear.

At this, Sigurdur Óli redoubled his efforts, arched himself and stood on tiptoe and shouted at the top of his voice at the very moment everything fell completely silent and his words echoed in all their glory around the walls of the gigantic warehouse and out into the yard:

"DID YOU SLEEP WITH HOLBERG?"

He was raking up leaves in his garden when Erlendur saw him. He didn't look up until Erlendur had been standing watching him for a long time as he toiled away with the slow movements of an old man. He wiped a drip from the end of his nose. It didn't seem to matter that it was raining and the leaves were stuck together and awkward to deal with. He did nothing hurriedly, hooked the leaves with his rake and tried to scrape them into little piles. He still lived in Keflavík. Born and bred there.

Erlendur had asked Elínborg to collect information about him and she'd dug up the main details about the old man whom Erlendur now watched in the garden; his police career, the numerous criticisms of his conduct and procedures during his many years in the force, the handling of Kolbrún's case and how he had been specifically reprimanded over it. She phoned back with the information while Erlendur was sitting over a meal, still in Keflavík. He considered saving the visit until the following day, then thought to himself that he couldn't be bothered driving there and back in a raging storm so he would just go direct.

The man was wearing a green parka and a baseball cap. His white, bony hands held the shaft of the rake. He was tall and had obviously once been sturdier and cut a more authoritative figure but he was old, wrinkled and runny-nosed now. Erlendur watched him, an old man pottering around in his garden. The man looked up from his leaves, but paid no particular attention to his observer. A good while passed like this until Erlendur decided to make a move.

"Why doesn't her sister want to talk to me?" he said and the old man looked up with a start.

"Eh? What was that?" The man stopped what he was doing. "Who are you?" he asked.

"How did you treat Kolbrún when she came to you to press charges?" Erlendur asked.

The old man looked at this stranger who had entered his garden, and he wiped his nose with the back of his hand. He looked Erlendur up and down.

"Do I know you?" he said. "What are you talking about? Who are you?"

"My name's Erlendur. I'm investigating the murder of a man from Reykjavík by the name of Holberg. He was accused of rape almost 40 years ago. You were in charge of the investigation. The woman who was raped was called Kolbrún. She's dead. Her sister won't talk to the police for reasons I'm trying to establish. She said to me, 'After what you did to her.' I'd like you to tell me what she's referring to."

The man looked at Erlendur without saying a word. Looked him in the eye and remained silent.

"What did you do to her?" Erlendur repeated.

"I can't remember . . . what right have you got? What kind of an insult is this anyway?" His voice was trembling slightly. "Get out of my garden or I'll call the police."

"No, Rúnar, I am the police. And I don't have time for any of this bollocks."

Rúnar thought it over. "Is this the new method? Attacking people with accusations and abuse?"

"Good of you to mention methods and abuse," Erlendur said. "At one time you ran up eight charges for breaches of duty, including brutality. I don't know who you had to serve to keep your job, but you didn't do him well enough towards the end because eventually you left the police in disgrace. Dismissed . . ."

"You shut up," said Rúnar, looking around shiftily. "How dare you."

". . . for repeated sexual harassment."

His white, bony hands tightened their grip on the rake, stretching his pallid skin until the knuckles stood out. His face closed up, hateful lines around his mouth, his stare narrowed until his eyes were half closed. On his way to see him, while the information from Elínborg was running through his mind like an electric shock, Erlendur had wondered whether Rúnar should be condemned for what he'd done in another life, when he was a different man. Erlendur had been in the police force long enough to have heard the stories about him, about the trouble he caused. He had in fact met Rúnar a couple of times many years before, but the man he now saw in the garden was so old and decrepit that it took Erlendur a while to be sure that it was the same person. Stories about Rúnar still circulated among the police. Erlendur had once read that the past was a different country and he could understand that. He understood that times change and people too. But he wasn't prepared to erase the past.

They stood in the garden facing one another.

"What about Kolbrún?" Erlendur said.

"Bugger off!"

"Not until you tell me about Kolbrún."

"She was a fucking whore!" Rúnar suddenly said between clenched teeth. "So take that and bugger off! Everything she said about me and to me was bloody lies. There wasn't any fucking rape. She lied the whole time!"

Erlendur visualised Kolbrún sitting in front of this man all those years ago when she filed the rape charge. He imagined her gradually mustering up her courage until finally she dared to go to the police to tell what had happened to her. He imagined the terror she'd experienced and, above all else, wanted to forget as if it had never occurred, as if it had merely been a nightmare from which she'd eventually wake. Then she realised she would never wake up. She had been defiled. She'd been attacked and she'd been plundered.

"She turned up three days after the incident and

accused the man of rape," Rúnar said. "It wasn't very convincing."

"So you threw her back out," Erlendur said.

"She was lying."

"And you laughed at her and belittled her and told her to forget it. But she didn't forget it, did she?"

The old man looked at Erlendur with loathing in his eyes.

"She went to Reykjavík, didn't she?" Erlendur said.

"Holberg was never convicted."

"Thanks to whom, do you reckon?"

Erlendur imagined Kolbrún wrangling with Rúnar at the office. Wrangling with him! That man! Arguing the truth of what she'd been through. Trying to convince him she was telling the truth as if he were the supreme judge in her case.

*

She had to summon all her strength to relate the events of that night to him and tried to give a systematic account, but it was just too painful. She couldn't describe it. Couldn't describe something indescribable, repulsive, hideous. Somehow she managed to piece together her disjointed story. Was that a grin? She didn't understand why the policeman was grinning. She had the impression it was a grin, but it couldn't be. Then he started questioning her about the details.

"Tell me exactly what it was like."

She looked at him, confused. Hesitantly began her story again.

"No, I've heard that. Tell me exactly what happened. You were wearing panties. How did he get your panties off? How did he get it inside you?"

Was he serious? Eventually she asked if there were any women working there.

"No. If you want to charge this man with rape, you have to be more precise than this, understand? Had you led him on somehow so he might have thought you were up for it?"

Up for it? She told him in an almost inaudible voice that she certainly had not.

"You'll have to speak up. How did he get your panties off?"

She was sure it was a grin. He questioned her brashly, queried what she said, was rude, some of the questions were downright abusive, filthy, he behaved as though she had provoked the assault, had wanted to have sex with the man, perhaps changed her mind but then it was too late, you know, too late to back out of that kind of thing. "There's no point in going to a dancehall, flirting with the man and then stopping halfway. No point at all," he said.

She was sobbing when she eventually opened her handbag, took out a plastic bag and handed it to him. He opened the bag and took out her ripped panties . . .

*

68

Rúnar let go of the rake and was about to walk past Erlendur, but Erlendur blocked his way and pinned him against the wall of the house. They looked each other in the eye.

"She gave you some evidence," Erlendur said. "The only evidence she had. She was certain Holberg had left something behind."

"She never gave me anything," Rúnar hissed. "Leave me alone."

"She gave you a pair of panties."

"She was lying."

"They should have fired you on the spot. You pathetic fucking beast." With an expression of revulsion Erlendur backed slowly away from the decrepit old man now huddled against the wall.

"I was just showing her what to expect if she pressed charges," he said in a squeaky voice. "I was doing her a favour. The courts laugh at that kind of case."

Erlendur turned around and walked away, wondering how God, if he existed, could possibly justify allowing someone like Rúnar live to an old age but taking the life of an innocent 4-year-old girl.

He planned to go back to see Kolbrún's sister but called in at the Keflavík library first. He walked among the bookshelves, running his eyes over the spines of the books until he found the Bible. Erlendur knew the Bible well. He opened it at the Psalms and found No. 64. He found the line that was inscribed on the headstone. "Preserve my life from fear of the enemy."

He had remembered correctly. The epitaph was a continuation of the first line of the Psalm. Erlendur read it over several times, pensively tracing his fingers across the lines, and quietly repeating the sentence to himself as he stood by the bookshelf.

The first line of the Psalm was a plea to the Lord. Erlendur could almost hear the woman's silent cry across the years.

"Hear my voice, O God, in my prayer."

11

Erlendur pulled up outside the corrugated-iron-clad white house and switched off the engine. He stayed in the car and finished his cigarette. He was trying to cut back on smoking and was down to five a day when things went well. This was number eight that day and it wasn't even 3 p.m.

He got out of the car, walked up the steps to the house and rang the bell. He waited a good while, but nothing happened. He rang again, but with no result. He put his face to the window and saw the green raincoat and umbrella and boots. He rang a third time, stood on the top step and tried to keep out of the rain. Suddenly, the door opened and Elín glared at him.

"Leave me alone, you hear? Go away! Get out!" She tried to slam the door but Erlendur blocked it with his foot.

"We're not all like Rúnar," he said. "I know your sister wasn't treated fairly. I went and talked to Rúnar. What he did is inexcusable, but it can't be changed now. He's senile and geriatric and he'll never see anything wrong in what he did."

"Will you leave me alone!"

"I have to talk to you. If it doesn't work like this I'll have to bring you in for questioning. I want to avoid that." He took the photograph from the cemetery out of his pocket and slipped it through the crack in the door. "I found this photo in Holberg's flat," he said.

Elín didn't answer him. A long while passed. Erlendur held the photo through the opening in the door, but he couldn't see Elín, who was still pushing against it. Gradually he felt the pressure on his foot easing and Elín took the photograph. Soon the door was open. She went inside holding the photograph. Erlendur stepped inside and closed the door carefully behind him.

Elín disappeared into a little sitting room and for a moment Erlendur wondered if he ought to take off his wet shoes. He wiped them on the mat and followed Elín into the sitting room, past the tidy kitchen and study. In the sitting room there were pictures and embroidery in gilded frames on the walls and a small electric organ in one corner.

"Do you recognise this photo?" Erlendur asked cautiously.

"I've never seen it before," she said.

"Did your sister have any contact with Holberg after the . . . incident?"

"None that I knew of. Never. You can imagine."

"Wasn't a blood test taken to determine if he was the father?"

"What for?"

"It would have backed up your sister's statement. That she was raped."

She looked up from the photo and gave him a long stare, then said, "You're all the same, you police. Too lazy to do your homework."

"Really?"

"Haven't you looked into the case?"

"The main details. I thought."

"Holberg didn't deny they had sex. He was smarter than that. He denied it was rape. He said my sister wanted him. Said she'd enticed him and invited him back to her place. That was his big defence. That Kolbrún had sex with him of her own free will. He played innocent. Played innocent, the bastard."

"But . . ."

"Kolbrún didn't care about proving paternity. She didn't want him to have anything to do with her child. Proving that Holberg was Audur's father wouldn't have made any difference to her rape claim so a blood test would have been futile."

"I hadn't realised."

"All my sister had was a pair of ripped panties," Elín went on. "She didn't look very roughed up. She wasn't strong, couldn't put up much of a fight, and she told me she was almost paralysed with fright when he started groping at her in the kitchen. He forced her into the bedroom and had his way with her there. Twice. Held her down and groped and talked filth until he was ready to do it again. It took her three days to pluck up the courage to go to the police. The medical examination they gave her later didn't help either. She never understood what made him attack her. She accused herself of provoking what he did. She thought she might have been leading him on at that party they went to after the dancehall closed. That she said something or suggested something that might have aroused him. She blamed herself. I expect that's a common reaction."

Elín stopped talking for a moment.

"When she finally acted, she ran into Rúnar," she continued. "I would have gone with her, but she was so ashamed that she didn't tell anyone what had happened until long afterwards. Holberg threatened her. Said that if she did anything about it he'd come back and torture her. When she went to the police she thought she was heading for safety. She'd be helped. They'd look after her. It wasn't until Rúnar sent her back home, after playing around with her and taking her panties and telling her to forget it, that she came to me."

"The panties were never found," Erlendur said. "Rúnar denied . . ."

"Kolbrún said she gave them to him and I never knew my sister to lie. I don't know what that man was thinking of. I see him walking around town here sometimes, in the supermarket or at the fish shop. I shouted at him once. Couldn't control myself. He looked as if he enjoyed it. Grinned. Kolbrún talked about that grin of his once. He said he'd never been given any panties and her statement

74

was so vague he thought she was under the influence. That's why he sent her home."

"He was given a warning in the end," Erlendur said, "but it didn't have much effect. Rúnar was always getting warnings. He was well known as a thug in the police but someone was protecting him, that is, until he couldn't be protected any more. Then he was dismissed."

"There were insufficient grounds for bringing charges, that's what they said. What Rúnar said was right, Kolbrún should just have forgotten it. Of course she dithered around for a long time, too long, and she was stupid enough to clean up the whole house from top to bottom, her bedclothes too, removed all the evidence. She kept the panties. After all that she still tried to keep some piece of evidence. As if she felt it would be enough. As if it was enough just to tell the truth. She wanted to wash the incident clean from her life. She didn't want to live with it. And, as I said, she didn't look too roughed up. She had a split lip where he held her mouth and one of her eyes was bloodshot but there were no other injuries."

"Did she get over it?"

"Never. She was a very sensitive woman, my sister. A beautiful soul and easy prey for anyone to harm. Like Holberg. Like Rúnar. They sensed that, both of them. They attacked her in their own separate ways. Savaged their prey." She looked down at the floor. "The beasts."

Erlendur waited for a moment before continuing.

"How did she react when she discovered she was pregnant?" he asked.

"Very sensibly, I thought. She decided straight-away to be happy about the child despite the circumstances, and she genuinely loved Audur. They were very attached to each other and my sister took particularly good care of her daughter. Did everything she could for her. That poor sweet girl."

"So Holberg knew the child was his?"

"Of course he knew, but he denied it completely. Said she was nothing to do with him. Accused my sister of sleeping around."

"They never kept in contact then, not about their daughter or . . ."

"Contact! Never. How could you imagine such a thing? That could never have happened."

"Kolbrún couldn't have sent him the photo?"

"No. No, I can't imagine that. That's out of the question."

"He could have taken it himself. Or someone who knew the background took it and sent it to him. Maybe he saw the death announcement in the papers. Were any obituaries written about Audur?"

"There was a death announcement in the local paper. I wrote a short obituary. He could have read that."

"Is Audur buried here in Keflavík?"

"No, we're from Sandgerdi, my sister and me, and there's a small cemetery at Hvalsnes, just outside it. Kolbrún wanted her to be buried there. It was the middle of winter. Took them ages to dig the grave."

76

"The death certificate says she had a brain tumour."

"That was the explanation they gave my sister. She just died. Died on us, poor little thing, and we couldn't do a thing, in her fourth year."

Elín looked up from the photograph to Erlendur. "She just died."

It was dark in the house and the words echoed through the gloom full of questioning and grief. Elín stood up slowly and switched on the dull light of a standard lamp as she walked out to the hallway and into the kitchen. Erlendur heard her turn on the tap, fill something with water, pour it, open a tin, he smelled the aroma of coffee. He stood up and looked at the pictures on the walls. They were drawings and paintings. A pastel by a child was in a thin black frame. Eventually he found what he was looking for. There were two, probably taken two years apart. Photographs of Audur.

The earlier photo had been taken at a studio. It was black-and-white. The girl was probably no more than one year old and was sitting on a big cushion wearing a pretty dress, with a ribbon in her hair and a rattle in one hand. She was half turned towards the photographer and was smiling, showing four little teeth. In the other she was aged about three. Erlendur imagined her mother had taken it. It was in colour. The girl was standing among some shrubs and the sun was shining straight down on her. She was wearing a thick red jumper and a little skirt, with white socks and black shoes with shiny buckles. She was looking directly into the camera. Her expression serious. Maybe she'd refused to smile.

"Kolbrún never got over it," said Elín, from the sitting-room doorway. Erlendur stood up straight.

"That must be the worst thing anyone could go through," he said, taking a cup of coffee. Elín sat back down on the sofa with her cup and Erlendur sat down facing her again and sipped his coffee.

"Do smoke if you want to," she said.

"I'm trying to stop," Erlendur said, trying not to sound apologetic. His thoughts turned to the pain he had in his chest but nevertheless he fished a crumpled pack out of his coat pocket and took one out. His ninth cigarette of the day. She pushed an ashtray towards him.

"Mercifully she didn't take long to die," Elín said. "Started feeling pains in her head. As if she had a headache, and the doctor who examined her only ever talked about child migraine. He gave her some pills, but they didn't do any good. He wasn't a good doctor. Kolbrún told me she smelled alcohol on his breath and she was worried about it. But then it all happened so suddenly. The girl's condition got worse. There was mention of a skin tumour that her doctor should have noticed. Marks. They called them *café au lait* at the hospital. Mainly under her arms. Finally she was sent to the hospital here in Keflavík where they decided it was some kind of neural tumour. It turned out to be a brain tumour. The whole thing took about six months."

Elín fell silent. "As I said, Kolbrún was never the same after that," she sighed. "I don't expect anyone could get over such a tragedy."

"Was an autopsy performed on Audur?" Erlendur asked, imagining the little body lit up by fluorescent lights on a cold steel table with a Y-cut across the chest.

"Kolbrún wouldn't entertain the idea," Elín said, "but she had no say in the matter. She went crazy when she found out they'd opened her up. Went mad with grief, of course, after her child died, and she wouldn't listen to anyone. She couldn't bear to think of her little girl being cut open. She was dead and nothing could change that. The autopsy confirmed the diagnosis. They found a malignant tumour in her brain."

"And your sister?"

"Kolbrún committed suicide three years later. She fell into an uncontrollable depression and needed medical care. Spent a while at a psychiatric ward in Reykjavík, then came back home to Keflavík. I tried to look after her as best I could but it was like she'd been switched off. She had no will to live. Audur had brought happiness into her life in spite of those terrible circumstances. But now she was gone."

Elín looked at Erlendur. "You're probably wondering how she went about it."

Erlendur didn't reply.

"She got into the bath and slashed both her wrists. Bought razor blades to do it with."

Elín stopped talking and the gloom in the sitting room enveloped them. "Do you know what comes into my mind when I think about that suicide? It's not the blood in the bath. Not my sister lying in the red water. Not the cuts. It's Kolbrún in the shop, buying the razor blades. Handing over the money for the razor blades. Counting out the coins."

Elín stopped talking.

"Don't you think it's funny the way your mind works?" she asked, as if she were talking to herself.

Erlendur didn't know how to answer her.

"I found her," Elín continued. "She set it up like that. Phoned me and asked me to come round that evening. We had a short chat. I was always on my guard because of her depression but she seemed to be improving towards the end. As if the fog was lifting. As if she was capable of tackling life again. There was no sign in her voice that evening that she was planning to kill herself. Far from it. We talked about the future. We were going to travel together. When I found her there she was at peace in a way I hadn't seen for ages. Peace and acceptance. But I know she didn't accept it in the slightest and she found no peace in her soul."

"I have to ask you one thing and then I'll leave you alone," Erlendur said. "I have to hear your answer."

"What's that."

"Do you have any knowledge about Holberg's murder?"

"No, I don't."

"And you had no part in it, directly or indirectly?"

"No."

They remained silent for a short while.

"The epitaph she chose for her daughter was about the enemy," Erlendur said.

"'Preserve my life from fear of the enemy.' She chose it herself, even though it didn't go on her own gravestone," Elín said. She stood up, walked over to a beautiful glass-fronted cabinet, opened a drawer in it and took out a little black box. She opened it with a key, lifted up some envelopes and took out a little piece of paper. "I found this on the kitchen table the night she died, but I'm not sure if she wanted me to have it inscribed on her gravestone. I doubt it. I don't think I realised how much she'd suffered until I saw this."

She handed Erlendur the piece of paper and he read the first five words from the Psalm he'd looked up in the Bible earlier: "Hear my voice, O God."

12

When Erlendur got home that evening his daughter, Eva Lind, was sitting up against the door to the flat, apparently asleep. He spoke to her and tried to wake her. She showed no response, so he put his hands under her arms, lifted her up and carried her inside. He didn't know whether she was sleeping or stoned. He lay her down on the sofa in the sitting room. Her breathing was regular. Her pulse seemed normal. He looked at her for a good while and wondered what to do. Most of all he wanted to put her in the bath. She gave off a stench, her hands were dirty and her hair matted with filth.

"Where have you been?" Erlendur whispered to himself.

He sat down in the chair beside her, still wearing his hat and coat, and thought about his daughter until he fell into a deep sleep.

He didn't want to wake up when Eva Lind shook him the next morning. Tried to hold on to the snatches of dreams that aroused the same discomfort within him as the one of the night before. He knew this was the same dream, but couldn't manage to fix it in his mind any more than last time, couldn't get a handle on it. All that remained was a lingering discomfort.

It was not yet 8 a.m. and it was still pitch dark outside. As far as Erlendur could tell the rain and autumn winds still hadn't let up. To his astonishment he smelled coffee from the kitchen and steam as if someone had been in the bath. He noticed Eva Lind was wearing one of his shirts and some old jeans that she tied tight around her thin waist with a belt. She was barefoot and clean.

"You were on good form last night," he said, and immediately regretted it. Then he thought that he should have given up being considerate towards her long ago.

"I've made a decision," Eva Lind said, walking into the kitchen. "I'm going to make you a grandfather. Grandad Erlendur."

"So were you having your final fling last night, or what?"

"Is it okay for me to stay here for a while, just until I find somewhere new?"

"For all I care."

He sat down at the kitchen table with her and sipped the coffee that she'd poured into a cup for him.

"And how did you reach this conclusion?"

"Just did."

"Just did?"

"Can I stay with you or not?"

"As long as you want. You know that."

"Will you stop asking me questions? Stop those

interrogations of yours. It's like you're always at work."

"I am always at work."

"Have you found the girl from Gardabaer?"

"No. It's not a priority case. I talked to her husband yesterday. He doesn't know anything. The girl left a note saying 'He's a monster what have I done?'"

"Someone must have been dissing her at the party."

"Dissing?" said Erlendur. "Is that a word?"

"What can you do to a bride at a wedding to make her do a runner?"

"I don't know," Erlendur said without interest. "My hunch is that the groom was touching up the bridesmaids and she saw him. I'm glad you're going to have the baby. Maybe it'll help you out of this vicious circle. It's about time."

He paused. "Strange how perky you are after the state you were in yesterday," he said eventually.

He phrased this as cautiously as he could, but he also knew that, under normal circumstances, Eva Lind shouldn't be shining like a summer's day, fresh out of the bath, making coffee and acting as if she'd never done anything but look after her father. She looked at him and he saw her weighing up the options and waited for her speech, waited for her to leap to her feet and give him a piece of her mind. She didn't.

"I brought some pills with me," she said very calmly. "It doesn't happen of its own accord. And not overnight. It happens slowly, over a long time, but it's the way I want to do it."

"And the baby?"

"It won't be harmed by what I use. I don't plan to harm the baby. I'm going to have it."

"What do you know about the effect that dope has on an embryo?"

"I know."

"Have it your own way. Take something, bring yourself down or whatever you call it, stay here in the flat, have a good think about yourself. I can . . ."

"No," Eva Lind said. "Don't you do anything. You go on with your life and stop spying on me. Don't think about what I'm doing. If I'm not here when you come home, it doesn't matter. If I come home late or don't come back to the flat at all, then don't interfere. If that happens, I'm gone, finito."

"So it's none of my business."

"It's never been any of your business," said Eva Lind, and sipped her coffee.

The phone rang and Erlendur got up and answered it. It was Sigurdur Óli, who was calling from home.

"I couldn't get hold of you yesterday," he said. Erlendur remembered he'd switched off his mobile while he was talking to Elín in Keflavík, and hadn't switched it back on.

"Are there any new developments?" Erlendur asked.

"I spoke to a man called Hilmar yesterday.

Another lorry driver who sometimes slept at Holberg's place in Nordurmýri. A rest stop or whatever they call it. He told me Holberg was a good pal, nothing to complain about, and everyone at work seemed to like him, helpful and sociable, blah blah blah. Couldn't imagine he had any enemies, but added that he didn't know him particularly well. Hilmar also told me Holberg hadn't been his usual self the last time he stayed with him, which was about ten days ago. Apparently he was acting strange."

"Strange in what way?"

"The way Hilmar described it, he was sort of afraid to answer the phone. Said there was some bugger who wouldn't leave him in peace, as he put it, always phoning him up. Hilmar said he stayed with him on the Saturday night and Holberg asked him to answer the phone for him once. Hilmar did, but when the caller realised it wasn't Holberg who'd answered he slammed the phone down."

"Can we find out who's been calling Holberg recently?"

"I'm having that checked. Then there's another thing. I've got a printout from the telephone company of the calls Holberg made, and something interesting came out of that."

"What?"

"You remember his computer?"

"Yes."

"We never looked at it."

"No. The technicians do that."

"Did you notice if it was plugged in to the telephone?"

"No."

"Most of Holberg's calls, almost all of them in fact, were to an Internet server. He used to spend days on end surfing the net."

"What does that mean?" asked Erlendur, who was particularly ill-informed about everything to do with computers.

"Maybe we'll see that when we switch on his computer," Sigurdur Óli replied.

They arrived at Holberg's flat in Nordurmýri at the same time. The yellow police tape had gone and there was no visible sign of a crime any more. No lights were on in the upper floors. The neighbours didn't appear to be at home. Erlendur had a key to the flat. They went straight over to the computer and switched it on. It started whirring.

"It's quite a powerful computer," Sigurdur Óli said, wondering for a moment whether he should explain to Erlendur about the size and type, but decided to give it a miss.

"Okay," he said, "I'll have a look to see what web addresses he had stored in his favourites. Loads of them, bloody loads of them. Maybe he's down-loaded some files. Wow!"

"What?" said Erlendur.

"His hard drive's jam-packed."

"Which means?"

"You need a hell of a lot of stuff to fill a hard

drive. There must be whole movies on here. Here's something he calls *avideo3*. Shall we see what it is?"

"Definitely."

Sigurdur Óli opened the file and a window popped up playing a video. They watched for a few seconds. It was a porn clip.

"Was that a goat they were holding over her?" Erlendur asked in disbelief.

"There are 312 *avideo* files," Sigurdur Óli said. "They could be clips like that one, even whole movies."

"*Avideo*?" said Erlendur.

"I don't know," said Sigurdur Óli. "Maybe animal videos. There's *gvideo* too. Should we look at, let's say, *gvideo*88? Double-click . . . maximise the window . . ."

"Double—?" said Erlendur, but stopped mid-sentence when four men having sex spread themselves across the 17-inch monitor.

"*Gvideo* must mean gay videos," said Sigurdur Óli when the scene was over.

"He was obviously obsessed then," Erlendur said. "How many films are there altogether?"

"There are more than a thousand files here, but there could be a lot more stored elsewhere on the drive."

Erlendur's mobile phone rang in his coat pocket. It was Elínborg. She'd been trying to trace the two men who went with Holberg to the party in Keflavík on the night that Kolbrún said she was assaulted.

Elínborg told Erlendur that one of them, Grétar, had disappeared years ago.

"Disappeared?" Erlendur said.

"Yes. One of our missing persons."

"And the other one?" Erlendur said.

"The other one's in prison," Elínborg said. "Always been in trouble. He's got one year left to serve of a four-year sentence."

"For what?"

"You name it."

13

Erlendur reminded forensics about the computer. It would take quite a while to investigate everything on it. He told them to look at every single file, list it and classify it and make a detailed report on the contents. Then he and Sigurdur Óli set off for Litla-Hraun prison, east of the city. It took them just over an hour to get there. Visibility was poor, the road was icy and the car still had summer tyres, so they had to be careful. The weather warmed up once they were through Threngslin Pass. They crossed the river Ölfusá and soon saw the two prison buildings rising up from the hard gravel banks in the hazy distance. The older building was three storeys high, in the gabled style. For years it had had a red corrugated-iron roof and, from a distance, looked like a gigantic old farmhouse. Now the roof had been painted grey to match the new building beside it. That was a steel-clad, cobalt-grey building with a watchtower, modern and fortified, not unlike a financial institution in Reykjavík.

How the times change, Erlendur thought to himself.

Elínborg had told the prison authorities to expect

them and which inmate they wanted to talk to. The prison governor welcomed the detectives and accompanied them to his office. He wanted them to have some details about the prisoner before talking to him. They had arrived at the worst possible time. The prisoner in question was in solitary confinement after he and two others had assaulted a recently convicted paedophile and left him for dead. He said he preferred not to go into details, but wanted to inform the police, to make it perfectly clear, that their visit was a breach of his solitary confinement and the prisoner would be, at best, in an unstable condition. After the meeting the inspectors were accompanied to the visiting hall. They sat and waited for the prisoner.

His name was Ellidi and he was a 56-year-old repeat offender. Erlendur knew him, he had in fact accompanied him to Litla-Hraun once himself. Ellidi had done various jobs during his miserable life: been at sea on fishing vessels and merchant ships, where he smuggled alcohol and drugs and was eventually convicted for it. He attempted an insurance fraud by setting fire to a 20-tonne boat off the south-west coast and sinking it. Three of them "survived". The fourth member of the group was left behind by mistake, locked in the engine room, and sank with the boat; the crime was discovered when divers went down to the wreck and it transpired that the fire had started in three places at once. Ellidi did four years at Litla-Hraun for insurance fraud, manslaughter and a number of minor offences of which he was convicted at the same time and that had been accumulating at the State Prosecutor's office. He spent two and a half years inside on that occasion.

Ellidi was notorious for violent physical assaults which in the worst cases left the victims maimed and permanently disabled. Erlendur remembered one case in particular and described it to Sigurdur Óli while they were driving over the moor. Ellidi had a score to settle with a young man in a house on Snorrabraut. By the time the police arrived on the scene he'd beaten the man so badly he was in intensive care for four days. Having tied the man to a chair he had amused himself by cutting his face with a broken bottle. Before they managed to overpower Ellidi he knocked one policeman out cold and broke another's arm. Icelandic judges were notoriously lenient. He received a two-year sentence for that offence and several accumulated minor ones as before. When the verdict was read out, he scoffed at it.

The door opened and Ellidi was brought into the hall by two wardens. He was powerfully built despite his age. Dark skinned, his head shaven bald. He had small ears with attached lobes but had nevertheless managed to pierce a hole in one from which a black swastika now dangled. His false teeth whistled when he spoke. He wore tattered jeans and a black T-shirt that revealed his thick biceps with tattoos up both arms. He towered well over six feet. They noticed he was handcuffed. One of his eyes was red, his face scratched and his upper lip swollen.

A psychopathic sadist, Erlendur said to himself.

The warders took up positions by the door and Ellidi went over to the table where he sat facing Erlendur and Sigurdur Óli. He sized them up with his grey, dull eyes, totally uninterested.

"Did you know a man called Holberg?" Erlendur asked.

Ellidi showed no response. Pretended he hadn't heard the question. He looked at Erlendur and Sigurdur Óli in turn with the same dull eyes. The warders spoke together in quiet voices by the door. Shouting could be heard from somewhere in the building. A door being slammed. Erlendur repeated his question, his words echoing around the empty hall. "Holberg! Do you remember him?"

Still he got no response from Ellidi, who looked aimlessly around the room, as though they weren't there. Some time elapsed in silence. Erlendur and Sigurdur Óli looked at one another and Erlendur asked the question a third time. Had he known Holberg, what was their relationship? Holberg was dead. Found murdered.

Ellidi's interest was aroused on hearing the last word. He put his stout arms on the table, rattling the handcuffs, unable to conceal his surprise. He looked inquisitively at Erlendur.

"Holberg was murdered at his home last weekend," Erlendur said. "We're talking to the people who knew him at various times and it seems the two of you were acquainted."

Ellidi had begun staring at Sigurdur Óli, who stared back. He didn't answer Erlendur.

"It's a routine . . ."

"I won't talk to you with these handcuffs on," Ellidi said suddenly, not taking his eyes off Sigurdur Óli. His voice was hoarse, rough and provocative. Erlendur thought for a moment, then stood up and went over to the two warders. He explained Ellidi's demand and asked whether his handcuffs could be removed. They hesitated, but then went over to him, undid the handcuffs and took up their posts at the door again.

"What can you tell us about Holberg?" Erlendur asked.

"They leave first," Ellidi said, nodding at the warders.

"Out of the question," Erlendur said.

"Are you a fucking poofter?" Ellidi asked, his gaze still fixed on Sigurdur Óli.

"Don't give us any of that crap," Erlendur said. Sigurdur Óli didn't answer him. They looked each other in the eye.

"Nothing's out of the question," Ellidi said. "Don't you go telling me anything's out of the question."

"They're not leaving," Erlendur said.

"Are you a poofter?" Ellidi said again, still staring at Sigurdur Óli, who showed no reaction.

They remained silent for a while. Eventually Erlendur stood up, went over to the two warders, repeated what Ellidi had said and asked if there was any chance of being left alone with him. The warders said that was impossible, they had orders not to leave the prisoner unattended. After some wrangling they let Erlendur talk to the governor over a two-way radio. Erlendur said it didn't make much difference which side of the door the warders stood, he and Sigurdur Óli had come all the way from Reykjavík and the prisoner was showing a degree of willingness to cooperate if certain conditions could be met. The governor talked to his men and said he'd take personal responsibility for the safety of the two detectives. The warders stepped outside and Erlendur went back to the table and sat down.

"Will you talk to us now?" he asked.

"I didn't know Holberg had been murdered," Ellidi said. "Those fascists put me in solitary for some shit I didn't do. How was he killed?" Ellidi was still glaring at Sigurdur Óli.

"None of your business," Erlendur said.

"My dad said I was the most curious bastard on earth. He was always saying that. None of your business. None of your business! He's dead. Was he stabbed? Was Holberg stabbed?"

"That's none of your business."

"None of my business!" Ellidi repeated and looked at Erlandur. "Fuck off then."

Erlendur thought for a moment. No-one outside the CID knew the details of the case. He was getting fed up with having to concede everything to this character.

"He was hit over the head. His skull was smashed. He died almost instantly."

"Was it a hammer?"

"An ashtray."

Ellidi slowly turned his gaze from Erlendur back to Sigurdur Óli.

"What kind of a wanker uses an ashtray?" he said. Erlendur noticed tiny beads of sweat forming on Sigurdur Óli's brow.

"That's what we're trying to find out," Erlendur said. "Have you been in touch with Holberg?"

"Did he suffer?"

"No."

"The jerk."

"Do you remember Grétar?" Erlendur asked. "He was with you and Holberg in Keflavík."

"Grétar?"

"Do you remember him?"

"What are you asking about him for?" Ellidi said. "What about him?"

"I understand Grétar went missing many years ago," Erlendur said. "Do you know anything about his disappearance?"

"What should I know about it?" Ellidi said. "What makes you think I know anything about it?"

"What were the three of you – you, Grétar and Holberg – doing in Keflavík . . ."

"Grétar was nuts," Ellidi said, interrupting Erlendur.

"What were you doing in Keflavík when . . ."

". . . he raped that pussy?" Ellidi cut in.

"What did you say?" Erlendur asked.

"Is that what you came here for? To ask about that pussy from Keflavík?"

"So you remember it?"

"What's that got to do with it?"

"I never said . . ."

"Holberg liked talking about it. Boasted. Got away with it. He did her twice, did you know that?" Ellidi said this bluntly and looked at them in turn.

"Are you talking about the rape in Keflavík?"

"What colour panties are you wearing, sweetie?" Ellidi turned on Sigurdur Óli, staring at him again. Erlendur looked at his colleague, whose eyes remained fixed on Ellidi.

"You watch your bloody mouth," Erlendur said.

"He asked her. Holberg. Asked about her panties. He was even madder than me." Ellidi giggled. "And they send me to the nick!"

"Who did he ask about the panties?"

"The chick from Keflavík."

"Did he tell you about it?"

"All the details," Ellidi said. "He was always talking about it. Anyway, what are you asking about Keflavík for? What's Keflavík got to do with it? And why are you asking about Grétar now? I don't get it."

"Just our boring routine work," Erlendur said.

"Right, so what do I get out of it?"

"You've got everything you want. We're sitting

alone here with you and your handcuffs are off. We have to listen to your filth. There's nothing else we can do for you. Either you answer the question now or we leave."

He couldn't resist the temptation. Reaching across the table he grabbed Ellidi's face in his strong hands and turned him towards him.

"Didn't your father ever tell you it's rude to stare?" he said. Sigurdur Óli looked at Erlendur.

"I can handle him. It's okay," he said.

Erlendur released his grip on Ellidi's face.

"How did you know Holberg?" he asked. Ellidi rubbed his jaw. He knew he'd just scored a minor victory. And he wasn't stopping there.

"Don't think I don't remember you," he said to Erlendur. "Don't think I don't know who you are. Don't think I don't know Eva."

Erlendur stared at the prisoner, thunderstruck. This wasn't the first time he'd heard this kind of thing from criminals, but he was never any less ill-prepared for it. He didn't know exactly who Eva Lind associated with but some of them were convicts, drug dealers, burglars, prostitutes, heavies. It was a long list. She'd been in trouble with the law herself. Once she was arrested after a tip-off from a parent for selling drugs at a school. She could easily know a man like Ellidi. A man like Ellidi could easily know her.

"How did you know Holberg?" Erlendur repeated.

"Eva's all right," Ellidi said. Erlendur could read countless meanings into his words.

"If you mention her again, we're gone," he said. "And then you won't have anyone to play with."

"Cigarettes, a telly in the cell, no fucking slavery and no more fucking solitary. Is that asking too much? Can't two supercops set that up? And it'd be nice to get a tart in here once a month or so. His chick for example," he said, pointing at Sigurdur Óli.

Erlendur stood up and Sigurdur Óli slowly rose to his feet. Ellidi started to laugh. A hoarse laugh that seethed inside him, progressed to a loud gurgling and culminated in him coughing up some yellow phlegm which he spat on the floor. They turned away from him and walked towards the door.

"He talked to me a lot about that rape in Keflavík!" he shouted after them. "Told me all about her. How that pussy squealed like a stuck pig and what he whispered in her ear while he waited to get it back up. Do you want to hear what that was? Do you want to hear what he said to her?! Fucking wankers! Do you want to hear what it was?!"

Erlendur and Sigurdur Óli stopped. They turned to see Ellidi shaking his head at them, foaming at the mouth and shrieking curses and oaths. He was on his feet, his hands on the table, leaning over it, stretching his big head in their direction and bellowing at them like a raging bull.

The hall door opened and the two warders stepped inside.

"He told her about the other one!" Ellidi screamed. "He told her what he did to the other fucking pussy he raped!"

14

When Ellidi saw the warders he went berserk. He leapt over the table, ran at the four men, screaming, and threw himself at them. He landed on top of Erlendur and Sigurdur Óli and they were both slammed to the ground before they could do a thing. He headbutted Sigurdur Óli, the blood spurted from both men's noses and his fist was raised to punch Erlendur's defenceless face when one of the warders took out a little black device and gave him an electric shock in his side. This slowed Ellidi down, but it didn't stop him. He raised his arm again. It was only when the other warder gave him a second electric shock that he slumped down and fell on top of Erlendur and Sigurdur Óli.

They crawled out from underneath him. Sigurdur Óli held a handkerchief to his nose to try to stop the bleeding. Ellidi was given a third electric shock and was finally still. The warders handcuffed him and, with great difficulty, lifted him up. They were going to take him out but Erlendur asked them to wait a moment. He went up to Ellidi.

"Which other one?" he asked.

Ellidi showed no reaction.

"Which other one that he raped?" Erlendur repeated.

Ellidi tried to smile, dazed by the electric shock, and a grimace moved across his face. Blood had run from his nose down into his mouth and his false teeth were bloody. Erlendur tried to conceal the eagerness in his voice, as if he couldn't care less what Ellidi knew. He tried not to make himself vulnerable. Tried not to show any expression. He knew that the slightest weakness made the heart of men like Ellidi pound, turned them into real men, gave them a purpose in their pitiful illusion of life. The slightest deviation would be enough. An eager tone in his voice, a sign in his eyes, a movement of his hands, a hint of impatience. Ellidi had managed to throw him off balance when he mentioned Eva Lind. Erlendur wasn't going to give him the pleasure of grovelling now.

They looked each other in the eye.

"Take him out," Erlendur said and turned away from Ellidi. The warders were about to lead the prisoner away but he stiffened and wouldn't budge when they tried to move him. He took a good, long look at Erlendur as if mulling something over, but eventually he gave in and allowed himself to be led from the room. Sigurdur Óli was still trying to stop the bleeding. His nose was swollen and his handkerchief was dripping with blood.

"That's a nasty nosebleed," Erlendur said and examined Sigurdur Óli's nose. "Nothing else though, nothing serious. There are no cuts and your nose isn't broken." He pinched it tight and Sigurdur Óli let out a shriek of pain.

"Oh, maybe it is broken, I'm no doctor," Erlendur said.

"That fucking bastard," Sigurdur Óli said. "That fucking bastard."

"Is he playing around with us or does he really know about another woman?" Erlendur said as they left the hall. "If there was one more perhaps there were others that Holberg raped who never came forward."

"There's no way to talk sense to that man," Sigurdur Óli said. "He was doing it for his own amusement, winding us up. He was playing with us. You can't trust a word he says. That jerk. That fucking jerk."

They went to the governor's office and gave him a brief report of what had happened. In their opinion, they said, the only place for Ellidi was a padded cell at a psychiatric ward. The governor agreed wearily, but said the only recourse available to the authorities was to keep him at Litla-Hraun. This wasn't the first time Ellidi had been confined to solitary for violence in the prison and it certainly wouldn't be the last.

They went out into the open air. As they were driving away from the prison and waiting for the big blue gate to the car park to open, Sigurdur Óli noticed a warder racing after them, waving to them to stop. They waited until he caught up with the car.

Erlendur wound down the window. "He wants to talk to you," the warder said, panting from running.

"Who?" Erlendur asked.

"Ellidi. Ellidi wants to talk to you."

"We've talked to Ellidi," Erlendur said. "Tell him to forget it."

"He says he's going to give you the information you want."

"He's lying."

"That's what he said."

Erlendur looked at Sigurdur Óli, who shrugged. He thought about it for a moment.

"Okay. We'll come then," he said eventually.

"He just wants you, not him," said the warder, looking at Sigurdur Óli.

Ellidi wasn't let out of his solitary cell again, so Erlendur had to talk to him through a small hole in the door. It was opened by sliding a panel to one side. The cell was dark, so Erlendur could not see in. He could only hear Ellidi's voice, hoarse and gurgling. The warder had led Erlendur to the door and then left him alone.

"How's the poofter?" was the first thing Ellidi asked. Instead of standing up at the hole in the door, he had retreated inside. Maybe he was lying on the bed. Maybe he was sitting up against a wall. Erlendur felt as if the voice was coming from deep inside the darkness. He had obviously calmed down.

"This isn't a tea party," Erlendur replied. "You wanted to talk to me."

"Who do you reckon killed Holberg?"

"We don't know. What about Holberg?"

"Her name was Kolbrún, the chick he did in Keflavík. He often talked about it. Talked about how close he was to getting caught when that pussy was stupid enough to press charges. He described all the details. Do you want to hear what he said?"

"No," said Erlendur. "What was your relationship with him?"

"We met up now and again. I sold him booze and bought porn for him while I was on the ships. We met when we were working together for the Harbour and Lighthouse Authority. Before he started lorry driving. We went into the towns together. You never get a lost fuck back. That was the first thing he taught me. He knew how to talk. Impressive. Good at talking women round. A fun bloke."

"You went into the towns?"

"That's why we were in Keflavík. We were painting the Reykjanes lighthouse. Fucking awful ghosts there. Ever been there? Screeching and howling all night. Worse than this shithole. Holberg wasn't scared of ghosts. He wasn't scared of anything."

"And he told you straightaway how he'd assaulted Kolbrún, when he'd only just met you?"

"He winked at me when he followed her out of the party. I knew what that meant. He could be a charmer. He thought it was funny to get away with it. Laughed a lot at some cop the girl went to and ruined her case for her."

"Did they know each other, Holberg and this cop?"

"I don't know."

"Did he ever talk about the daughter Kolbrún gave birth to after the rape?"

"Daughter? No. Did he get her pregnant?"

"You know about another rape," Erlendur said without answering him. "Another woman he raped. Who was it? What was her name?"

"I don't know."

"So why did you call me back?"

"I don't know who it was but I know when it was and where she lived. More or less. That's enough for you to find her."

"When? And where?"

"Yeah, right, what do I get?"

"You?"

"What can you do for me?"

"I can't do anything for you and I don't want to do anything for you."

"Sure you do. Then I'll tell you what I know."

Erlendur pondered.

"I can't promise anything," he said.

"I can't stand being in solitary."

"Was that why you called me back?"

"You don't know what it does to you. I'm going mad in this cell. They never put the light on. I don't know what day it is. You're kept here like an animal in a cage. They treat you like a beast."

"And what, you're the Count of Monte Cristo!" Erlendur said sarcastically. "You're a sadist, Ellidi.

The worst sort of psychopath and sadist there is. A dumb idiot who likes violence. A homophobe and a racist. You're the worst type of retard I know. I don't care if they keep you locked up in here for the rest of your life. I'm going upstairs to recommend just that."

"I'll tell you where she lived if you get me out of here."

"I can't get you out of here, you idiot. I don't have the authority to and, even if I did, I wouldn't. If you want to cut your solitary short perhaps you should stop attacking people."

"You could do a deal on it. Say you wound me up. Say that poofter started it. I was cooperative, but he was making smart-arse remarks. And I helped you with your enquiries. They'll listen to you. I know who you are. They'll listen to you."

"Did Holberg talk about any others apart from those two?"

"Are you going to do that for me?"

Erlendur thought about it. "I'll see what I can do. Did he talk about any others?"

"No. Never. I only knew about those two."

"Are you lying?"

"I'm not lying. The other one never pressed charges. It was in the early '6os. He never went back to that place."

"What place?"

"Are you going to get me out of here?"

"What place?"

"Promise!"

"I can't promise anything," Erlendur said. "I'll talk to them. What place was it?"

"Húsavík."

"How old was she?"

"It was the same sort of job as the one in Keflavík, only more ferocious," Ellidi said.

"Ferocious?"

"Don't you want to hear it?" Ellidi said, unable to conceal his eagerness. "Do you want to hear what he did?"

Ellidi didn't wait for an answer. His voice poured out through the hole in the door and Erlendur stood there, listening to the hoarse confession coming from the darkness.

Sigurdur Óli was waiting for him in the car. As they drove away from the prison Erlendur gave a short account of his conversation with Ellidi but kept quiet about the monologue at the end. They decided to look at the register of people who lived in Húsavík in the years around 1960. If the woman was a similar age to Kolbrún, as Ellidi had implied, it was just possible she could be found.

"And what about Ellidi?" Sigurdur Óli asked when they were back in the Threngslin Pass on their way to Reykjavík.

"I asked if they'd reduce his solitary confinement and they refused. There was nothing else I could do."

"You kept your promise at least," Sigurdur Óli

smiled. "If Holberg raped those two, couldn't there have been more?"

"There could have been," Erlendur said vacantly.

"What are you thinking about now?"

"There are two things that bother me," Erlendur said. "I'd like to know precisely what it was that the little girl died of." He could hear Sigurdur Óli heave a sigh beside him. "And I'd like to know if she was definitely Holberg's child."

"So what's puzzling you about that?"

"Ellidi told me Holberg had a sister."

"A sister?"

"Who died young. We need to find her medical records. Look for them at the hospitals. See what you can come up with."

"What did she die of? Holberg's sister?"

"Possibly something similar to Audur. Holberg mentioned something about her head once. Or that was how Ellidi described it. I asked if it could have been a brain tumour, but Ellidi didn't know."

"And how does that help our case?" Sigurdur Óli asked.

"I think there could be a kinship connection," Erlendur said.

"Kinship? What, because of the message we found?"

"Yes," Erlendur said, "because of the message. Maybe it's a question of kinship and heredity."

15

The doctor lived in a town house on the west side of the Grafarvogur suburb. He no longer held a regular medical practice. He welcomed Erlendur at the door himself and showed him into the spacious hallway that he used as an office. He explained to Erlendur that he now did occasional work for lawyers on cases of disability assessment. The office area was simply furnished, tidy, with a little desk and type-writer. The doctor was a short, rather thin man with sharp features. He had a sprightly manner about him. He carried two pens in the breast pocket of the shirt he was wearing. His name was Frank.

Erlendur had phoned beforehand to arrange an appointment. The afternoon was wearing on and it was beginning to get dark. Back at the station, Sigurdur Óli and Elínborg huddled over a photo-copy of a 40-year-old register of the inhabitants of Húsavík which had been faxed to them by the local government office in the north. The doctor asked Erlendur to sit down.

"Isn't it just a pack of liars who come to see you?" Erlendur asked, looking around the office.

"Liars?" the doctor said. "I wouldn't say that.

Some of them, undoubtedly. Neck injuries are the most tricky. You really can't do anything but believe patients who complain of neck injuries after a car accident. They're the most difficult to handle. Some feel more pain than others but I don't think there are many who aren't genuinely in a great deal of discomfort."

"When I phoned you remembered the girl in Keflavík immediately."

"That sort of thing's difficult to forget. Difficult to forget the mother. Kolbrún, wasn't that her name? I understand she committed suicide."

"It's a bloody tragedy from start to finish," Erlendur said. He wondered whether to ask the doctor about the pain he felt in his chest when he woke up in the mornings, but decided this was not the time. The doctor was bound to discover he was fatally ill, send him to hospital and he'd be playing the harp with the angels by the weekend. Erlendur tried to avoid bad news whenever possible and, as he didn't expect to hear any good news about himself, he kept quiet.

"You said it was to do with the murder in Nordurmýri," the doctor said, snapping Erlendur back to reality.

"Yes, Holberg, the murder victim, may have been the father of the girl in Keflavík," Erlendur said. "The mother claimed so all along. Holberg neither confirmed nor denied it. He admitted having sex with Kolbrún so rape couldn't be proved against him. Often there's very little evidence on which to base that kind of case. We're investigating the man's past. The girl fell ill and died in her fourth year. Can you tell me what happened?"

"I don't see how that could have anything to do with the murder case."

"Well, we'll see. Could you answer my question please?"

The doctor took a good long look at Erlendur.

"It's probably best for me to tell you straight-away, Inspector," the doctor said, as if steeling himself for something. "I was a different man at that time."

"A different man?"

"And a worse one. I haven't touched alcohol for almost 30 years now. I'll be honest about this up front, so you don't need to put yourself to any more bother, I had my GP licence suspended from 1969 to 1972."

"Because of the little girl?"

"No, no, not because of her, though that would have been ample reason in its own right. It was because of drinking and negligence. I'd rather not go into that unless it's absolutely necessary."

Erlendur wanted to let the matter rest there, but couldn't restrain himself.

"So you were drunk more or less all those years, you mean?"

"More or less."

"Was your GP licence reinstated?"

"Yes."

"And no other trouble since then?"

"No, no other trouble since then," the doctor said, shaking his head. "But, as I say, I wasn't in a good state when I looked after Kolbrún's girl. Audur. She had head pains and I thought it was child migraine. She used to vomit in the mornings. When the pain got worse I gave her stronger medication. It's all rather a blur to me. I've chosen to forget as much as I can from that time. Everyone can make mistakes, doctors too."

"What was the cause of death?"

"It probably wouldn't have made any difference if I'd acted faster and sent her to hospital," the doctor said thoughtfully. "At least that's what I tried to tell myself. There weren't many paediatricians around then and we didn't have those brain scans. We had to act much more on what we felt and knew and, as I said, I didn't feel anything much except the need to drink in those years. A messy divorce didn't help. I'm not making excuses for myself," he said with a look at Erlendur, although he obviously was.

Erlendur nodded.

"After about two months, I think, I started to suspect it could be something more serious than child migraine. The girl didn't get any better. It didn't let up. She just got worse and worse. Withered away, got very skinny. There were a number of possibilities. I thought it might be something like a tubercular infection of the head. At one time the stock diagnosis was to call it a head cold when actually no-one had a clue. Then the hypothesis was meningitis, but various symptoms were absent; it works much faster too. The girl got what they call *café au lait* on her skin and I finally started thinking about an oncogenic disease."

"*Café au lait*?" Erlendur said, remembering he had heard this mentioned before.

"It can accompany oncogenic diseases."

"You sent her to Keflavík hospital then?"

"She died there," the doctor said. "I remember what a tragic loss it was for the mother. She went out of her mind. We had to tranquillise her. She flatly refused to let them do an autopsy on the girl. Screamed at us not to do it."

"But they did an autopsy all the same."

The doctor hesitated.

"It couldn't be avoided. There was no way."

"And what transpired?"

"An oncogenic disease, like I said."

"What do you mean by an oncogenic disease?"

"A brain tumour," the doctor said. "She died of a brain tumour."

"What kind of brain tumour?"

"I'm not sure," the doctor said. "I don't know whether they studied it in depth though I expect they probably did. I seem to recall mention of some kind of genetic disease."

"Genetic disease!" Erlendur said, raising his voice.

"Isn't that the fashion these days? What does this

have to do with Holberg's murder?" the doctor
asked.

Erlendur sat there deep in thought.

"Why are you asking about this girl?"

"I have these dreams," Erlendur said.

16

Eva Lind wasn't in the flat when Erlendur returned home that evening. He tried to follow her advice not to dwell on where she was, whether she'd come back and what kind of state she'd be in if she did. He'd called in at a takeaway and picked up a bag of fried chicken for dinner. He threw it down on a chair and was taking off his coat when he smelled the familiar old aroma of cooking. He hadn't smelled something being cooked in his kitchen for a very long time. Chicken like that lying on the chair was his food, hamburgers, takeaways from the greasy spoon, ready meals from the supermarket, cold boiled sheep head, tubs of curds, tasteless microwave dinners. He couldn't remember the last time he'd actually cooked himself a proper meal in the kitchen. He couldn't remember when he'd last even wanted to.

Erlendur carefully made his way to the kitchen as if expecting to find an intruder there and saw that the table had been laid for two with beautiful plates that he vaguely recalled owning. Wine glasses on high stalks stood beside each plate, there were serviettes and red candles burning in two candleholders that didn't match and which Erlendur had never seen before.

Slowly he made his way further into the kitchen and saw something simmering in a big pot. Lifting the lid, he looked down at a particularly delicious-looking meat stew. A slick of cooking oil was floating above turnips, potatoes, cubes of meat and spices, the whole thing giving off an aroma that filled his flat with the smell of real home cooking. He stooped over the pot and inhaled the smell of boiled meat and vegetables.

"I needed some more veg," Eva Lind said at the kitchen door. Erlendur hadn't noticed her enter the flat. She was wearing his anorak and holding a bag of carrots.

"Where did you learn to make meat stew?" Erlendur asked.

"Mum was always making meat stew," Eva Lind said. "Once when she wasn't bad-mouthing you she said her meat stew used to be your favourite meal. Then she said you were a bastard."

"Right on both counts," Erlendur said. He watched Eva Lind chop up the carrots and add them to the pot with the other vegetables. The thought occurred to him that he was experiencing proper family life and it made him both sad and happy at the same time. He didn't allow himself the luxury of expecting this joy to last.

"Have you found the murderer?" Eva Lind asked.

"Ellidi sends his regards," Erlendur said. The words had escaped before he could entertain the notion that a beast like Ellidi didn't belong in this environment.

"Ellidi. He's at Litla-Hraun. Does he know who I am?"

"The scumbags I talk to mention you by name sometimes," Erlendur said. "They think they're scoring points off me."

"And are they?"

"Some of them. Like Ellidi. How do you know him?" Erlendur asked cautiously.

"I've heard stories about him. Met him once years ago. He'd stuck his false teeth in with plastic glue. But I don't really know him."

"He's an incredible idiot."

They didn't talk about Ellidi any more that evening. When they sat down to eat, Eva Lind poured water into the wine glasses and Erlendur ate so much that he could barely stagger into the sitting room afterwards. He fell asleep there in his clothes and slept badly until the morning.

This time he remembered most of the dream. He knew it was the same dream that had visited him in recent nights but which he had failed to get hold of before the waking state turned it into nothing.

Eva Lind appeared to him as he had never seen her before enveloped in a light coming from somewhere he couldn't tell in a beautiful summer dress reaching down to her ankles and with long dark hair down to her back and the vision was perfect almost scented with summer and she walked towards him or maybe

*she floated because he thought to himself that she
never touched the ground he could not identify the
surroundings all he could see was that glaring light
and Eva Lind in the middle of the light approached
him smiling from ear to ear and he saw himself open
his arms to greet her and wait to be able to hold her
and he felt his impatience but she never entered his
arms but handed him a photograph and the light
disappeared and Eva Lind disappeared and he was
holding the photo he knew so well that was taken in
the cemetery and the photograph came to life and he
was inside it and looked up at the dark sky and felt
the raining pounding down on his face and when he
looked down he saw the tombstone drop back and
the grave opened into the darkness until the coffin
appeared and it opened and he saw the girl in the
coffin cut along the middle of her torso and up to
her shoulders and suddenly the girl opened her eyes
and stared up towards him and she opened her
mouth and he heard her pitiful cry of anguish from
the grave*

He woke with a start gasping for breath and
stared into space while he collected himself. He
called out to Eva Lind but received no reply. He
walked to her room but sensed the emptiness there
before he even opened the door. He knew she had
left.

After examining the register of the inhabitants of
Húsavík, Elínborg and Sigurdur Óli had compiled a

list of 176 women who were potential victims of rape by Holberg. All they had to go on was Ellidi's word that it had been "the same sort of job", so they used Kolbrún's age as a reference with a ten-year deviation either side. On first examination it emerged that the women could be roughly divided into three groups: a quarter of them still lived in Húsavík, half had moved to Reykjavík and the remaining quarter was scattered throughout Iceland.

"Enough to drive you mad," Elínborg sighed, looking down the list before she handed it to Erlendur. She noticed he was scruffier than usual. The stubble on his face was several days old, his bushy ginger hair stood out in all directions, his tatty and crumpled suit needed dry-cleaning: Elínborg was wondering whether to offer to point this out to him, but Erlendur's expression didn't invite any joking.

"How are you sleeping these days, Erlendur?" she asked guardedly.

"On my arse," Erlendur said.

"And then what?" Sigurdur Óli said. "Should we just walk up to each of these women and ask if they were raped 40 years ago? Isn't that a bit . . . brash?"

"I can't see any other way to do it. Let's start with the ones who've moved away from Húsavík," Erlendur said. "We'll start looking in Reykjavík and see if we can't gather any more information about this woman in the process. If that stupid bugger Ellidi isn't lying, Holberg mentioned her to Kolbrún.

She may well have repeated it, to her sister, maybe to Rúnar. I need to go back to Keflavík."

"Maybe we can narrow the group down a bit," he said, after a moment's thought.

"Narrow it down? How?" said Elínborg. "What are you thinking?"

"I just had an idea."

"What?" Elínborg was impatient already. She'd turned up for work in a new, pale green dress suit that no-one seemed likely to pay any attention to.

"Kinship, heredity and diseases," Erlendur said.

"Right," Sigurdur Óli said.

"Let's assume Holberg was the rapist. We have no idea how many women he raped. We know about two and actually about only one for certain. Even though he denied it, everything points to the fact that he did rape Kolbrún. He was Audur's father, or, at least, we should work on that assumption, but he could equally have had another child with the woman from Húsavík."

"Another child?" Elínborg said.

"Before Audur," Erlendur said.

"Isn't that unlikely?" Sigurdur Óli said.

Erlendur shrugged.

"Do you want us to narrow the group down to women who had children just before, what was it, 1964?"

"I don't think that would be such a bad idea."

"He could have kids all over the place," Elínborg said.

"True. He didn't necessarily commit more than

121

one rape either so it's a long shot," Erlendur said. "Did you find out what his sister died of?"

"No, I'm working on it," Sigurdur Óli said. "I tried to find out about their family, but nothing came out of it."

"I checked on Grétar," Elínborg said. "He disappeared suddenly, like the ground had opened up and swallowed him. No-one missed him in the slightest. When his mother hadn't heard from him for two whole months she finally phoned the police. They put his picture in the papers and on TV but drew a blank. It was in 1974, the year of the big festival to commemorate the settlement of Iceland. In the summer. Did you go to the festival at Thingvellir then?"

"I was there," Erlendur said. "What about Thingvellir? Do you think that's where he went missing?"

"Perhaps, but that's all I know," Elínborg said. "They made a routine missing-persons investigation and talked to people his mother knew that he knew, including Holberg and Ellidi. They questioned three others too but no-one knew anything. No-one missed Grétar except his mother and sister. He was born in Reykjavík, no wife or children, no girlfriend, no extended family. The case was left open for a few months and then it just died. He was 34."

"If he was as pleasant as his mates Ellidi and Holberg, I'm not surprised nobody missed him," Sigurdur Óli said.

"Thirteen people went missing in Iceland in the 1970s when Grétar disappeared," Elínborg said.

"Twelve in the 1980s, not counting fishermen lost at sea."

"Thirteen disappearances," Sigurdur Óli said, "isn't that rather a lot? None of them solved?"

"There doesn't have to be anything criminal behind it," Elínborg said. "People disappear, want to disappear, make themselves disappear."

"If I understand correctly," Erlendur said, "the scenario is like this: Ellidi, Holberg and Grétar are having a night out at a dance in the Cross one weekend in the autumn of 1963."

He saw that Sigurdur Óli's face was one huge question mark.

"The Cross was an old military hospital post that was converted into a dancehall. They used to hold really raunchy dances there."

"I think that was where the Icelandic Beatles started playing," Elínborg interjected.

"They meet some women at the dance and one of the women has a party at her house afterwards," Erlendur went on. "We need to try to find these women. Holberg walks one of them home and rapes her. Apparently he'd played the same trick before. He whispers to her what he did to another woman. She might have lived in Húsavík and in all likelihood never pressed charges. Three days later Kolbrún has finally plucked up the courage to report the crime but runs into a policeman who has no sympathy for women who invite men in after a dance and then shout rape. Kolbrún has a baby girl. Holberg could have known about the baby, we find a photo of her gravestone in his desk. Who took it? Why? The girl dies from a fatal illness and her mother commits suicide three years later. Three years after that, one of Holberg's mates disappears. Holberg is murdered a few days ago and an incomprehensible message is left behind.

"Why was Holberg murdered now, in his old age? Was his attacker connected to this background? And, if so, why wasn't Holberg attacked before? Why all the wait? Or didn't his murder have anything to do with the fact, if it is a fact, that Holberg was a rapist?"

"It doesn't look like premeditated murder, I don't think we can ignore that," Sigurdur Óli interjected. "As Ellidi put it, what kind of wanker uses an ashtray? It's not as if there was a long historical build-up to it. The message is just a joke, indecipherable. Holberg's murder doesn't have anything to do with any rape. We should probably be looking for the young man in the green army jacket."

"Holberg was no angel," Elínborg said. "Maybe it's a revenge murder. Someone probably thought he deserved it."

"The only person we know for certain who hated Holberg is Kolbrún's sister in Keflavík," Erlendur said. "I can't imagine her killing anyone with an ashtray."

"Couldn't she have got someone else to do it?" said Sigurdur Óli.

"Who?" Erlendur asked.

"I don't know. Anyway, I'm coming round to the

idea that someone was prowling around the neighbourhood planning to break in somewhere, burgle the place and maybe smash it up, Holberg caught him and got hit over the head with the ashtray. It was some junkie who couldn't tell his arse from his elbow. Nothing to do with the past, just the present. Reykjavík the way it is these days."

"At least, someone thought the right thing to do was to bump him off," Elínborg said. "We have to take the message seriously. It's no joke."

Sigurdur Óli looked at Erlendur. "When you talked about wanting to know precisely what the girl died of, do you mean what I think you mean?" he asked.

"I have a nasty feeling I might," Erlendur said.

17

Rúnar answered the door himself and looked at Erlendur for a good while without being able to place his face. Erlendur was standing in a communal hallway, soaking wet after running from the car to building. To his right was a staircase leading to the upper flat. The stairs were carpeted but the carpet was worn through where it had been walked on the most. There was a musty smell in the air and Erlendur wondered whether horse-lovers lived in the house. Erlendur asked Rúnar whether he remembered him and Rúnar seemed to do so, because he immediately tried to slam the door, but Erlendur was too fast for him. He was inside the flat before Rúnar could do a thing about it.

"Cosy," Erlendur said, looking around the dim interior.

"Will you leave me alone!" Rúnar tried to shout at Erlendur, but his voice cracked and squeaked.

"Watch your blood pressure. I'd hate to have to give you the kiss of life if you dropped dead on me. I need to get some details from you and then I'm gone and you can get back to dying in here. Shouldn't take you very long. You don't exactly look like Super Senior of the Year."

"Bugger off!" Rúnar said, as angrily as his age allowed him, turned round, walked into the sitting room and sat down on the sofa. Erlendur followed him and sat down heavily in a chair facing him. Rúnar didn't look at him.

"Did Kolbrún talk about another rape when she came to you about Holberg?"

Rúnar didn't answer him.

"The sooner you answer, the sooner you get rid of me."

Rúnar looked up and stared at Erlendur.

"She never mentioned any other rape. Will you leave now?"

"We have reason to believe that Holberg had raped someone before he met Kolbrún. He may have played the same trick again after her raped her, we don't know. Kolbrún is the only woman who pressed charges against him even if nothing ever came of it, thanks to you."

"Get out!"

"Are you sure she didn't mention any other woman? It's conceivable that Holberg bragged to Kolbrún about another rape."

"She didn't say a thing about that," Rúnar said, looking down at the table.

"Holberg was with two of his friends that night. One of them was Ellidi, an old lag you might know of. He's in prison, fighting ghosts and monsters in solitary confinement. The other one was Grétar. He vanished off the face of the earth the summer the national festival was held. Do you know anything about the company Holberg kept?"

"No. Leave me alone!"

"What were they doing in town here the night Kolbrún was raped?"

"I don't know."

"Didn't you ever talk to them?"

"No."

"Who handled the investigation in Reykjavík?"

Rúnar looked Erlendur in the face for the first time.

"It was Marion Briem."

"Marion Briem!"

"That bloody idiot."

Elín wasn't at home when Erlendur knocked on her door, so he got back inside his car, lit a cigarette and pondered whether to continue on his journey to Sandgerði. The rain beat down on the car and Erlendur, who never watched the weather forecasts, wondered whether the wet spell would ever come to an end. Maybe this was a mini-version of Noah's flood, he thought to himself through the blue cigarette smoke. Maybe it was necessary to wash people's sins away every now and again.

Erlendur was apprehensive about meeting Elín again and was half relieved when it turned out she wasn't home. He knew she'd turn on him and the last thing he wanted was to provoke her, as when she called him a "bloody cop". But it couldn't be avoided. Either now or later. He heaved a deep sigh and burnt his cigarette down until he felt the heat against his fingertips. He held down the smoke while he stubbed out the cigarette, then exhaled heavily. A line from an anti-smoking campaign ran through his mind: It only takes one cell to start cancer.

He'd felt the pain in his chest that morning, but it had gone now.

Erlendur was backing away from the house when Elín knocked on his window.

"Were you coming to see me?" she asked from under her umbrella when he wound down the window.

Erlendur put on an inscrutable smile and gave a slight nod. She opened the door to her house for him and he suddenly felt like a traitor. The others had already set off for the cemetery.

He took off his hat and hung it on a peg, took off his coat and shoes and went into the sitting room in his crumpled suit. He was wearing a brown sleeveless cardigan under his jacket but hadn't done it up properly, so there was no hole for the bottom button. He sat in the same chair as when he had visited the house the last time. Elín had gone into the kitchen to switch on the coffee maker and the aroma began to fill the house. When she returned she sat in a chair facing him.

The traitor cleared his throat. "One of the people out on the town with Holberg the night he raped Kolbrún is called Ellidi and he's a prisoner at Litla-Hraun. It's a long time now since we started calling him 'one of the usual suspects'. The third man was called Grétar. He disappeared off the face of the earth in 1974. The year of the national festival."

"I was at Thingvellir then," Elín said. "I saw the poets there."

Erlendur cleared his throat again.

"And did you talk to this Ellidi?" Elín went on.

"A particularly nasty piece of work," Erlendur said.

Elín excused herself, stood up and went into the kitchen. He heard cups clinking. Erlendur's mobile phone rang in his jacket pocket and he held his breath as he answered it. He could see from the caller ID that it was Sigurdur Óli.

"We're ready," Sigurdur Óli said. Erlendur could hear it raining over the phone.

"Don't do anything until I get back to you," Erlendur said. "You understand? Don't make a move until you hear from me or I turn up there."

"Have you talked to the old bag?"

Without answering, Erlendur hung up and put the phone back in his pocket. Elín came in carrying a tray, put cups on the table in front of Erlendur and poured coffee for them both. They both took it black. She put the coffee pot on the table and sat down facing Erlendur. He began again.

"Ellidi told us Holberg had raped another woman before Kolbrún and probably bragged about it to her." He saw the look of astonishment on Elín's face.

"If Kolbrún knew about someone else, she never

told me," she said and shook her head thoughtfully. "Could he be telling the truth?"

"We have to act on that assumption," Erlendur said. "Ellidi's so strung out he could lie about that sort of thing. But we haven't got our hands on anything to refute what he says."

"We didn't talk about the rape very often," Elín said. "I think that was because of Audur. Among other things. Kolbrún was a very reticent woman, shy, withdrawn, and she closed up even more after what happened. And of course it was repulsive to talk about that awful experience when she was pregnant by it, not to mention after the child was born. Kolbrún did everything she could to forget that the rape ever happened. Everything to do with it."

"I imagine if Kolbrún knew about another woman she'd have told the police to back up her own statement, if nothing else. But she didn't mention a word of it in any of the reports I've read."

"Maybe she wanted to spare the woman," Elín said.

"Spare her?"

"Kolbrún knew what it was like to suffer a rape. She knew what it was like to report a rape. She hesitated about it a lot herself and all that seemed to come out of it was humiliation. If the other woman didn't want to come forward, Kolbrún may have respected her wishes. I'd imagine so. But it's difficult to say, I'm not sure exactly what you're talking about."

"She may not have known any details, no name, maybe just a vague suspicion. If he only implied something through what he said."

"She never talked about anything like that to me."

"When you talked about the rape, in what terms was it?"

"It wasn't exactly about the act itself," Elín said.

The phone in Erlendur's pocket rang again and Elín stopped talking. Erlendur pulled the phone out and saw that it was Sigurdur Óli. Erlendur just switched it off and put it away.

"Sorry," he said.

"Aren't they a real pest, those phones?"

"Absolutely," Erlendur said. He was running out of time. "Please, go on."

"She talked about how much she loved her daughter, Audur. They had a very special relationship despite those awful circumstances. Audur meant the world to Kolbrún. I know it's a terrible thing to say, but I don't think she would have wanted to miss out on being a mother. Do you understand that? I even thought she regarded Audur as some kind of compensation, or something, for the rape. I know it's a clumsy way to put it, but it was as if the girl was some kind of godsend amidst all that misfortune. I can't say what my sister thought, how she felt or what feelings she kept to herself, I only have a limited picture of that and I wouldn't presume to speak for her. But as time went by she came to worship her little girl and never let her out of her sight. Never. Their relationship was strongly coloured by what had happened, but Kolbrún never thought of her in terms of the beast who ruined her life. She only saw the beautiful child that Audur was. My sister was overprotective of her daughter and that went beyond death and the grave, as the epitaph shows. 'Preserve my life from fear of the enemy.' "

"Do you know exactly what your sister meant by those words?"

"It was a plea to God, as you'll see if you read the Psalm. Naturally, the little girl's death had something to do with it. How it happened and how tragic it was. Kolbrún couldn't bear the thought of Audur having an autopsy. She wouldn't think of it."

Erlendur looked awkwardly at the floor but Elín didn't notice.

"You could easily imagine," Elín said, "how those terrible things that Kolbrún went through, the rape and then her daughter's death, had a serious effect on her mental health. She had a nervous breakdown. When they started talking about an autopsy her paranoia built up, and in her need to protect Audur she saw the doctors as enemies. She had her daughter in those terrible circumstances and lost her so soon. She saw that as God's will. My sister wanted her daughter to be left in peace."

Erlendur waited a moment before he made his move.

"I think I'm one of those enemies."

Elín looked at him, not understanding what he meant.

"I think we need to dig up the coffin and do a more precise autopsy, if that's possible."

Erlendur said this as carefully as he could. It took Elín a while to understand his words and put them in context, and when their meaning had sunk in she gave him a blank look.

"What are you saying?"

"We may be able to find an explanation for why she died."

"Explanation? It was a brain tumour!"

"It could be . . ."

"What are you talking about? Dig her up? The child? I don't believe it! I was just telling you . . ."

"We have two reasons."

"Two reasons?"

"For the autopsy," Erlendur said.

Elín had stood up and was pacing the room in a frenzy. Erlendur sat tight and had sunk deeper into the soft armchair.

"I've talked to the doctors at the hospital here in Keflavík. They couldn't find any reports about Audur except a provisional post-mortem by the doctor who performed the autopsy. He's dead now. The year Audur died was his last year as a doctor at the hospital. He mentioned only the brain tumour and ascribed her death to that. I want to know what kind of disease it was that caused her death.

I want to know if it could have been a hereditary disease."

"A hereditary disease! I don't know about any hereditary diseases."

"We're also looking for it in Holberg," Erlendur said. "Another reason for an exhumation is to make sure that Audur was Holberg's daughter. They do it with DNA tests."

"Do you doubt that she is?"

"Not necessarily, but it has to be confirmed."

"Why?"

"Holberg denied the child was his. He said he'd had sex with Kolbrún with her consent but denied the paternity. When the case was dropped they didn't see any particular grounds for proving it or otherwise. Your sister never insisted on anything like that. She'd obviously had enough and wanted Holberg out of her life."

"Who else could have been the father?"

"We need confirmation because of Holberg's murder. It might help us find some answers."

"Holberg's murder?"

"Yes."

Elín stood over Erlendur, staring at him.

"Is that monster going to torment us all beyond the grave?"

Erlendur was about to answer, but she went on.

"You still think my sister was lying," Elín said. "You're never going to believe her. You're no better than that idiot Rúnar. Not in the slightest."

She bent over him where he was sitting in the chair.

"Bloody cop!" she hissed. "I should never have let you into my house."

18

Sigurdur Óli saw the car headlights approaching in the rain and knew it was Erlendur. The hydraulic digger rumbled as it took up a position by the grave, ready to start digging when the signal was given. It was a mini-digger that had chugged between the graves with jerks and starts. Its caterpillar tracks slid in the mud. It spewed out clouds of black smoke and filled the air with a thick stench of oil.

Sigurdur Óli and Elínborg stood by the grave with a pathologist, a lawyer from the Public Prosecutor's office, a minister and churchwarden, several policemen from Keflavík and two council workers. The group stood in the rain, envying Elínborg, who was the only one with an umbrella, and Sigurdur Óli, who had been allowed to stand half under it. They noticed Erlendur was alone when he got out of his car and slowly walked towards them. They had papers authorising the exhumation, which was not to begin until Erlendur gave his permission.

Erlendur surveyed the area, silently rueing the disruption, the damage, the desecration. The gravestone had been removed and laid on a pathway near the grave. Beside it was a green jar with a long point on the base that could be stuck down into the soil. The jar contained a withered bunch of roses and Erlendur thought to himself that Elín must have put it on the grave. He stopped, read the epitaph once again and shook his head. The white wooden pegging to mark out the grave, which had stood barely eight inches up from the ground, now lay broken beside the headstone. Erlendur had seen that kind of fencing around children's graves, and it pained him to see it discarded this way. He looked up into the black sky. Water dripped from the brim of his hat onto his shoulders and he squinted against the falling rain. He scanned the group standing by the digger, finally looked at Sigurdur Óli and nodded. Sigurdur Óli made a sign to the digger operator. The bucket rose into the air then plunged deep into the porous soil.

Erlendur watched the digger tear up 30-year-old wounds. He winced at each thrust of the bucket. The pile of soil steadily grew and the deeper the hole became, the more darkness it consumed. Erlendur stood some distance away and watched the bucket digging deeper and deeper into the wound. Suddenly he felt a sensation of déjà-vu, as if he had seen this all before in a dream, and for an instant the scene in front of him took on a dreamlike atmosphere: his colleagues standing there looking into the grave, the council workers in their orange overalls leaning forward onto their shovels, the minister in the big black overcoat, the rain that poured down into the grave and came back up in the bucket as if the hole were bleeding.

Had he dreamt it exactly like this?

Then the sensation disappeared and as always when something like that happened he couldn't begin to understand where it had come from; why he felt he was reliving events that had never happened before. Erlendur didn't believe in premonitions, visions or dreams, nor reincarnation or karma, he didn't believe in God although he'd often read the Bible, nor in eternal life or that his conduct in this world would affect whether he went to heaven or hell. He felt that life itself offered a mixture of the two.

Then sometimes he experienced this incomprehensible and supernatural déjà-vu, experienced time and place as if he'd seen it all before, as if he stepped outside himself, became an onlooker to his own life. There was no way he could explain what it was that happened or why his mind played tricks on him like this.

Erlendur came back to his senses when the bucket struck the lid of the coffin and a hollow clunk was heard from inside the grave. He moved a step closer. Through the rainwater pouring down into the hole he saw the vague outline of the coffin.

"Careful!" Erlendur shouted at the digger operator, throwing his hands up in the air.

Out of the corner of his eye he saw car headlights approaching. They all looked up in the direction of the lights and saw a car crawling along in the rain until it stopped by the cemetery gate. An old lady in a green coat got out. They noticed the taxi sign on the car roof. The taxi drove off and the lady stormed towards the grave. As soon as Erlendur was within earshot she started shouting and waving her fist at him.

"Grave-robber!" he heard Elín shout. "Grave-robbers! Body-snatchers!"

"Keep her back," Erlendur said calmly to the policemen who walked over to Elín and stopped her when she was only a few yards from the grave. She tried to fight them off in her frenzy of rage but they held her arms and restrained her.

The two council workers climbed into the grave with their shovels, dug around the coffin and put ropes around the ends of it. It was fairly intact. The rain pounded on the lid with a hollow thudding, washing the soil from it. Erlendur imagined it would have been white. A tiny white casket with brass handles and a cross on the lid. The men tied the ropes to the bucket of the digger which very carefully lifted Audur's coffin out of the ground. It was still in one piece but looked extremely fragile. Erlendur saw Elín had stopped struggling and shouting at him. She'd started to cry when the white casket emerged and hung motionless in the ropes above the grave before being lowered to the ground. The minister went up to it, made the sign of the cross over it and moved his lips in prayer. A small van backed slowly along the path and stopped. The council workers untied the ropes, lifted the coffin into the van and closed the doors. Elínborg got into the front seat beside the driver, who set off out of the cemetery, through the gate and down the road until the red rear lights disappeared in the rain and the gloom.

The minister went over to Elín and asked the policemen to let her go. They did so at once. The minister asked if there was anything he could do for her. They clearly knew each other well and spoke together in whispers. Elín appeared calmer. Erlendur and Sigurdur Óli exchanged glances and looked down into the grave. The rainwater had already started to collect in the bottom.

"I wanted to try to stop this repulsive desecration," Erlendur heard Elín say to the minister. He was somewhat relieved to see that Elín had collected herself. He walked over to her with Sigurdur Óli following close behind.

"I'll never forgive you for this," Elín said to Erlendur. The minister was standing by her side. "Never!"

"I do understand," Erlendur said, "but the investigation takes priority."

"Investigation? Bugger your investigation," Elín shouted. "Where are you taking the body?"

"To Reykjavík."

"And when are you bringing it back?"

"Two days from now."

"Look what you've done to her grave," Elín said in a puzzled tone of resignation, as if she hadn't yet completely taken in what had happened. She walked past Erlendur towards the headstone and what remained of the fencing, the vase of flowers and the open grave.

Erlendur decided to tell her about the message that was found in Holberg's flat.

"A note was left behind at Holberg's place when we found him," Erlendur said, walking after Elín. "We couldn't make much of it until Audur entered the picture and we talked to her old doctor. Icelandic murderers generally don't leave anything behind but a mess, but the one who killed Holberg wanted to give us something to rack our brains over. When the doctor talked about the possibility of a hereditary disease the message suddenly took on a certain meaning. Also after what Ellidi told me in the prison. Holberg has no living relatives. He had a sister who died at the age of nine. Sigurdur Óli here", Erlendur said, pointing to his colleague, "found the medical reports about her – Ellidi was right. Like Audur, Holberg's sister died of a brain tumour. Very probably from the same disease."

"What is it you're saying? What was the message?" Elín asked.

Erlendur hesitated. He looked at Sigurdur Óli who looked first at Elín and then back at Erlendur.

"I am him," Erlendur said.

"What do you mean?"

"That was the message: 'I am him' with the final word, 'him', in capitals."

"I am him," Elín repeated. "What does that mean?"

"It's impossible to say really but I've been wondering if it doesn't imply some kind of relation," Erlendur said. "The person who wrote 'I am him' would have felt he had something in common with Holberg. It could be a fantasy by some nutcase who didn't even know him. Just nonsense. But I don't think so. I think the disease will help us. I think we have to find out exactly what it was."

"What kind of relation?"

"According to the records, Holberg didn't have any children. Audur wasn't named after him. Her last name was Kolbrúnardóttir. But if Ellidi's telling the truth when he says Holberg raped more women besides Kolbrún, women who didn't come forward, it could be just as likely that he's had other children. That Kolbrún wasn't the only victim who had his child. We've narrowed down the search for a possible victim in Húsavík to the women who had children over a certain period and we're hoping something will come out of this soon."

"Húsavík?"

"Holberg's previous victim was from there, apparently."

"What do you mean by a hereditary disease?" Elín said. "What sort of disease? Is it the one that killed Audur?"

"We have to examine Holberg, confirm that he was Audur's father and piece everything together. But if this theory is correct, it's probably a rare, genetically transmitted disease."

"And did Audur have it?"

"She may have died too long ago to give a satisfactory result but that's what we want to find out."

By now they had walked to the church, Elín by Erlendur's side and Sigurdur Óli following behind them. Elín led the way. The church was open; they went in out of the rain and stood in the vestibule looking out at the gloomy autumn day.

"I think Holberg was Audur's father," Erlendur said. "Actually I have no reason to doubt your word and what your sister told you. But we need confirmation. It's vital from the point of view of the police investigation. If a genetic disease is involved which Audur got from Holberg, it could be some-where else too. It's possible that the disease is linked to Holberg's murder."

They didn't notice a car driving slowly away from the cemetery along the rough old track of a road, its lights switched off and barely visible in the darkness. When it reached Sandgerdi it picked up speed, the headlights were switched on and it had soon caught up with the van carrying the body. On the Keflavík road the driver made sure he kept two or three cars behind the van. In this way, he followed the coffin all the way to Reykjavík.

When the van stopped in front of the morgue on Barónsstígur he parked the car some distance away and watched as the coffin was carried into the building and the doors closed behind it. He watched the van drive away and saw when the woman who'd accompanied the coffin left the morgue and got into a taxi.

When everything was quiet again, he drove away.

19

Marion Briem opened the door for him. Erlendur
hadn't said he was coming. He'd come straight from
Sandgerdi and decided to talk to Marion before
going home. It was 6 p.m. and it was pitch dark
outside. Marion invited Erlendur in and asked him
to excuse the mess. It was a small flat, a sitting
room, bedroom, bathroom and kitchen, and it was
an example of how careless people can be when they
live alone, not unlike Erlendur's flat. Newspapers,
magazines and books were spread all over, the
carpet was worn and dirty, unwashed dishes were
piled up beside the kitchen sink. The light from a
table lamp made a feeble attempt to illuminate the
dark room. Marion told Erlendur to sweep the
newspapers on one of the chairs onto the floor and
take a seat.

"You didn't tell me you were involved in the case
at the time," Erlendur said.

"Not one of my great achievements," Marion
said, taking a cigarillo from a box, with small, slight
hands, a pained expression, a large head on what
was in other respects a delicately built body.
Erlendur declined the offer of one. He knew that

Marion still kept an eye on interesting cases, sought information from colleagues who still worked for the police and even occasionally chipped in on them.

"You want to know more about Holberg," Marion said.

"And his friends," Erlendur said and sat down after sweeping the pile of newspapers aside. "And about Rúnar from Keflavík."

"Yes, Rúnar from Keflavík," Marion said. "He was going to kill me once."

"He's not likely to today, the old wreck," Erlendur said.

"So you met him," Marion said. "He's got cancer, did you know that? A question of weeks rather than months."

"I didn't know," Erlendur said, and visualised Rúnar's thin and bony face. The drip on the end of his nose while he raked up the leaves in his garden.

"He had incredibly powerful friends at the ministry. That's why he hung on. I recommended dismissal. He was given a warning."

"Do you remember Kolbrún at all?"

"The most miserable victim I've seen in my life," Marion said. "I didn't get to know her well, but I do know she could never tell a lie about anything. She made her accusations against Holberg and described the treatment she got from Rúnar, as you know. It was her word against his in Rúnar's case, but her statement was convincing. He shouldn't have sent her home, panties or no panties. Holberg raped her.

That was obvious. I made them confront each other, Holberg and Kolbrún. And there was no question."

"You made them confront each other?"

"It was a mistake. I thought it would help. That poor woman."

"How?"

"I made it look like a coincidence or an accident. I didn't realise . . . I shouldn't be telling you this. I'd reached a dead-end in the investigation. She said one thing and he said something else. I called them both in at once and made sure they'd meet."

"What happened?"

"She had hysterics and we had to call a doctor. I'd never seen anything like it before, or since."

"What about him?"

"Just stood there grinning."

Erlendur was silent for a moment.

"Do you think it was his child?"

Marion shrugged. "Kolbrún always claimed it was."

"Did Kolbrún ever talk to you about another woman that Holberg raped?"

"Was there another one?"

Erlendur repeated what Ellidi had said and had soon outlined the whole investigation. Marion Briem sat smoking the cigarillo, listening. Staring at Erlendur with small eyes, alert and piercing. They never missed anything. They saw a tired middle-aged man with dark lines under his eyes, several days' stubble on his cheeks, thick eyebrows that stuck out, his bushy ginger hair that was all in a tangle, strong teeth that sometimes showed behind pallid lips, a weary expression that had witnessed all the worst dregs of human filth. Marion Briem's eyes revealed clear pity and a sad certainty that they were looking at their own reflection.

Erlendur had been under Marion Briem's guidance when he joined the CID and everything he had learned in those first years, Marion taught him. Like Erlendur, Marion had never been a senior officer and always worked on routine investigations but had enormous experience. An infallible memory that hadn't deteriorated in the slightest with age. Everything seen and heard was classified, recorded and saved in the infinite storage space of Marion's brain, then called up without the slightest effort when needed. Marion could recall old cases in the minutest detail, a fountain of wisdom about every aspect of Icelandic criminology. Sharp powers of deduction and a logical mind.

To work with, Marion Briem was an intolerably pedantic, stringent and insufferable old bastard, as Erlendur once put it to Eva Lind when the topic arose. A deep rift had developed between him and his old mentor for many years which reached the point where they hardly said a word to each other. Erlendur felt that in some inexplicable way he had disappointed Marion. He thought this was becoming increasingly obvious until his mentor eventually retired, much to Erlendur's relief.

After Marion left work it was as if their relationship returned to normal. The tension eased and the rivalry more or less disappeared.

"So that's why it occurred to me to drop in on you and see what you remembered about Holberg, Ellidi and Grétar," Erlendur said in the end.

"You're not hoping to find Grétar after all these years?" Marion said in a tone of astonishment. Erlendur discerned a look of worry.

"How far did you get with it?"

"I never got anywhere, it was only a part-time assignment," Marion said. Erlendur cheered up for a moment when he felt he could sense a hint of apology. "He probably disappeared over the weekend of the national festival at Thingvellir. I talked to his mother and friends, Ellidi and Holberg, and his workmates. Grétar worked for Eimskip as a stevedore. Everyone thought he'd probably fallen into the sea. If he'd fallen into the cargo hold they said they couldn't have failed to find him."

"Where were Holberg and Ellidi around the time Grétar disappeared? Do you remember?"

"They both said they were at the festival and we could verify that. But of course the exact time of Grétar's disappearance was uncertain. No-one had seen him for two weeks when his mother contacted us. What are you thinking? Have you got a new lead on Grétar?"

"No," Erlendur said. "And I'm not looking for him. So long as he hasn't appeared out of the blue and murdered his old friend Holberg in Nordurmýri then he can be gone for ever for all I care. I'm trying to work out what kind of a group they were, Holberg, Ellidi and Grétar."

"They were scum. All three of them. You know Ellidi yourself. Grétar wasn't a bit better. More of a wimp. I had to deal with him once over a burglary and it looked to me like the start of a pathetic small-time criminal career. They worked together at the Harbour and Lighthouse Authority. That's how they met. Ellidi was the dumb sadist. Picked fights whenever he got the chance. Attacked weaker people. Hasn't changed either, so I believe. Holberg was a kind of ringleader. The most intelligent one. He got off lightly over Kolbrún. When I started asking about him at the time, people were reluctant to talk. Grétar was the wimp who latched onto them, unassertive, cowardly, but I had the feeling there was more to him than met the eye."

"Did Rúnar and Holberg know each other previously?"

"I don't think so."

"We haven't announced it yet," Erlendur said, "but we found a note on top of the body."

"A note?"

"The murderer wrote 'I am him' on a piece of paper and left it on top of Holberg."

"I am him?"

"Doesn't that suggest they were related?"

"Unless it's a Messiah complex. A religious maniac."

"I'd rather put it down to kinship."

" 'I am him'? What's he saying by that? What's the meaning?"

"I wish I knew," Erlendur said.

He stood up and put on his hat, saying he had to get home. Marion asked how Eva Lind was, Erlendur said she was dealing with her problems and left it at that. Marion accompanied him to the door and showed him out. They shook hands. When Erlendur went down the steps, Marion called out to him.

"Erlendur! Wait a minute, Erlendur."

Erlendur turned around and looked up to Marion standing in the doorway and he saw how age had left its mark on that air of respectability, how rounded shoulders could diminish dignity and a wrinkled face bear witness to a difficult life. It was a long time since he'd been to that flat and he had been thinking, while he sat facing Marion in the chair, about the treatment that time hands out to people.

"Don't let anything you find out about Holberg have too much effect on you," Marion Briem said. "Don't let him kill any part of you that you don't want rid of anyway. Don't let him win. That was all."

Erlendur stood still in the rain, unsure of what this advice was supposed to mean. Marion Briem nodded at him.

"What burglary was it?"

"Burglary?" Marion asked opening the door again.

"That Grétar did. What did he burgle?"

"A photographic shop. He had some kind of fixation with photographs," Marion Briem said. "He took pictures."

Two men, both wearing leather jackets and black leather boots laced up to their calves, knocked at Erlendur's door and disturbed him as he was nodding off in his armchair later that evening. He'd come home, called out to Eva Lind without getting a reply and sat down on the chicken portions that had lain on the chair ever since he'd slept sitting on them the night before. The two men asked for Eva Lind. Erlendur had never seen them before and hadn't seen his daughter since she had cooked him the meat stew. Their expressions were ruthless when they asked Erlendur where they could get hold of her and they tried to see inside the flat without actually pushing past him. Erlendur asked what they wanted his daughter for. They asked if he was hiding her inside his flat, the dirty old sod. Erlendur asked if they'd come to collect a debt. They told him to fuck off. He told them to bugger off. They told him to eat shit. When he was about to close the door, one of them stuck his knee in past the doorframe. "Your daughter's a fucking cunt," he shouted. He was wearing leather trousers.

Erlendur sighed. It had been a long, dull day.

He heard the knee crack and splinter when the door slammed against it with such force that the upper hinges ripped out of the frame.

20

Sigurdur Óli was wondering how to phrase the question. He was holding a list with the names of ten women who'd lived in Húsavík before and after 1960 but had since moved to Reykjavík. Two on the list were dead. Two had never had any children. The remaining six had all become mothers during the period when the rape was likely to have occurred. Sigurdur Óli was on his way to visit the first one. She lived on Barmahlíd. Divorced. She had three grown-up sons.

But how was he supposed to put the question to these middle-aged women? "Excuse me, madam, I'm from the police and I've been sent to ask you whether you were ever raped in Húsavík when you lived there." He talked it over with Elínborg, who had a list with the names of ten other women, but she didn't understand the problem.

Sigurdur Óli regarded it as a futile operation that Erlendur had launched. Even if Ellidi happened to be telling the truth and the time and place fitted and they finally found the right woman after a long search, what guarantees were there that she would talk about the rape at all? She'd kept quiet about it all her life. Why should she start talking about it now? All she needed to say, when Sigurdur Óli or any of the five detectives who were carrying the same kind of list knocked on her door, was "no", and they could say little more than "sorry to bother you." Even if they did find the woman, there were no guarantees that she had in fact had a child as a result of the rape.

"It's a question of responses, you should use psychology," Erlendur had said when Sigurdur Óli tried to make him see the problem. "Try to get into their homes, sit down, accept a coffee, chat, be a bit of a gossip."

"Psychology!" Sigurdur Óli snorted when he got out of his car on Barmahlíd and he thought about his partner, Bergthóra. He didn't even know how to use psychology on her. They'd met under unusual circumstances some years before, when Bergthóra was a witness in a difficult case and after a short romance they decided to start living together. It turned out that they were well suited, had similar interests and both wanted to make a beautiful home for themselves with exclusive furniture and *objets d'art*, yuppies at heart. They always kissed when they met after a long day at work. Gave each other little presents. Even opened a bottle of wine. Sometimes they went straight to bed when they got home from work, but there'd been considerably less of that recently.

That was after she had given him a pair of very ordinary Finnish wellington boots for his birthday.

He tried to beam with delight but the expression of disbelief stayed on his face for too long and she saw there was something wrong. When he finally smiled, it was false.

"Because you didn't have any," she said.

"I haven't had a pair of wellington boots since I was . . . 10," he said.

"Aren't you pleased?"

"I think they're great," Sigurdur Óli said, knowing that he hadn't answered the question. She knew it too. "No, seriously," he added and could tell he was digging himself a cold grave. "It's fantastic."

"You're not pleased with them," she said morosely.

"Sure I am," he said, still at a total loss because he couldn't stop thinking about the 30,000-króna wristwatch he'd given her for her birthday, bought after a week of explorations all over town and discussions with watchmakers about brands, gold plating, mechanisms, straps, water-tightness, Switzerland and cuckoo clocks. He'd applied all his detective skills to find the right watch, found it in the end and she was ecstatic, her joy and delight were genuine.

Then he was sitting in front of her with his smile frozen on his face and tried to pretend to be overjoyed, but he simply couldn't do it for all his life was worth.

"Psychology?" Sigurdur Óli snorted again.

He rang the bell when he'd arrived at the door of the first lady he was visiting on Barmahlíd and asked the question with as much psychological depth as he could muster, but failed miserably. Before he knew it, in a fluster he'd asked the woman on the landing whether she might ever have been raped.

"What the bloody hell are you on about?" the lady said, war paint on her face, finery on her fingers and a ferocious expression which did not look likely to ease up. "Who are you? What kind of a pervert are you anyway?"

"No, sorry," Sigurdur Óli said and was back down the stairs in a split second.

Elínborg had more luck, since she had her mind more on her work and wasn't shy about chatting away to gain people's confidence. Her speciality was cooking, she was an exceptionally interested and capable cook and had no trouble finding a talking point. If the chance presented itself she'd ask what that gorgeous aroma emanating from the kitchen was and even people who'd lived on nothing but popcorn for the past week would welcome her indoors.

She was in the sitting room of a basement flat in Breidholt and accepted a cup of coffee from a lady from Húsavík, widowed many years before and the mother of two grown-up children. Her name was Sigurlaug and she was last on Elínborg's list. She'd found it easy to phrase the sensitive question and asked the people she interviewed to contact her if they heard anything in their circle, gossip from Húsavík if there was nothing better to be had.

". . . and that's why we're looking for a woman of your age from Húsavík who might have known Holberg at that time and even maybe had some trouble from him."

"I don't remember anyone called Holberg from Húsavík," the woman said. "What kind of trouble do you mean?"

"Holberg just stayed in Húsavík for a while," Elínborg said. "So you won't necessarily remember anything about him. He never lived there. And it was physical assault. We know he attacked a woman in the town several decades ago and we're trying to locate her."

"You must have that in your reports."

"The assault was never reported."

"What sort of assault?"

"Rape."

The woman instinctively put her hand to her mouth and her eyes grew to the size of saucers.

"Good Lord!" she said. "I don't know anything about that. Rape! My God! I've never heard about anything like that."

"No, it seems to have been a closely guarded secret," Elínborg said. She deftly dodged probing questions from the woman who wanted to know the details, and talked about preliminary enquiries and mere hearsay. "I was wondering", she said then, "whether you know anyone who might know about this matter." The woman gave her the names of two of her friends from Húsavík and said they never missed anything. Elínborg wrote down their names, sat a while longer so as not to be rude, and then took her leave.

Erlendur had a cut on his forehead on which he had put a plaster. One of his two visitors from the previous night was out of action after Erlendur slammed the door on his knee and sent him howling to the floor. The other stared in astonishment at this treatment until the next thing he knew was that Erlendur was up against him on the landing and pushed him, without flinching for a moment, backwards down the stairs. He managed to grab the banister and stop himself falling the whole way down. He didn't fancy tackling Erlendur, who stood at the top of the stairs, with his swollen and bruised forehead; he looked for an instant at his companion lying on the floor roaring in pain, then back at Erlendur, and decided to make himself scarce. He was hardly more than 20.

Erlendur phoned an ambulance and while they waited for it he found out what the men wanted from Eva Lind. The man was reluctant at first, but when Erlendur offered to take a look at his knee he immediately became more talkative. They were debt collectors. Eva Lind owed both money and dope to some man Erlendur had never heard of before.

Erlendur didn't explain his plaster to anyone when he went to work the next day, and no-one dared ask him about it. The door had almost knocked him out when it bounced back off the debt collector's leg and hit him on the head. His forehead still ached, he was anxious about Eva Lind and hadn't been able to sleep much that night, dozing in the chair for the odd hour and hoping his daughter would come back before the situation got out of hand. He stopped in his office just long enough to find out that Grétar had had a sister and his mother was still alive, living at Grund old people's home.

As he'd told Marion Briem, he wasn't looking for Grétar in particular, any more than for the lost girl from Gardabaer, but he didn't think it would do any harm to know more about him. Grétar had been at the party the night Kolbrún was raped. Maybe he'd left behind a memory of that night, a stray detail he'd blurted out. Erlendur didn't expect to find out anything new about his disappearance, Grétar could rest in peace for all he cared, but he'd been interested in missing persons for a long time. Behind each and every one was a horror story, but to his mind there was also something intriguing about people vanishing without trace and no-one knowing why.

Grétar's mother was 90 and blind. Erlendur spoke briefly to the director of the home, who had difficulty in taking her eyes off his forehead, and told him that Theodóra was one of the oldest and longest-standing residents there, a perfect member of the community in all respects, loved and admired by the staff and everyone else.

Erlendur was led in to see Theodóra and introduced to her. The old woman was sitting in a wheelchair in her room, wearing a dressing gown, covered with a woollen blanket, her long grey hair in a plait running down the back of the chair, her body hunched up, her hands bony and her face kindly. There were few personal belongings there. A framed photograph of John F. Kennedy hung above her bed. Erlendur sat in a chair in front of her, looked into the eyes that could no longer see, and said he wanted to talk about Grétar. Her hearing seemed to be fine and her mind was sharp. She showed no sign of surprise but got straight to the point. Erlendur could tell she was from Skagafjördur. She spoke with a thick northern accent.

"My Grétar wasn't a perfect lad," she said. "To tell you the truth he was an awful wretch. I don't know where he got it from. A cheap wretch. Going around with other wretches, layabouts, riff-raff the lot of them. Have you found him?"

"No," Erlendur said. "One of his friends was murdered recently. Holberg. Maybe you've heard about it."

"I didn't know. He got bumped off, you say?"

Erlendur was amused and for the first time in a long while he saw reason to smile.

"At home. They used to work together in the old days, Holberg and your son. At the Harbour and Lighthouse Authority."

"The last I saw of my Grétar, and I still had decent sight then, was when he came home to see me the same summer as the national festival and stole some money from my purse and a bit of silver. I didn't find out until he'd left again and the money had disappeared. And then Grétar disappeared himself. Like he'd been stolen too. Do you know who stole him?"

"No," Erlendur said. "Do you know what he was up to before he went missing? Who he was in touch with?"

"No idea," the old woman said. "I never knew what Grétar was up to. I told you so at the time."

"Did you know he took photographs?"

"Yes. He took photographs. He was always taking those pictures. I don't know why. He told me once that photos were the mirrors of time, but I didn't have a clue what he was talking about."

"Wasn't that a bit highbrow for Grétar?"

"I'd never heard him talk like that."

"His last address was on Bergstadastraeti where he rented a room. Do you know what happened to his belongings, the camera and films, do you know that?"

"Maybe Klara knows," Theodóra said. "My daughter. She cleaned out his room. Threw all that rubbish away, I think."

Erlendur stood up and she followed his movements with her head. He thanked her for her assistance, said she'd been very valuable and he wanted to praise her for how well she looked and how sharp her mind was, but he didn't. He didn't want to patronise her. He looked up along the wall above her bed at the photograph of Kennedy and couldn't restrain himself from asking.

"Why have you got a photograph of Kennedy

above your bed?" he said, looking into her vacant eyes.

"Oh," Theodóra sighed, "I was so fond of him while he was alive."

21

The bodies lay side by side on the cold slabs in the morgue on Barónsstígur. Erlendur tried not to think about how he had brought the father and daughter together in death. An autopsy and tests had already been performed on Holberg's body, but it was awaiting further studies which would focus on genetic diseases and whether he was related to Audur. Erlendur noticed that the body's fingers were black. He'd been fingerprinted after his death. Audur's body lay wrapped in a white canvas sheet on a table beside Holberg. She was still untouched.

Erlendur didn't know the pathologist and saw little of him. He was tall, with large hands. He wore thin plastic gloves, wearing a white apron over a green gown, tied at the back, and wearing green trousers of the same material. He had a gauze over his mouth and a blue plastic cap on his head and white trainers.

Erlendur had been to the morgue often enough before and always felt equally bad there. The smell of death filled his senses and settled in his clothes, the smell of formalin and sterilising agents and the horrifying stench of dead bodies that had been opened. Bright fluorescent lamps were suspended from the ceiling, casting a pure white light around the windowless room. There were large white tiles on the floor and the walls were partly tiled, the upper half painted with white plastic paint. Standing up against them were tables with microscopes and other research equipment. On the walls were many cupboards, some with glass doors, revealing instruments and jars that were beyond Erlendur's comprehension. However, he did understand the function of the scalpels, tongs and saws that were spread out in a neat row on a long instrument table.

Erlendur noticed a scent card hanging down from a fluorescent lamp above one of the two operating tables. It showed a girl in a red bikini running along a white sandy beach. There was a tape recorder on one of the tables and several cassettes beside it. It was playing classical music. Mahler, Erlendur thought. The pathologist's lunch box was on a table beside one of the microscopes.

"She stopped giving off any scent long ago, but her body's still in good shape," the pathologist said and looked over to Erlendur, who was standing by the door as if hesitant about entering the brightly lit chamber of death and decay.

"Eh?" Erlendur said, unable to take his eyes off the white heap. There was a tone of gleeful anticipation in the pathologist's voice that he could not fathom.

"The girl in the bikini, I mean," the pathologist said with a nod at the scent card. "I need to get a new card. You probably never get used to the smell. Do come in. Don't be afraid. It's just meat. He waved the knife over Holberg's body. No soul, no life, just a carcass of meat. Do you believe in ghosts?"

"Eh?" Erlendur said again.

"Do you think their souls are watching us? Do you think they're hovering around the room here or do you think they've taken up residence in another body? Been reincarnated. Do you believe in life after death?"

"No, I don't," Erlendur replied.

"This man died after a heavy blow to the head that punctured his scalp, smashed his skull and forced its way through to the brain. It looks to me as if the person who delivered the blow was standing facing him. It's not unlikely that they looked each other in the eye. The attacker is probably right-handed, the wound's on the left side. And he's in good physical shape, a young man or middle-aged at most, hardly a woman unless she's done manual labour. The blow would have killed him almost instantaneously. He would have seen the tunnel and the bright lights."

"It's quite probable he took the other route," Erlendur said.

"Well. The intestine is almost empty, remains of eggs and coffee, the rectum is full. He suffered, if that isn't too strong a word, from constipation. Not uncommon at that age. No-one has claimed the body, I understand, so we've applied for permission to use it for teaching purposes. How does that grab you?"

"So he's more use dead than alive."

The pathologist looked at Erlendur, walked up to a table, took a red slice of meat from a metal tray and held it up with one hand.

"I can't tell whether people were good or bad," he said. "This could just as easily be the heart of a saint. What we need to find out, if I understand you correctly, is whether it pumped bad blood."

Erlendur looked in astonishment at the pathologist holding Holberg's heart and examining it. Watched him handling the dead muscle as if nothing could be more natural in the world.

"It's a strong heart," the pathologist went on. "It could have gone on pumping for a good few years, could have taken its owner past a hundred."

The pathologist put the heart back on the metal tray.

"There's something quite interesting about this Holberg, though I haven't examined him particularly in that respect. You probably want me to. He has various mild symptoms of a specific disease. I found a small tumour in his brain, a benign tumour which would have troubled him a little, and there's *café au lait* on his skin, especially here under his arms."

"*Café au lait*?" Erlendur said.

"*Café au lait* is what it's called in the textbooks. It looks like coffee stains. Do you know anything about it?"

"Nothing at all."

"I'll undoubtedly find more symptoms when I look at him more closely."

"There was talk of *café au lait* on the girl. She developed a brain tumour. Malignant. Do you know what the disease is?"

"I can't say anything about it yet."

"Are we talking about a genetic disease?"

"I don't know."

The pathologist went over to the table where Audur lay.

"Have you heard the story about Einstein?" he asked.

"Einstein?" Erlendur said.

"Albert Einstein."

"What story?"

"A weird story. True. Thomas Harvey? Never heard of him? A pathologist."

"No."

"He was on duty when Einstein died," the pathologist continued. "A curious chap. Performed the autopsy, but because it was Einstein he couldn't resist and opened up his head and looked at the brain. And he did more than that. He stole Einstein's brain."

Erlendur said nothing. He couldn't make head or tail of what the pathologist was talking about.

"He took it home. That strange urge to collect things that some people have, especially when famous people are involved. Harvey lost his job when the theft was discovered and over the years he became a mysterious figure, a legend really. All kinds of stories circulated about him. He always kept the brain in his house. I don't know how he got away with it. Einstein's relatives were always trying to recover the brain from him, but in vain. Eventually in his old age he made his peace with the relatives and decided to return the brain to them. Put it in the boot of his car and drove right across America to Einstein's grandchild in California."

"Is this true?"

"True as daylight."

"Why are you telling me this?" Erlendur asked.

The pathologist lifted up the sheet from the child's body and looked underneath it.

"Her brain's missing," he said, and the look of nonchalance vanished from his face.

"What?"

"The brain," the pathologist said, "isn't where it belongs."

22

Erlendur didn't immediately understand what the pathologist had said and looked at him as if he hadn't heard. He couldn't fathom what he was talking about. For a moment he looked down at the body, then looked up quickly again when he saw a bone from a little hand protruding from beneath the sheet. He didn't think he could handle the image of what was lying underneath it. He didn't want to know what the girl's earthly remains looked like. Didn't want that image to appear every time he thought about her.

"She's been opened up before," the pathologist said.

"Is the brain missing?" Erlendur groaned.

"An autopsy was performed before."

"Yes, at Keflavík hospital."

"When did she die?"

"1968," Erlendur said.

"And, if I understand correctly, Holberg was her father, but they didn't live together, her parents?"

"The girl only had her mother."

"Was permission given to use her organs for research purposes?" the pathologist continued. "Do you know about that at all? Did the mother give her permission?"

"She wouldn't have done," Erlendur said.

"It could have been taken without her permission. Who was looking after her when she died? Who was her doctor?"

Erlendur named Frank. The pathologist was silent for a while.

"I can't say that I'm entirely unfamiliar with such incidents. Relatives are sometimes asked whether organs may be removed for research purposes. All in the name of science, of course. We need that. For teaching, too. I know of instances when, if there is no next of kin, certain organs are removed for research before the body is buried. But I don't know many cases of organs being stolen outright when the relatives have been consulted."

"How could the brain be missing?" Erlendur went on asking.

"The head's been sawn in half and it was removed in one piece."

"No, I mean . . ."

"A neat job," the pathologist continued. "A skilled person at work. You cut through the spinal cord, through the neck from the rear here and take the brain out."

"I know the brain was studied in connection with a tumour," Erlendur said. "Do you mean that it wasn't put back?"

"That's one explanation," the pathologist said, covering up the body. "If they removed the brain to study it they would hardly have been able to return it in time for the funeral. It needs to be fixed."

"Fixed?"

"To make it better to work on. It turns like cheese. Brains take a while to fix."

"Wouldn't it have been enough just to take samples?"

"I don't know," the pathologist said. "All I know is that the brain isn't in place, which makes it difficult to determine the cause of death. Maybe we can see with DNA tests on the bones. That could tell us something."

There was no mistaking the look of astonishment on Frank's face when he opened the door and saw Erlendur standing on the steps again in a torrential downpour.

"We exhumed the girl", Erlendur said without any preamble, "and the brain's missing. Do you know anything about it?"

"Exhumed her? The brain?" the doctor said and showed Erlendur into his office. "What do you mean, the brain's missing?"

"What I say. The brain's been removed. Probably to study it in connection with the cause of death, but it wasn't returned. You were her doctor. Do you know what happened? Do you know anything about the matter?"

"I was her general practitioner, as I think I explained to you the last time you came. She was under the supervision of Keflavík hospital and the doctors there."

"The person who performed the autopsy is dead. We were given a copy of his pathologist's report, which is very curt and mentions only a brain tumour. If he did any more studies of it, there's no record of them. Wouldn't it have been enough just to take samples? Did they need to remove the whole brain?"

The doctor shrugged. "I'm not sure." He hesitated for a moment. "Were more organs missing?" he asked.

"More organs?" Erlendur said.

"Besides the brain. Was that all that was missing?"

"What do you mean?"

"Nothing else was touched?"

"I don't think so. The pathologist didn't mention anything. What are you getting at?"

Frank looked at Erlendur, thoughtfully. "I don't expect you've ever heard Jar City mentioned, have you?"

"What Jar City?"

"It's now been closed, I believe, not so very long ago in fact. The room was called that. Jar City."

"What room?"

"Upstairs on Barónsstígur. Where they kept the organs."

"Go on."

"They were kept in formalin in glass jars. All kinds of organs that were sent there from the hospitals. For teaching. In the faculty of medicine. They were kept in a room the medical students called Jar City. Preserved innards. Hearts, livers and limbs. Brains too."

"From the hospitals?"

"People die in hospitals. They're given autopsies. The organs are examined. They're not always returned, some are kept for teaching purposes. At one time the organs were stored in Jar City."

"What are you telling me this for?"

"The brain needn't be lost for ever. It might still be in some Jar City. Samples that are preserved for teaching purposes are all documented and classified, for example. If you need to locate the brain there's a chance that you still can."

"I've never heard about this before. Are the organs taken without permission or do they obtain the relatives' consent . . . what's the arrangement?"

The doctor shrugged. "To tell the truth, I don't know. Naturally it all depends. Organs are extremely important for medical teaching. All university hospitals have large collections of organs. I've even heard that some doctors, medical researchers, have their own private collections, but I can't vouch for that."

"Organ collectors?"

"There are such people."

"What happened to this . . . Jar City? If it's not around any more?"

"I don't know."

"So you think that's where the brain could have ended up? Preserved in formalin?"

"Quite easily. Why did you exhume the girl?"

"Maybe it was a mistake," Erlendur sighed. "Maybe the whole case is one big mistake."

23

Elínborg located Klara, Grétar's sister. Her search for Holberg's other victim, the Húsavík woman as Erlendur called her, had produced no results. All the women she had approached showed the same reaction: enormous and genuine surprise followed by such a zealous interest that Elínborg had to use every trick in the book to avoid giving away any details of the case. She knew that no matter how much she and the other policemen who were looking for the woman emphasised that it was a sensitive case and not to be discussed with anyone, that wouldn't prevent the gossip lines from glowing red hot when evening came around.

Klara greeted Elínborg at the door of her neat flat in the Seljahverfi district of Breidholt suburb. She was a slender woman in her fifties, dark-haired, wearing jeans and a blue sweater. She was smoking a cigarette.

"Did you talk to Mum?" she said when Elínborg had introduced herself and Klara had invited her inside, friendly and interested.

"That was Erlendur," Elínborg said, "who works with me."

"She said he wasn't feeling very well," Klara said, walking in front of Elínborg into the sitting room and offering her a seat. "She's always making remarks you can't figure out."

Elínborg didn't answer her.

"I'm off work today," she said as if to explain why she was hanging around at home in the middle of the day, smoking cigarettes. She said she worked at a travel agency. Her husband was at work, the two children had flown the nest; the daughter studying medicine, she said, proudly. She'd hardly put out one cigarette before she took out another and lit it. Elínborg gave a polite cough, but Klara didn't take the hint.

"I read about Holberg in the papers," Klara said as if she wanted to stop herself rambling on. "Mum said the man asked about Grétar. We were half-brother and -sister. Mum forgot to tell him that. We had the same mother. Our fathers are both long since dead."

"We didn't know that," Elínborg said.

"Do you want to see the stuff I cleared out of Grétar's flat?"

"If you don't mind," Elínborg said.

"A filthy hole he lived in. Have you found him?"

Klara looked at Elínborg and hungrily sucked the smoke down into her lungs.

"We haven't found him," Elínborg said, "and I don't think we're looking for him especially." She gave another polite cough. "It's more than a quarter of a century since he disappeared, so . . ."

"I have no idea what happened," Klara interrupted, exhaling a thick cloud of smoke. "We weren't often in touch. He was quite a bit older than me, selfish, a real pain actually. You could never get a word out of him, he swore at Mum and stole from both of us if he got the chance. Then he left home."

"So you didn't know Holberg?" Elínborg asked.

"No."

"Or Ellidi?" she added.

"Who's Ellidi?"

"Never mind."

"I didn't know who Grétar went around with. When he went missing someone called Marion contacted me and took me to where he'd been living. It was a filthy hole. A disgusting smell in the room and the floor covered with rubbish, and the half-eaten sheep heads and mouldy mashed turnips that he used to live on."

"Marion?" Elínborg asked. She hadn't been working for the CID long enough to recognise the name.

"Yes, that was the name."

"Do you remember a camera among your brother's belongings?"

"That was the only thing in the room in one piece. I took it but I've never used it. The police thought it was stolen and I don't approve of that sort of thing. I keep it down in the storeroom in the basement. Do you want to see it? Did you come about the camera?"

"Could I have a look at it?" Elínborg asked.

Klara stood up. She asked Elínborg to wait a moment and went into the kitchen to fetch a key ring. They walked out into the corridor and down to the basement. Klara opened the door that led to the storerooms, switched on the light, went up to one of the doors and opened it. Inside, old rubbish was piled everywhere, deckchairs and sleeping bags, skiing equipment and camping gear. Elínborg noticed a blue foot-massage device and a Soda-stream drinks maker.

"I had it in a box here," Klara said after squeezing her way, past the rubbish, halfway into the store-room. She bent down and picked up a little brown cardboard box. "I put all Grétar's stuff in this. He didn't own anything except that camera." She opened the box and was about to empty it when Elínborg stopped her.

"Don't take anything out of the box," she said and put out her hands to take it. "You never know what significance the contents might have for us," she added by way of explanation.

Klara handed her the box with a half-insulted expression and Elínborg opened it. It contained three tattered paperback thrillers, a penknife, a few coins and a camera – a pocket-size Kodak Insta-matic that Elínborg recalled had been a popular Christmas and confirmation present years before. Not a remarkable possession for someone with a burning interest in photography, but it undoubtedly served its purpose. She couldn't see any films in the box. Erlendur had asked her to check specifically whether Grétar had left behind any films. She took out a handkerchief and turned the camera round and saw there was no film in it. There were no photos in the box either.

"Then there are all kinds of trays and liquids here," Klara said and pointed inside the storeroom. "I think he developed the photos himself. There's some photographic paper too. It must be useless by now, mustn't it?"

"I should take that too," Elínborg said and Klara dived back into the rubbish.

"Do you know if he kept his rolls of film, or did you see any at his place?" Elínborg asked.

"No, none," Klara said as she bent over for the trays.

"Do you know where he might have kept them?"

"No."

"So do you know what this photography was all about?"

"Well, he enjoyed it, I expect," Klara said.

"I mean the subjects: did you see any of his photos?"

"No, he never showed me anything. As I said, we didn't have much contact. I don't know where his photos are. Grétar was a damn layabout," she said, uncertain whether she was repeating herself, then shrugged as if deciding you can't say a good thing too often.

"I'd like to take this box away with me," Elínborg said. "I hope that's okay. It'll be returned shortly."

"What's going on?" Klara asked, for the first time

showing an interest in the police inquiry and the questions about her brother. "Do you know where Grétar is?"

"No," Elínborg stressed, trying to dispel all doubt. "Nothing new has emerged. Nothing."

The two women who were with Kolbrún the night Holberg attacked her were named in the police investigation documents. Erlendur had launched a search for them and it turned out that both were from Keflavík, but neither lived there any more.

One of them had married an American from the NATO base shortly after the incident and now lived in the USA, while the other had moved from Keflavík to Stykkishólmur five years later. She was still registered as living there. Erlendur wondered whether he should spend the whole day on a trip out west to Stykkishólmur or phone her and hope that would be enough.

Erlendur's English was poor so he asked Sigurdur Óli to locate the woman in America. He spoke to her husband. She had died 15 years earlier. From cancer. The woman was buried in America.

Erlendur phoned Stykkishólmur and had no difficulty making contact with the second woman. First he phoned her home and was told that she was at work. She was a nurse at the hospital there.

The woman listened to Erlendur's questions but said unfortunately she couldn't help him. She hadn't been able to help the police at the time and nothing had changed.

"Holberg has been murdered", Erlendur said, "and we think it might even be connected with this incident."

"I saw that on the news," the voice on the phone said. The woman's name was Agnes and Erlendur tried to visualise her from the sound of her voice. At first he imagined an efficient, firm woman in her sixties, overweight because she was short of breath. Then he noticed her smoker's cough and Agnes assumed a different image in his mind, turned thin as a rake, her skin yellow and wrinkled. She coughed with a nasty, gravelly sound at regular intervals.

"Do you remember that night in Keflavík?" Erlendur asked.

"I went home before them," Agnes said.

"There were three men with you."

"I went home with a man called Grétar. I told the police at the time. I find it rather uncomfortable to talk about."

"It's news to me that you went home with Grétar," Erlendur said, riffling through the reports in front of him.

"I told them when they asked me the same question all those years ago." She coughed again but tried to spare Erlendur the throaty noises. "Sorry. I've never been able to give up those damn cigarettes. He was a bit of a loser. That Grétar. I never saw him after that."

"How did you and Kolbrún know each other?"

"We used to work together. That was before I

studied nursing. We were working in a shop in Keflavík which closed down long ago. That was the first and only time we went out anywhere together. Understandably."

"Did you believe Kolbrún when she talked about a rape?"

"I didn't hear about it until the police suddenly turned up at my house and started asking me about that night. I can't imagine she'd have lied about something like that. Kolbrún was very respectable. Thoroughly honest about everything she did, although a bit feeble perhaps. Delicate and sickly. Not a strong character. Maybe it's an awful thing to say, but she wasn't the fun type, if you know what I mean. Not a lot of action going on around her."

Agnes stopped talking and Erlendur waited for her to start again.

"She wasn't fond of going out and I really had to cajole her to come out with me and my friend Helga that evening. She moved to America but passed away many years ago, maybe you know that. Kolbrún was so reserved and sort of lonely and I wanted to do something for her. She agreed to go to the dance, then came back with us to Helga's afterwards, but she wanted to go home soon after that. I left before her so I don't really know what happened there. She didn't turn up for work on the Monday and I remember phoning her, but she didn't answer. A few days later the police came to ask about Kolbrún. I didn't know what to think. I didn't notice anything about Holberg that was abnormal in any way. He was quite a charmer if I remember right. I was very surprised when the police started talking about rape."

"He apparently made a good impression," Erlendur said. "A ladies' man, I think he was described as."

"I remember him coming into the shop."

"Him? Holberg?"

"Yes, Holberg. I think that was why they sat down with us that night. He said he was an accountant from Reykjavík, but that was just a lie, wasn't it?"

"They all worked at the Harbour and Lighthouse Authority. What kind of a shop was it?"

"A boutique. We sold ladieswear. Lingerie too."

"And he came to the shop?"

"Yes. The day before. On the Friday. I had to go back through all this at the time and I still remember it well. He said he was looking for something for his wife. I served him and when we met at the dance he behaved as though we knew each other."

"Did you have any contact with Kolbrún after the incident? Did you talk to her about what happened?"

"She never came back to the shop and, as I say, I didn't know what happened until the police started questioning me. I didn't know her that well. I tried to phone her a few times when she didn't turn up for work and I went to where she lived once, but didn't catch her in. I didn't want to interfere too much. She was like that. Mysterious. Then her sister came in and said Kolbrún had quit her job. I heard she died a few years afterwards. By then I'd moved up here to Stykkishólmur. Was it suicide? That's what I heard."

"She died," Erlendur said, and thanked Agnes politely for talking to him.

His thoughts turned to a man called Sveinn he'd been reading about. He survived a storm on Mosfellsheidi. His companions' suffering and deaths seemed to have little effect on Sveinn. He was the best equipped of the travellers and the only one who reached civilisation safe and sound, and the first thing he did after they'd tended to him on the closest farm to the heath was to put on ice skates and amuse himself by skating on a nearby lake.

At the same time his companions were still freezing to death on the heath.

After that he was never called anything but Sveinn the Soulless.

24

The search for the woman from Húsavík had still not led anywhere when towards evening Sigurdur Óli and Elínborg sat down at Erlendur's office to talk things over before going home. Sigurdur Óli said he wasn't surprised, they'd never find the woman this way. When Erlendur asked peevishly if he knew a better method, he shook his head.

"I don't feel as if we're looking for Holberg's murderer," Elínborg said, staring at Erlendur. "It's as if we're looking for something completely different and I'm unclear what it is. You've exhumed a little girl's body and I, for one, have no idea why. You've started looking for a man who went missing a generation ago and who I can't see has anything to do with the case. I don't think we're asking ourselves the obvious question: either the murderer was someone close to Holberg or a total stranger, someone who broke in intending to burgle him. Personally I think that's the most likely explanation. I think we ought to step up the search for that person. Some dopehead. The green army jacket. We haven't really done anything about that."

"Maybe it's someone Holberg paid for his services," Sigurdur Óli said. "With all that porn on his computer there's a good chance he paid for sex."

Erlendur sat through the criticism in silence and stared into his lap. He knew that most of what Elínborg had said was true. Maybe his judgment had been distorted by worrying about Eva Lind. He didn't know where she was, he didn't know what state she was in, she was being chased by people who wanted to harm her and he was helpless to protect her. He told neither Sigurdur Óli nor Elínborg of what he had discovered from the pathologist.

"We have the note," he said. "It's no coincidence we found it with the body."

The door suddenly opened and the head of forensics peeped inside.

"I'm leaving," he said. "I just wanted to let you know they're still examining the camera and they'll call you as soon as they find anything worth reporting."

He closed the door behind him without saying goodbye.

"Maybe we can't see the wood for the trees," Erlendur said. "Maybe there's a terribly simple solution to the whole thing. Maybe it was some nutcase. But maybe, and this is what I think to be the case, the murder has much deeper roots than we realise. Maybe there's nothing simple about it. Maybe the explanation lies in Holberg's character and what he did in his past."

Erlendur paused.

"And the note," he said. "'I am him.' What do you want to do with that?"

"It could be from some 'friend'," Sigurdur Óli said, making quotation marks with his fingers. "Or a workmate. We haven't applied ourselves much in those areas. To tell the truth I don't know where all this searching for an old woman is supposed to lead us. I don't have a clue how to ask them if they've been raped without getting hit over the head with a rolling pin."

"And hasn't Ellidi told that sort of lie before in his life?" Elínborg said. "Isn't that precisely what he wants, to make fools of us? Have you considered that?"

"Oh, come on," Erlendur said as if he couldn't be bothered to listen to this nagging any more. "The inquiry has led us onto this path. It would be wrong for us not to investigate the clues we get, wherever they come from. I know Icelandic murders aren't complicated, but there's something about this one that doesn't fit if you just want to put it down to coincidence. I don't think it's a mindless act of brutality."

The telephone on Erlendur's desk rang. He answered, listened for a short while and then nodded and said thank you before putting the phone down. His suspicion had been confirmed.

"Forensics," he said, looking at Elínborg and Sigurdur Óli. "Grétar's camera was used to take the photo of Audur's grave in the cemetery. We took a photograph using his camera and the same kind of scratches came out. So now we know there's at least a strong probability that Grétar took the picture. Possibly someone else used his camera, but the alternative is much more likely."

"And what does that tell us?" Sigurdur Óli asked, looking at the clock. He had invited Bergthóra out for a meal that evening and intended to make up for his clumsiness on his birthday.

"For example, it tells us that Grétar knew Audur was Holberg's daughter. Not many people were aware of that. And it also tells us that Grétar saw particular reason, a) to locate the grave, and b) to take a photo of it. Did he do it because Holberg asked him to? Did he do it to spite him? Is Grétar's disappearance connected with the photograph? If so, how? What did Grétar want with the photo? Why did we find it hidden in Holberg's desk? What sort of person takes pictures of children's graves?"

Elínborg and Sigurdur Óli watched Erlendur asking these questions. They noticed how his voice turned into a half-whisper and saw that he wasn't talking to them any more, but had disappeared inside himself, vacant and remote. He put his hand on his chest and instinctually rubbed it, apparently without realising what he was doing. They looked at one another but didn't dare to ask.

"What sort of person takes pictures of children's graves?" Erlendur said again.

Later that evening Erlendur found the man who had sent the debt collectors for Eva Lind. He

received information from the narcotics squad, who
had a fairly thick file on him, and found out he
frequented a pub by the name of Napoleon, in the
city centre. Erlendur went there and sat down facing
the man. His name was Eddi and he looked about
40, chubby and bald. His few remaining teeth were
stained yellow.

"Did you expect Eva to get special treatment
because you're a cop?" Eddi said when Erlendur sat
down with him. He seemed to know at once who
Erlendur was even though they'd never met before.
Erlendur had the feeling he'd been expecting him.

"Have you found her?" Erlendur asked and
looked all around the darkened room at the handful
of unfortunates who were sitting at tables and
making tough-guy gestures and expressions. Suddenly the name of the pub assumed significance in
his mind.

"You understand that I'm her friend," Eddi said.
"I give her what she wants. Sometimes she pays me.
Sometimes she takes too long about it. The guy with
the knee sends his regards."

"He grassed on you."

"It's difficult to find decent people," Eddi said,
pointing around the room.

"How much is it?"

"Eva? Two hundred thousand. And she doesn't
just owe me."

"Can we make a deal?"

"As you please."

Erlendur took out 20,000 crowns, which he'd

taken out of a cash machine on his way there, and put it on the table. Eddi took the money, counted it carefully and put it in his pocket.

"I can let you have some more after a week or so."

"That's cool."

Eddi gave Erlendur a probing look.

"I thought you were going to give me some lip," he said.

"For what?" Erlendur said.

"I know where she is," Eddi said, "but you'll never be able to save Eva."

Erlendur located the house. He'd been in that kind of house before on the same business. Eva Lind lay on a mattress in the hovel surrounded by other people. Some were her age, others much older. The house was open and the only obstacle was a man, whom Erlendur took to be about 20, who met him in the doorway waving his arms. Erlendur slammed him against the wall and threw him out. A naked light bulb hung from the ceiling of one of the rooms. He bent down to Eva and tried to wake her. Her breathing was regular and normal, her heartbeat a little fast. He shook her and slapped her lightly across the cheek and soon Eva opened her eyes.

"Grandad," she said, and her eyes closed again. He lifted Eva up and carried her out of the room, taking care not to tread on the other motionless bodies lying on the floor. He couldn't tell whether they were awake or asleep. She opened her eyes again.

"She's here," she whispered, but Erlendur didn't know what she was talking about and kept on walking with Eva out to his car. The sooner he got her out of there the better. He put her down on her feet to open the car door and she leaned up against him.

"Did you find her?" she asked

"Find who? What are you talking about?" He lay her down on the front seat, fastened her seatbelt, sat in the driver's seat and was about to drive away.

"Is she with you?" Eva Lind asked without opening her eyes.

"Who, dammit?" Erlendur shouted.

"The bride," Eva Lind said. "The babe from Gardabaer. I was lying next to her."

25

Erlendur was eventually woken up by the phone ringing. It resounded in his head until he opened his eyes and looked around everywhere. He'd slept in the armchair in the sitting room. His coat and hat were lying on the sofa. It was dark in the flat. Erlendur got to his feet slowly and wondered whether he could wear the same clothes for yet another day. He couldn't remember the last time he had undressed. He looked into the bedroom before answering the phone and saw that the two girls were lying in his bed where he'd put them the night before. He pulled the door to.

"The fingerprints on the camera match the ones on the photograph," Sigurdur Óli said when Erlendur eventually answered. He had to repeat the sentence twice more before Erlendur realised what he was talking about.

"Do you mean Grétar's fingerprints?"

"Yes, Grétar's."

"And Holberg's prints were on the photo too?" Erlendur said. "What the hell were they up to?"

"Beats my balls off," Sigurdur Óli said.

"Pardon?"

"Nothing. So Grétar took the photo then. We can assume that. He showed it to Holberg or Holberg found it. We'll go on looking for the Húsavík woman today, won't we?" Sigurdur Óli asked. "You don't have any new leads?"

"Yes," Erlendur said. "And no."

"I'm on my way up to Grafarvogur. We've almost finished the women in Reykjavík. Are we going to send someone up to Húsavík when we've finished here?"

"Yes," Erlendur said and put down the phone. Eva Lind was in the kitchen. She'd been woken up by the phone ringing. She was still dressed, as was the girl from Gardabaer. Erlendur had gone back into the hovel, carried her out and driven them both to his flat.

Eva Lind went into the toilet without saying a word and Erlendur heard her retching violently. He went into the kitchen and made some strong coffee, the only solution he knew in that situation, sat down at the kitchen table and waited for his daughter to come back out. Quite a while passed, he filled two cups. Eva Lind came out at last. She had wiped her face. Erlendur thought she looked terrible. Her body was so scrawny it barely hung together.

"I knew she did dope sometimes," Eva Lind said in a hoarse voice when she sat down with Erlendur, "but I met her by pure chance."

"What happened to you?" Erlendur asked.

She looked at her father.

"I'm trying," she said, "but it's difficult."

"Two lads came here asking for you. Filthy-mouthed. I gave some Eddi character some money you owed him. It was him who told me where that the hovel was."

"Eddi's okay."

"Are you going to keep trying?"

"Should I get rid of it?" Eva Lind stared down at the floor.

"I don't know."

"I'm so scared I've damaged it."

"Maybe you're trying on purpose."

Eva Lind looked up at her father.

"You're fucking pathetic," she said.

"Me!"

"Yes, you."

"What am I supposed to think? Tell me that!" Erlendur shouted. "Can you possibly handle this endless self-pity? What a bloody loser you can be sometimes. Do you really feel so good in that company you keep that you can't think there's anything better for you? What right do you have to treat your life like that? What right do you have to treat the life inside you like that? Do you really think things are so horrible for you? Do you really think no-one in the world feels as bad as you? I'm investigating the death of a girl who didn't even reach the age of five. She fell ill and died. Something no-one understands destroyed her and killed her. Her coffin was three feet long. Can you hear what I'm saying? What right have you got to live? Tell me that!"

Erlendur was shouting. He stood up and hammered on the kitchen table with such a force that the cups started jumping around and when he saw that he picked one up and threw it at the wall behind Eva Lind. His rage flared up and for a moment he lost control of himself. He overturned the table, swept everything off the kitchen surfaces, pots and glasses slammed into the walls and floor. Eva Lind sat still in her chair, watched her father go berserk and her eyes filled with tears.

Finally Erlendur's rage abated, he turned to Eva Lind and saw her shoulders were shaking and she was hiding her face in her hands. He looked at his daughter, her dirty hair, thin arms, wrists hardly thicker than his fingers, her skinny, trembling body. She was barefoot and there was dirt under all her nails. He went over to her and tried to pull her hands away from her face, but she wouldn't let him. He wanted to apologise to her. Wanted to take her in his arms. He did neither.

Instead, he sat down on the floor beside her. The phone rang but he didn't answer it. There was no sign of the other girl from the bedroom. The phone stopped ringing and the flat fell silent again. The only sound was Eva Lind sobbing. Erlendur knew he was no model father and the speech he'd delivered could just as easily have been directed at himself. Probably he was talking just as much to himself and was as angry with himself as with Eva Lind. A psychologist would say he'd been venting his anger on the girl. But maybe what he said did have some effect. He hadn't seen Eva Lind cry before. Not since she was a small child. He left her when she was two.

At last Eva Lind took her hands away from her face, sniffed and wiped her face.

"It was her dad," she said.

"Her dad?" Erlendur said.

"Who was a monster," Eva Lind said. " 'He's a monster. What have I done?' It was her dad. He started touching her up when she started growing breasts and he kept going further and further. Couldn't even keep his hands off her at her own wedding. Took her off to some empty part of the house. Told her she looked so sexy in her wedding dress he couldn't control himself. Couldn't stand the thought of her leaving him. Started goosing her. She freaked out."

"What a crowd!" Erlendur groaned.

"I knew she did dope sometimes. She's asked me to score for her before. She totally flipped and went to see Eddi. She's been lying in that dump ever since."

Eva Lind stopped. "I think her mother knew about it," she said afterwards. "All the time. She didn't do anything. The house was too flash. Too many cars."

"Doesn't the girl want to go to the police?"

"Wow!"

"What?"

"Go through all that crap for a three-month

suspended sentence if anyone believes her? Come on!"

"What's she going to do?"

"She'll go back to the bloke. Her husband. I think she likes him."

"She blamed herself then, did she?"

"She doesn't know what to think."

"Because she wrote 'What have I done?' She took the blame on herself."

"It's not surprising she's a bit screwed up."

"It always seems to be the bloody perverts who seem happiest of all. Smile at the world as if there's never anything gnawing away at their bloody consciences."

"Don't talk to me like that again," Eva Lind said. "Never talk to me like that again."

"Do you owe more people than Eddi?" Erlendur asked.

"A few. But Eddi's the main problem."

The phone rang yet again. The girl in the bedroom stirred and sat up, looked all around and got out of bed. Erlendur wondered whether to bother answering. Whether to bother going to work. Whether he ought to spend the day with Eva Lind. Keep her company, maybe get her to go to the doctor with him and have the embryo looked at, if you could call it an embryo. Find out if everything was all right. Stand by her.

But the phone refused to stop ringing. The girl had come out into the corridor and looked all around in confusion. She called out to ask if anyone was in the flat. Eva Lind called back that they were in the kitchen. Erlendur stood up, met the girl in the kitchen doorway and said hello. He received no reply. They'd both slept in their clothes just like Erlendur. The girl looked around the kitchen that Erlendur had smashed up and cast a sideways glance at him.

Erlendur answered the phone at last.

"What was the smell in Holberg's flat like?" Erlendur took a while to realise it was Marion Briem's voice.

"The smell?" Erlendur repeated.

"What was the smell in his flat like?" Marion Briem repeated.

"It was a sort of nasty basement smell," Erlendur said. "A smell of damp. A stench. I don't know. Like horses?"

"No, it's not horses," Marion Briem said. "I was reading about Nordurmýri. I talked to a plumber friend of mine and he referred me to another plumber. I've talked to a lot of plumbers."

"Why plumbers?"

"Very interesting, the whole business. You didn't tell me about the fingerprints on the photo." There was a hint of accusation in Marion's voice.

"No," Erlendur said. "I didn't get round to it."

"I heard about Grétar and Holberg. Grétar knew the girl was Holberg's daughter. Maybe he knew something else."

Erlendur remained silent.

"What do you mean?" he said eventually.

"Do you know the most important thing about Nordurmýri?" Marion Briem asked.

"No," Erlendur said, finding it difficult to follow Marion's train of thought.

"It's so obvious that I missed it at the time."

"What is it?"

Marion paused for a moment as if to give extra weight to the words.

"Nordurmýri. North Mire."

"And?"

"The houses were built on marsh land."

26

Sigurdur Óli was surprised that the woman who answered the door knew what his business was before he explained it. He was standing on yet another staircase, this time in a three-storey block of flats in Grafarvogur. He had barely introduced himself and was halfway through explaining his presence there when the woman invited him to come inside, adding that she'd been expecting him.

It was early morning. Outside it was overcast with fine drizzle and the autumn gloom spread over the city as if in confirmation that it would very soon be winter, get darker and colder. On the radio, people had described it as the worst rainy spell for decades.

The woman offered to take his coat. Sigurdur Óli handed it to her and she hung it in a wardrobe. A man of a similar age to the woman came out of their kitchenette and greeted him with a handshake. They were both around 70, wearing some kind of track-suit and white socks as if they were on their way for a jog. He had interrupted them in the middle of morning coffee.

The flat was very small but efficiently furnished, with a small bathroom, kitchenette and sitting room and a spacious bedroom. It was boiling hot inside the flat. Sigurdur Óli accepted the offer of coffee and asked for a glass of water as well. His throat had immediately become parched. They exchanged a few words about the weather until Sigurdur Óli couldn't wait any longer.

"It looks as if you were expecting me," he said, sipping at the coffee. It was watery and tasted foul.

"Well, no-one's talking about anything except that poor woman you're looking for," she said.

Sigurdur Óli gave her a blank look.

"Everyone from Húsavík," the woman said, as if she shouldn't need to explain something so obvious. "We haven't talked about anything else since you started looking for her. We've got a very big club for people from Húsavík here in the city. I'm sure everyone knows you're looking for that woman."

"So it's the talk of the town?" Sigurdur Óli asked.

"Three of my friends from the north who now live here have phoned me since last night and this morning I had a call from Húsavík. They're gossiping about it all the time."

"And have you come to any conclusions?"

"Not really," she said and looked at her husband. "What was this man supposed to have done to her?"

She didn't try to conceal her curiosity. Didn't try to hide her nosiness. Sigurdur Óli was disgusted by how eager she was to find out the details and instinctively tried to guard his words.

"It's a question of an act of violence," he said.

"We're looking for the victim, but you probably know that already."

"Oh yes. But why? What did he do to her? And why now? I think, or we think," she said, looking at her husband, who was sitting silently following the conversation, "it's so strange how it matters after all these years. I heard she was raped. Was that it?"

"Unfortunately I can't divulge any details about the inquiry," Sigurdur Óli said. "And maybe it doesn't matter. I don't think you should make too much fuss about it. When you're talking to other people, I mean. Is there anything you could tell me that might be useful?"

The couple looked at each other.

"Make too much fuss about it?" she said, surprised. "We're not making any fuss about it. Do you think we're making any fuss about it, Eyvi?" She looked at her husband, who seemed unaware how to answer. "Go on, answer me!" she said sharply and he gave a start.

"No, I wouldn't say that, that's not right."

Sigurdur Óli's mobile phone rang. He didn't keep it loose in his pocket like Erlendur, but in a smart holder attached to the belt around his stiffly pressed trousers. Sigurdur Óli asked the couple to excuse him, stood up and answered the phone. It was Erlendur.

"Can you meet me at Holberg's flat?" he asked.

"What's going on?" Sigurdur Óli said.

"More digging," Erlendur said and rang off.

When Sigurdur Óli drove into Nordurmýri, Erlendur and Elínborg were already there. Erlendur was standing in the doorway to the basement smoking a cigarette. Elínborg was inside the flat. As far as Sigurdur Óli could see she was having a good sniff around, she stuck her head out and sniffed, exhaled and then tried somewhere else. He looked at Erlendur who shrugged and threw his cigarette into the garden and they went inside the flat together.

"What kind of smell do you think there is in here?" Erlendur asked Sigurdur Óli, and Sigurdur Óli started sniffing at the air like Elínborg. They walked from room to room with their noses in the air, except Erlendur who had a particularly poor sense of smell after so many years of smoking.

"When I first came in here," Elínborg said, "I thought that horsey people must live in the building or in this flat. The smell reminded me of horses, riding boots, saddles, or that sort of thing. Horse dung. Stables, really. It was the same smell that was in the first flat my husband and I bought. But there weren't any horse-lovers living there either. It was a combination of filth and rising damp. The radiators had been leaking onto the carpet and parquet for years and no-one had done anything about it. We also had the spare bathroom converted but the plumbers did it so badly, just stuffed straw into the hole and put a thin layer of concrete over it. So there was always a smell of sewers that came up through the repair."

"Which means?" Erlendur said.

"I think it's the same smell, except it's worse here. Rising damp and filth and sewer rats."

"I had a meeting with Marion Briem," Erlendur said, uncertain whether they knew the name. "Naturally Marion read up on Nordurmýri and reached the conclusion that the fact it's a marsh is important."

Elínborg and Sigurdur Óli exchanged glances.

"Nordurmýri used to be like a distinct village in the middle of Reykjavík," Erlendur went on. "The houses were built during or just after the war. Iceland had become a republic and they named the streets after the saga heroes, Gunnarsbraut, Skeggjagata and all that. It was a wide cross-section of society who gathered here, ranging from the reasonably well-off, even the rich, to those who barely had a penny to their name so they rented cheap basement flats like this one. A lot of old people like Holberg live in Nordurmýri, though most of them are more civilised than he was, and many of them live in precisely this type of basement flat. Marion told me all this."

Erlendur paused.

"Another feature of Nordurmýri is this sort of basement flat. Originally there weren't any basement flats, the owners had them converted, installed kitchens and walls, made rooms, made places to live. Previously these basements were where the work was done for, what did Marion call them? Self-contained homes. Do you know what that is?"

They both shook their heads.

"You're too young, of course," Erlendur said, well aware that they would hate him saying that. "In basements like this were the girls' rooms. They were maids in the homes of the more wealthy people. They had rooms in holes like this. There was a laundry room too, a room for making haggis, for example, and other food, storerooms, a bathroom and all that."

"Not forgetting that it's a marsh." Sigurdur Óli said sarcastically.

"Are you trying to tell us something important?" Elínborg said.

"Under these basements are foundations . . ." Erlendur said.

"That's quite unusual," Sigurdur Óli said to Elínborg.

". . . just like under all other houses," Erlendur continued, not letting Sigurdur Óli's quips disturb him. "If you talk to a plumber, as Marion Briem did . . ."

"What's all this Marion Briem bullshit anyway?" Sigurdur Óli said.

". . . you'll find out they've often been called out to Nordurmýri to deal with a problem that can arise years, decades after houses have been built on marsh land. It happens in some places but not others. You can see it happening on the outside of some houses. A lot of them are coated with pebbledash and you can see where the pebbledash ends and the bare wall of the house starts at ground level. A strip of maybe one or two feet. The point is that the ground subsides indoors too."

Erlendur noticed they'd stopped grinning.

"In the estate-agency business it's called a concealed fault and it's difficult to know how to deal with this sort of thing. When the houses subside it puts pressure on the sewage pipes and they burst under the floor. Before you know it, you're flushing your toilet straight into the foundations. It can go on for ages because the smell can't get through the concrete. But damp patches form because the hot-water outflow in many old houses is connected into the sewage pipe and leaks into the basement when the pipe breaks, it gets hot and the steam reaches the surface. The parquet warps."

Erlendur had their complete attention by now.

"And Marion told you all that?" Sigurdur Óli said.

"To fix it you have to break up the floor," Erlendur continued, "and go down into the foundations to mend the pipe. The plumbers told Marion that sometimes when they drilled through the floor they'd hit a hollow. The base plate is fairly thin in some places and underneath there's an air pocket. The ground has subsided by half a yard, maybe even a whole yard. All because of the marsh."

Sigurdur Óli and Elínborg looked at each other.

"So is it hollow under the floor here?" Elínborg asked, stamping with one foot.

Erlendur smiled.

"Marion even managed to locate a plumber who

came to this house the same year as the national festival. Everyone remembers that year and this plumber clearly recalled coming here because of the damp in the floor."

"What are you trying to tell us?" Sigurdur Óli asked.

"The plumber broke up the floor in here. The base plate isn't very thick. It's hollow underneath in a lot of places. The plumber remembers the job so clearly because he was shocked that Holberg wouldn't let him finish."

"How come?"

"He opened up the floor and mended the pipe, then Holberg threw him out and said he'd finish it himself. And he did."

They stood in silence until Sigurdur Óli couldn't resist the temptation any longer.

"Marion Briem?" he said. "Marion Briem!" He said the name over and again as if struggling to understand it. Erlendur was right. He was too young to remember Marion from the force. He repeated the name like it was some kind of conundrum, then suddenly stopped and looked thoughtful and finally asked:

"Wait a minute. Who is this Marion? What kind of name is that anyway? Is it a man or a woman?"

Sigurdur Óli gave Erlendur a questioning look.

"I sometimes wonder myself," Erlendur replied and took out his mobile phone.

27

Forensics began by tearing away the flooring in each room of the flat, the kitchen and bathroom and the den. It had taken all day to get the necessary permission for the operation. Erlendur had argued his case at a meeting with the police commissioner who agreed, though reluctantly, that there were sufficient suspicions to justify breaking up the floor in Holberg's flat. The matter was rushed through because of the murder that had been committed in the building.

Erlendur presented the excavation as a link to the search for Holberg's murderer; he implied that Grétar could well be alive and might conceivably have been the killer. The police would doubly benefit from the excavation. If Marion Briem's hunch was correct, it would rule out Grétar as a suspect and solve the riddle of a person missing for more than a quarter of a century.

They ordered the largest available size of transit van into which to load the whole of Holberg's household effects, apart from the fixtures and their contents. It was starting to get dark when the van backed up to the house and shortly afterwards a tractor pulled up with a pneumatic drill. A team of forensics experts gathered there and more detectives joined them. The residents were nowhere to be seen.

It had been raining all day, as on the previous days. But now it was only a fine drizzle that rippled in the cold autumn breeze and settled on Erlendur's face where he stood to one side, a cigarette between his fingers. Sigurdur Óli and Elínborg stood with him. A crowd had gathered in front of the house but seemed reluctant to get too close. It included reporters, television cameramen and newspaper photographers. Cars of all sizes marked with newspaper and television company logos were spread all around the neighbourhood and Erlendur, who had prohibited all contact with the media, wondered whether to have them removed.

Holberg's flat was soon empty. The big van remained in the forecourt while it was being decided what to do with the effects. Eventually Erlendur ordered them to be sent to the police storage depot. Erlendur saw the linoleum and carpets being carried out of the flat and loaded into the van, which then rumbled off, out of the street.

The head of forensics greeted Erlendur with a handshake. He was about 50, named Ragnar, rather fat and with a black mop of hair standing out in all directions. He was educated in Britain, read only British thrillers and was a particular devotee of British detective series on television.

"What bloody nonsense have you got us into now?" he asked, looking over towards the media crews. There was a hint of humour in his voice. He thought it was marvellous that they were tearing up the floor to look for a body.

"How does it look?" Erlendur asked.

"All the floors have a thick coat of some kind of ship's paint," Ragnar said. "It's impossible to tell if they've been tampered with. We can't see any concrete of a different age or anything that might be a repair to it. We're banging on the floor with hammers, but it sounds hollow almost everywhere. Whether it's subsidence or something else, I don't know. The concrete in the building itself is thick, quality stuff. None of that alkaline bollocks. But there are a lot of damp patches on the floor. Couldn't that plumber you were in touch with help us?"

"He's in a retirement home in Akureyri and says he's not coming back south in this life. He gave us a fairly accurate description of where he opened the floor."

"We're also inserting a camera down the sewage pipe. Looking at the plumbing, seeing if it's all right, to find out if we can see the old repair."

"Do you really need a drill that big?" Erlendur asked, nodding towards the tractor.

"I haven't the faintest idea. We've got smaller electric drills, but they couldn't penetrate wet shit. We've got smaller pneumatics and if we find a hollow we can drill through the base plate and slip a little camera through it like they use for inspecting damaged sewage pipes."

"Hopefully that will do. We don't want to have to smash the whole house down."

"There's a bloody stench in that dump anyway," the head of forensics said, and they walked off towards the basement. Three forensic experts wearing white paper overalls, with plastic gloves and hammers, were walking around the flat, banging on the stone floor and marking with blue felt-tip pens where they thought it sounded hollow.

"According to the buildings surveyors' office the basement was converted into a flat in 1959," Erlendur said. "Holberg bought it in 1962 and probably moved in straightaway. He'd lived here ever since."

One of the forensics people came up to them and greeted Erlendur. He had a set of drawings of the building, one for each floor.

"The toilets are in the centre of each floor. The sewage pipes come down from the floors above and enter the foundations where the basement toilet is. It was already in the basement before the conversion, and you could imagine the flat being designed around it. The toilet's linked up to the sewage pipe in the bathroom, then the pipe continues due east through part of the sitting room, under the bedroom and out into the street."

"The search isn't confined to the sewage pipe," the head of forensics said.

"No, but we've put a camera into the drain from the street. They were just telling me the pipe's split where it enters the bedroom and we thought we'd take a look there first. It's in a similar place to where I understand the floor was opened."

Ragnar nodded and looked at Erlendur, who shrugged as if what forensics did was none of his business.

"It can't be a very old split," the head of forensics said. "The smell must be coming from there. Are you saying this man was buried in the foundations over 25 years ago?"

"He disappeared then, at least," Erlendur said.

Their words merged into the hammering that became a continuous din echoing between the empty walls. The forensics expert took some ear defenders out of a black case the size of a small suitcase and put them on, then picked up one of the small electric drills and plugged it in. He pressed the trigger a few times to test it, then thrust it down on the floor and started breaking it up. The noise was awful and the rest of the forensic team put on ear defenders too. He made little headway. The solid concrete barely flaked. He gave up trying and shook his head.

"We need to start up the tractor," he said, fine dust covering his face. "And bring the pneumatic in. And we need masks. What bloody idiot had this brilliant idea anyway?" he said and spat on the floor.

"Holberg would hardly have used a pneumatic drill under cover of darkness," the head of forensics said.

"He didn't need to do anything under cover of

darkness," Erlendur said. "The plumber made the hole in the floor for him."

"Do you reckon he put him down the shithole?"

"We'll see. Maybe he needed to rearrange things in the foundations. Maybe it's all a misunderstanding."

Erlendur went out into the night air. Sigurdur Óli and Elínborg were sitting in the car eating hotdogs that Sigurdur Óli had bought from the nearest kiosk. A hotdog was waiting for Erlendur on the dashboard. He wolfed it down.

"If we find Grétar's body here, what does that tell us?" Elínborg asked Erlendur and wiped her mouth.

"I wish I knew," Erlendur said thoughtfully. "I just wish I knew."

At that moment the chief superintendent came hurrying over, banged on the window, opened the door and told Erlendur to come with him for a moment. Sigurdur Óli and Elínborg got out of the car as well. The chief superintendent's name was Hrólfur and he'd been off sick during the day but seemed fit as a fiddle now. He was very fat and the way he dressed hid it badly. He was the lethargic type and rarely contributed anything to the investigations. He was off sick for weeks every year.

"Why wasn't I contacted about these operations?" he asked, visibly angry.

"You're ill," Erlendur said.

"Bollocks," Hrólfur said. "Don't you think you can go running the department as you please. I'm your superior. You talk to me about this kind of operation before you go putting your bloody stupid brainwaves into practice!"

"Wait a minute, I thought you were ill," Erlendur repeated, feigning surprise.

"And how did it ever occur to you to hoodwink the police commissioner like that?" Hrólfur hissed. "How did it occur to you that there's a man under the floor here? You've got nothing to go on. Absolutely nothing except some crap about house foundations and a smell. Have you gone mad?"

Sigurdur Óli walked hesitantly over to them.

"There's a woman here I think you ought to talk to, Erlendur," he said, holding out the phone which Erlendur had left behind in the car. "It's personal. She's quite worked up."

Hrólfur turned to Sigurdur Óli and told him to piss off and leave them alone.

Sigurdur Óli didn't give way.

"You ought to talk to her immediately, Erlendur," he said.

"What's the meaning of this? You act as if I don't exist!" Hrólfur shouted, stamping his foot. "Is this a bloody conspiracy? Erlendur, if we're going to smash up the foundations of people's houses because they smell, we'll end up never doing anything else. It's totally absurd! It's ridiculous."

"Marion Briem had this interesting idea," Erlendur said as calmly as before, "and I thought it was worth investigating. The police commissioner thought so too. Do excuse me for not contacting you, but I'm pleased to see you're back on your feet.

And I really must say, Hrólfur, that you're looking exceptionally perky. Please excuse me."

Erlendur walked past Hrólfur, who stared at him and Sigurdur Óli, ready to say something, but not knowing what it ought to be.

"One thing occurred to me," Erlendur said. "I should have done it ages ago."

"What?" Sigurdur Óli said.

"Contact the Harbour and Lighthouse Authority and find out if they can tell whether Holberg was in Húsavík or thereabouts in the early '60s."

"Okay. Here, talk to this woman."

"Which woman?" Erlendur said and took the phone. "I don't know any woman."

"They put her through to your mobile. She'd been asking for you at the office. They told her you were busy, but she wouldn't take no for an answer."

At that moment the pneumatic drill on the tractor started up. A deafening noise came from the basement and they saw a thick cloud of dust billowing out. The police had covered all the windows so no-one could see inside. Everyone apart from the drill operator had gone outside and they all stood at a distance, waiting. They looked at their watches and seemed to be discussing how late it was. They knew they couldn't go on making that noise all evening in the middle of a residential area. They'd have to stop soon and continue the next morning or take other action.

Erlendur hurried into the car with his phone and

closed the door on the noise. He recognised the voice immediately.

"He's here," Elín said, as soon as she heard Erlendur's voice on the phone. She seemed very agitated.

"Relax, Elín," Erlendur said. "Who are you talking about?"

"He's standing in front of the house in the rain, staring in at me." Her voice turned to a whisper.

"Who, Elín? Are you at home? In Keflavík?"

"I don't know when he came, I don't know how long he's been standing there. I just noticed him. They wouldn't put me through to you."

"I don't quite follow. Who are you talking about, Elín?"

"The man of course. It's that beast. I'm sure of it."

"Who?"

"That brute who attacked Kolbrún!"

"Kolbrún? What are you talking about?"

"I know. It can't be, but he's standing here all the same."

"Aren't you getting things mixed up?"

"Don't say I'm getting anything mixed up. Don't say that! I know exactly what I'm saying."

"Which man who attacked Kolbrún?"

"Well, HOLBERG!" Instead of raising her voice, Elín hissed down the phone. "He's standing outside my house!"

Erlendur said nothing.

"Are you there?" Elín whispered. "What are you going to do?"

"Elín," Erlendur said emphatically. "It can't be Holberg. Holberg's dead. It must be someone else."

"Don't talk to me like I'm a baby. He's standing out here in the rain, staring at me. That beast."

28

The connection broke off and Erlendur started the engine. Sigurdur Óli and Elínborg watched him reverse through the crowd and disappear off down the street. They looked at each other and shrugged as if they'd given up trying to figure him out ages ago.

Before he was even out of the street he had already contacted the Keflavík police and sent them off to Elín's house to apprehend a man in the vicinity who was wearing a blue anorak, jeans and white trainers. Elín had described the man. He told the sergeant not to switch on the sirens or flashing lights, but to approach as quietly as possible so as not to scare him off.

"Stupid old bag," Erlendur said to himself and hung up his phone.

He drove out of Reykjavík as fast as he could, through Hafnarfjördur and onto the Keflavík road. The traffic was heavy and visibility was poor, but he zig-zagged between the cars and even onto a traffic island to overtake. He disregarded all the traffic lights and made it to Keflavík in half an hour. It helped him that the CID had recently been issued with blue police lights that they could put on the roofs of their unmarked cars in emergencies. He'd laughed at the time. Recalled the apparatus on a detective programme on television and thought it was ridiculous to go around using thriller props in Reykjavík.

Two police cars were parked outside Elín's house when he pulled up. Elín was waiting for him inside with three policemen. She said the man had vanished into the dark just before the police cars pulled up at the house. She pointed out where he'd been standing and the direction he ran, but the police could not find any trace of him. The police were baffled about how to deal with Elín, who refused to tell them who the man was and why he was dangerous; his only crime, apparently, was that he had been standing outside her house in the rain. When they put their questions to Erlendur, he told them the man was connected with a murder inquiry in Reykjavík. He told them to inform the Reykjavík police if they came across anyone matching the man's description.

Elín was fairly agitated and Erlendur decided the wisest move would be to get the police out of her house as quickly as possible. He managed without much effort. They said they had better things to do than chase around after figments of an old woman's imagination, though they made sure Elín didn't hear them say it.

"I swear it was him outside," she said to Erlendur

when they were alone in the house. "I don't know how, but it was him!"

Erlendur looked at her and heard what she was saying and could see that she meant it in all seriousness. He knew she'd been under great strain recently.

"It just doesn't make sense, Elín. Holberg's dead. I saw him in the morgue." He paused to think, then added, "I saw his heart."

Elín looked at him.

"You think I'm nuts. You think I'm imagining it all. That it's a way of getting attention because . . ."

"Holberg's dead," Erlendur interrupted her. "What am I supposed to think?"

"Then it was the spitting image of him," Elín said.

"Describe this man to me in more detail."

Elín stood up, went to the sitting-room window and pointed out at the rain.

"He was standing there, by the path that leads out to the street between the houses. Stood completely still and looked in at me. I don't know if he saw me. I tried to hide from him. I was reading and I got up when it started to get dark in the sitting room and I was going to switch on the light when I happened to look out of the window. His head was bare and it was like he couldn't care less if he got soaked through. Even though he was standing just there, somehow he still seemed miles away."

Elín thought for a moment. "He had black hair and looked around 40. Average height."

"Elín," Erlendur said. "It's dark outside. Pouring

rain. You can hardly see out of the window. The path isn't lit. You wear glasses. Are you telling me that . . ."

"It was only just starting to get dark then and I didn't run for the phone straightaway. I had a good look at the man out of this window and the kitchen window. It took me quite a while to realise it was Holberg, or someone like him. The path isn't lit, but there's a fair amount of traffic in the street and every time a car went past it lit him up so I could see his face clearly."

"How can you be so sure?"

"He was the image of Holberg when he was younger," Elín said. "Not the old bloke in the photo in the papers."

"Did you see Holberg when he was younger?"

"Yes, I saw him. Kolbrún was called down to the CID once, out of the blue. They told her they needed a more detailed explanation about some part of her statement. All bloody lies. Someone called Marion Briem was handling the case. What kind of a name is that anyway? Marion Briem? They told Kolbrún to go to Reykjavík. She asked me to go with her and I did. She had an appointment, I think it was in the morning. We went in there and that Marion met us and showed us into a room. We'd been sitting there a while when the door suddenly opened and Holberg walked in. That Marion was standing behind him by the door."

Elín paused.

"And what happened?" Erlendur asked.

"My sister had a breakdown. Holberg was grinning and he made some obscene gesture with his tongue and Kolbrún grabbed me like she was drowning. She couldn't breathe. Holberg started laughing and Kolbrún had a fit. She rolled her eyes, started foaming at the mouth and fell on the floor. Marion took Holberg back out but I saw that beast there for the first and only time and I'll never forget that ugly mug of his."

"And you saw that same face outside your window tonight?"

Elín nodded.

"I was shocked, I admit that, and of course it can't have been Holberg in person, but the man looked exactly like him."

Erlendur wondered whether he should tell Elín about his recent train of thought. He weighed up how much he could tell her and whether there was any certainty that what he would say had any foundation in reality. They sat in silence while he thought it over. It was late evening and Erlendur's thoughts turned to Eva Lind. He felt the pain in his chest again and stroked it as if that would make it go away.

"Are you all right?" Elín asked.

"We've been working on something recently, but I haven't got a clue if there's anything behind it," Erlendur said. "But what happened here supports the theory. If Holberg had another victim, if he raped another woman, there's a chance she had his child just like Kolbrún did. I've been wondering about that possibility because of the note we found with Holberg's body. It's possible he had a son. If the rape took place before 1964 that son would be close to 40 today. And it could have been him standing outside your house here tonight."

Elín looked at Erlendur, thunderstruck.

"Holberg's son? Could that be?"

"You said he was the spitting image of him."

"Yes, but . . ."

"I'm sort of turning it over in my mind. Somewhere in this case there's a missing link and I think this man could well be it."

"But why? What's he doing here?"

"Don't you think that's obvious?"

"What's obvious?"

"You're his sister's aunt," Erlendur said and watched the expression on Elín's face change as it gradually dawned on her what Erlendur meant.

"Audur was his sister," she said. "But how could he know about me? How could he know where I live? How could he link Holberg with me? There's been nothing about his past in the papers, nothing about his rapes or him having a daughter. No-one knew about Audur. How does that man know who I am?"

"Maybe he'll tell us that when we find him."

"Is he Holberg's killer, do you reckon?"

"Now you're asking me if he murdered his own father," Erlendur said.

Elín thought. "My God," she said.

"I don't know," Erlendur said. "If you see him outside again, call me."

Elín had stood up and gone to the window facing the path as if expecting to see him there again.

"I know I was a bit hysterical when I phoned you and said Holberg was here because I felt for a moment that it could be him. It was such a terrible shock seeing him. But I didn't feel scared. I was angry more than anything, but there was something about the man, the way he was standing, the way he bowed his head. There was something sad about him, in his face, some kind of sorrow. I thought to myself that he couldn't be feeling well. He can't feel well. Was he in touch with his father? Do you know?"

"I don't know for sure that he actually exists," Erlendur said. "What you saw supports one theory. We have no leads on that man. There aren't any photos of him at Holberg's flat if that's what you mean. But someone did phone Holberg several times shortly before he was murdered and he was nervous about those calls. We don't know any more than that."

Erlendur took out his mobile phone and asked Elín to excuse him for a moment.

"What the bloody hell have you got us into now?" Sigurdur Óli shouted in a clearly furious voice. "They hit the shit pipe and it was swarming with filthy bugs, millions of disgusting little bugs under the sodding floor. It's disgusting. Where the hell are you?"

"Keflavík. Any sign of Grétar?"

"No, there's no sodding sign of any fucking Grétar," Sigurdur Óli said and rang off.

"There's one more thing, Inspector," Elín said, "I just realised it when you talked about him being related to Audur. I can see now that I was right. I didn't understand it then, but there was another look on his face that I thought I'd never see again. It was a face from the past that I've never forgotten."

"What was it?" Erlendur said.

"That was why I didn't feel scared of him. I didn't realise at first. He reminded me of Audur too. There was something about him that reminded me of Audur."

29

Sigurdur Óli returned his mobile phone to the holder on his belt and walked back to the house. He'd been inside with several other policemen when the pneumatic drill penetrated the base plate and the stench that came out was so overpowering that he retched. He rushed for the door like everyone else inside and thought he would vomit before he made it out into the fresh air. When they went back in they wore goggles and masks over their mouths, but the horrendous smell still penetrated them.

The drill operator widened the hole over the broken sewage pipe. It was easy going once he was through the floor. Sigurdur Óli dreaded to think how long ago the pipe had been broken. It looked as if waste had been collecting in a large area under the floor. There was a faintly discernable steam rising up from the hole. He shone a torch down at the patch of filth and from what he could see the ground had subsided by at least half a yard from the base plate.

The patch of filth was like a thick, swarming trunk of little black bugs. He jumped back when he saw some kind of creature dart past the beam of light.

"Watch out!" he shouted and strode out of the basement. "There are rats under that bloody thing. Close up the hole and call in pest control. Let's stop here. Stop everything this minute!"

No-one objected. One of the forensic team spread a plastic sheet over the hole in the floor and the basement was empty in a flash. Sigurdur Óli tore off his mask when he came out of the basement and voraciously gulped down the fresh air. They all did.

On his way home from Keflavík, Erlendur heard about the progress of the investigation in Nordur-mýri. A pest-control officer had been called out, but the police would take no further action until the following morning when everything that was living in the foundations had been exterminated. Sigurdur Óli had gone home and was getting out of the shower when Erlendur called him for an update. Elínborg had gone home too. A guard was mounted outside Holberg's flat while the pest-control officer did his work. Two police cars stood outside the house all night.

Eva Lind met her father at the door when he got home. It was past 9 p.m. The bride had left. Before she went she had told Eva Lind she was going to talk to her husband and find out how he was feeling. She wasn't sure whether she would tell him the real reason for running out of their wedding. Eva Lind urged her to, said she shouldn't cover up for that bastard of a father of hers. The last thing she should do was cover up for him.

They sat down in the sitting room. Erlendur told Eva Lind all about the murder investigation, where it had led him and what was going through his mind. He did so not least to gain some kind of understanding of the case for his own benefit, a clearer picture of what had been happening over the past few days. He told her almost everything, from the moment they found Holberg's body in the basement, the smell in his flat, the note, the old photograph in the drawer, the pornography on his computer, the epitaph on the gravestone, Kolbrún and her sister, Elín, Audur and her unexplained death, the dreams that haunted him, Ellidi in prison and Grétar's disappearance, Marion Briem, the search for Holberg's other victim and the man in front of Elín's house, conceivably Holberg's son. He tried to give a systematic account and discussed with himself various theories and questions, until he reached a dead end and stopped talking.

He didn't tell Eva Lind the brain was missing from the child's body. He hadn't yet begun to understand how that could have happened.

Eva Lind listened to him without interrupting and she noticed how Erlendur rubbed his chest while he talked. She could feel how the Holberg case was affecting him. She could sense an air of resignation about him that she'd never noticed before. She could sense his weariness when he talked about the little girl. It was as if he withdrew inside himself, his voice went quieter and he became increasingly remote.

"Is Audur the girl you told me about when you were shouting at me this morning?" Eva Lind asked.

"She was, I don't know, maybe some kind of godsend to her mother," Erlendur said. "She loved the girl beyond death and the grave. Sorry if I've been nasty to you. I didn't intend to, but when I see the way you live, when I see your careless attitude and your lack of self-respect, when I see the destruction, everything you do to yourself and then I watch the little coffin coming up out of the ground, then I can't understand anything any more. I can't understand what's happening and I want to . . ."

Erlendur fell silent.

"Beat the shit out of me," Eva Lind finished the sentence for him.

Erlendur shrugged.

"I don't know what I want to do. Maybe the best thing is to do nothing. Maybe it's best to let life run its course. Forget the whole business. Start doing something sensible. Why should I want to get involved in all this? All this filth. Talking to people like Ellidi. Doing deals with shits like Eddi. Seeing how people like Holberg get their kicks. Reading rape reports. Digging up the foundations of a house full of bugs and shit. Digging up little coffins."

Erlendur stroked his chest even harder.

"You think it won't affect you. You reckon you're strong enough to withstand that sort of thing. You think you can put on armour against it over the years and can watch all the filth from a distance as if it's none of your business, and try to keep your senses. But there isn't any distance. And there's no armour. No-one's strong enough. The repulsion haunts you like an evil spirit that burrows into your mind and doesn't leave you in peace until you believe that the filth is life itself because you've forgotten how ordinary people live. This case is like that. Like an evil spirit that's been unleashed to run riot in your mind and ends up leaving you crippled."

Erlendur heaved a deep sigh. "It's all one great big bloody mire."

He stopped talking and Eva Lind sat silently with him.

Some time passed like this until she got up, sat down beside her father, put her arm round him and sidled up against him. She could hear his heart beating rhythmically, like a soothing clock, and eventually fell asleep with a contented smile on her face.

30

Around 9 a.m. the following day the forensic and CID teams gathered at Holberg's house. There was hardly a glimpse of daylight even at that time in the morning. The sky was gloomy and it was still raining. The radio had said the rain in Reykjavík was approaching the record of October 1926.

The sewage pipe had been cleaned and there was nothing left alive in the foundations. The hole in the base plate had been widened so that two men could go down through it at once. The owners of the flats above were standing in a group outside the basement door. They had ordered a plumber to mend the pipe and were waiting to call him in as soon as the police gave permission.

It soon emerged that the hollow area around the sewage pipe was relatively small. It measured about three square yards and was contained because the ground hadn't sunk away from the base plate everywhere. The pipe had broken in the same place as before. The old repair was visible and there was a different kind of gravel underneath the pipe from that around it. The forensic technicians discussed whether to widen the hole even further, dig up the gravel from the foundations and empty it out until they could see everywhere under the base plate. After some argument they decided that the plate might break if what was under it was removed completely, so they opted for a safer and more technically advanced method, drilling holes through the floor here and there and putting a miniature camera down into the foundations.

Sigurdur Óli watched when they started drilling holes into the floor and then set up two monitors that were connected to the two cameras that forensics were using. The cameras were little more than pipes with a light on the front which were slipped into the holes and could be moved by remote control. Holes were drilled in the floor where it was thought to be hollow underneath, they slipped the cameras inside and switched on the two monitors. The picture came out in black-and-white and seemed of very poor quality to Sigurdur Óli, who owned a German television set costing half a million crowns.

Erlendur arrived at the basement just as they were starting to probe with the cameras and shortly afterwards Elínborg turned up. Sigurdur Óli noticed Erlendur had shaved and was wearing clean clothes which looked almost as though they'd been ironed.

"Anything happening?" Erlendur asked and lit a cigarette, to Sigurdur Óli's chagrin.

"They're going to do a camera probe," Sigurdur Óli said. "We can watch it on the screen."

"Nothing in the sewage?" Erlendur said, sucking down the smoke.

"Bugs and rats, nothing else."

"Filthy stench down here," Elínborg said and took out a perfumed handkerchief that she carried in her handbag. Erlendur offered her a cigarette, but she declined.

"Holberg could have used the hole the plumber made to put Grétar under the floor," Erlendur said. "He would have seen it was hollow under the base plate and could have moved the gravel around once he'd put Grétar wherever he wanted."

They gathered around the screen but couldn't make out very much of what they saw. A little glow of light moved back and forth, up and down and to the sides. Sometimes they thought they could see the outline of the base plate and sometimes they appeared to see gravel. The ground had subsided to varying degrees. In some places it was right up to the plate, but elsewhere there was a gap of up to three feet.

They stood for a good while watching the cameras. It was noisy in the basement because the forensic team was continually drilling new holes and Erlendur soon lost his patience and walked out. Elínborg quickly followed him and then Sigurdur Óli. They all got into Erlendur's car. He had told them the previous evening why he suddenly left for Keflavík, but they hadn't had the opportunity to discuss it any further.

"Of course it fits in with the message that was left

behind in Nordurmýri. And if the man Elín saw in Keflavík looks so much like Holberg, that fits in with the theory about his second child."

"Holberg may not have had a son after the rape," Sigurdur Óli said. "We've got no evidence as such to support that, except that Ellidi knew about another woman. That's all there is. Besides which, Ellidi's a moron."

"No-one we've talked to who knew Holberg has mentioned he had a son," Elínborg said.

"No-one we've talked to knew Holberg in the first place," Sigurdur Óli said. "That's the point. He was a loner, socialised with a few workmates, down-loaded porn from the Internet, went around with jerks like Ellidi and Grétar. No-one knows anything about the guy."

"What I'm wondering is this," Erlendur said. "If Holberg's son does exist, how does he know about Elín, Audur's aunt? Doesn't that mean he must also know about Audur, his sister? If he knows about Elín, I presume he knows about Kolbrún and the rape as well, and I can't work out how. There haven't been any details about the investigation in the media. Where would he get his information from?"

"Couldn't he have got this out of Holberg before he bumped him off?" Sigurdur Óli said. "Isn't that likely?"

"Maybe he tortured him to make him confess," Elínborg said.

"First of all, we don't know whether this man

even exists," Erlendur said. "Elín was very emotional when she saw him. Even assuming he is real, we don't have any idea if he killed Holberg. Nor whether he even knew of his father's existence, having been born under those circumstances, after a rape. Ellidi said there was a woman before Kolbrún who got the same treatment, maybe worse. If she got pregnant by it, I doubt that the mother would have been too eager to name the father. She didn't notify the police about what happened. We don't have anything about Holberg's other rapes in our files. We still have to find this woman, if she exists . . ."

"And we're smashing up the foundations of a house to look for a man who probably has nothing to do with the case," Sigurdur Óli said.

"Maybe Grétar isn't under the foundations here," Elínborg said.

"How come?" Erlendur said.

"Maybe he's still alive, you mean?" Sigurdur Óli said.

"He knew all about Holberg, I'd imagine," Elínborg said. "He knew about the daughter, otherwise he wouldn't have taken a photograph of her grave. He definitely knew how she came into the world. If Holberg had another child, a son, he would have known about him too."

Erlendur and Sigurdur Óli looked at her with growing interest.

"Maybe Grétar's still with us," she continued, "and in touch with the son. That's one explanation for how the son could know about Elín and Audur."

"But Grétar went missing a good 25 years ago and hasn't been heard of since," Sigurdur Óli said.

"Just because he went missing doesn't necessarily mean he's dead," Elínborg said.

"So that . . ." Erlendur began, but Elínborg interrupted him.

"I don't think we can rule him out. Why not allow for the possibility that Grétar is still alive? No body was ever found. He could have left the country. It could have been enough for him to move to the countryside. No-one gave a damn. No-one missed him."

"I don't remember any instance of that," Erlendur said.

"Of what?" Sigurdur Óli asked.

"A missing person returning a whole generation later. When people disappear in Iceland it's always for good. No-one ever comes back after an absence of more than 25 years. Never."

31

Erlendur left his colleagues in Nordurmýri and went up to Barónsstígur to meet the pathologist. The pathologist was completing his autopsy on Holberg and was covering up the body when Erlendur went up to him. Audur's body was nowhere to be seen.

"Have you found the girl's brain?" the pathologist asked straight out when Erlendur walked in on him.

"No," Erlendur said.

"I talked to a professor, an old girlfriend of mine from the university, and explained it to her, I hope that was all right, and she wasn't surprised about our little discovery. That short story by Halldór Laxness, have you read it?"

"The one about Nebuchadnezzar? It has crossed my mind in the past couple of days," Erlendur said.

"Isn't it called 'Lily', that story? It's a long time since I read it, but it's about some medical students who snatch a body and put rocks in the coffin, and basically that's what happens. No-one kept any real tabs on that in the old days, just as the story describes. People who died in hospital had autopsies unless it was forbidden and of course the autopsy was used for teaching purposes. Sometimes samples were removed and they could be anything really, from whole organs to minor tissue samples. Then everything was wrapped up and the person in question was given a decent burial. These days it's rather different. An autopsy is performed only if the relatives give their consent and organs are removed for research and teaching purposes only if certain conditions are met. I don't think anything is stolen nowadays."

"You don't think so?"

The pathologist shrugged.

"We're not talking about organ transplants, are we?" Erlendur said.

"A completely different matter. People are generally prepared to help others if it's a question of life and death."

"And where's the organ bank?"

"There are thousands of samples in this building alone," the pathologist said. "Here on Barónsstígur. The largest part of it is the Dungal collection, which is the largest bio-sample bank in Iceland."

"Could you show it to me?" Erlendur asked. "Is there a register of where the samples come from?"

"It's all carefully documented. I took the liberty of checking for our sample but I couldn't find it."

"Where is it then?"

"You ought to talk to the professor and hear what she has to say. I think there are some registers up at the university."

"Why didn't you tell me this straightaway?"

Erlendur asked. "When you discovered the brain had been removed? You knew about it?"

"Talk to her and come back. I've probably told you far too much already."

"Are the registers for the collection in the university?"

"As far as I know," the pathologist said, gave him the professor's name and told him to let him get on with his work.

"So you know about Jar City then," Erlendur said.

"They used to call one room here Jar City," the pathologist said. "It's closed now. Don't ask me what happened to the jars, I haven't got the faintest idea."

"Do you find this uncomfortable to talk about?"

"Will you stop this."

"What?"

"Stop it."

The professor, Hanna, who was head of the University of Iceland's Faculty of Medicine, stared across the desk at Erlendur as if he were a cancerous growth that needed to be removed from her office at the earliest possible opportunity. She was somewhat younger than Erlendur but extremely firm, spoke fast and was quick to reply, and gave the impression that she couldn't stand any nonsense or unnecessary digressions. She asked Erlendur quite brashly to get to the point when he embarked upon a long speech about his reasons for being in her office. Erlendur smiled to himself. He took an immediate liking to her and knew they'd be at each other's throats before their meeting was over. She was wearing a dark suit, plump, no make-up, short, blond hair, her hands practical, her expression serious and profound. Erlendur would have liked to see her smile. His wish was not granted.

He had disturbed her during a lecture. Knocked on the door to ask for her as if he'd lost his way. She came to the door and asked him kindly to wait until the lecture was over. Erlendur stood in the corridor, as if he had been caught playing truant, for a quarter of an hour before the door opened. Hanna strode out into the corridor and past Erlendur and told him to follow her. He had trouble doing so. She seemed to take two steps for every one of his.

"I can't understand what the CID wants of me," she said as she breezed along, turning her head slightly as if to reassure herself that Erlendur was keeping up with her.

"You'll find out," Erlendur panted.

"I certainly hope so," Hanna said and showed him into her office.

When Erlendur told her his business she sat and thought about it for a long time. Erlendur managed to slow her down a little with the account of Audur and her mother and the autopsy, the diagnosis and the brain that had been removed.

"Which hospital did you say the girl was admitted to?" she asked eventually.

"Keflavík. How do you obtain organs for teaching?"

Hanna stared at Erlendur.

"I don't see what you're getting at."

"You use human organs for teaching purposes," Erlendur said. "Bio-samples, I think they're called, I'm no expert, but the question is very simple. Where do you get them from?"

"I don't think I need to tell you anything about that," she said and started to fiddle with some papers lying on her desk as if she was too busy to pay proper attention to Erlendur.

"It's quite important to us," Erlendur said, "to us at the police, to find out if the brain still exists. Conceivably it's in your records. It was studied at the time but not returned to its rightful place. There may be a perfectly straightforward explanation. The tumour took time to examine and the body had to be buried. The university and hospitals are the most likely places for storing organs. You can sit there with your poker face, but I can do a couple of things to cause a bit of aggro for you, the university and the hospitals. Just think what a pain the media can be sometimes, and I just happen to have a couple of friends on the papers."

Hanna took a long look at Erlendur, who stared back.

"A crow starves sitting," she said eventually.

"But finds flying," Erlendur completed the proverb.

"That was really the only rule in this respect, but I

can't tell you anything, as you can possibly imagine. These are fairly sensitive issues."

"I'm not investigating it as a criminal act," Erlendur said. "I don't even know whether an organ theft was involved. What you do to dead people is none of my business, if it's kept within reasonable limits."

Hanna's expression turned even more ferocious.

"If this is what the medical profession needs, I'm sure it can be justified to some people. I need to locate a specific organ from a specific individual to study it again and if we can trace its history from the time it was removed until the present day I'd be extremely grateful. This is private information for my own purposes."

"What kind of private information?"

"I'm not interested in letting this go any further. We need to get the organ back if possible. What I was wondering is whether it wouldn't have sufficed to take a sample, whether the whole organ needed to be removed."

"Of course I don't know the specific case to which you're referring but there are stricter rules in force about autopsies now than in the old days," Hanna said after some thought. "If this case was in the '60s it could have happened, I wouldn't rule that out. You say the girl was given an autopsy against her mother's will. It's hardly the first instance of that. Today, the relatives are asked immediately after a death if an autopsy can be performed. I think I can say that their wishes are honoured apart from absolutely exceptional cases. That would have applied in this case. Child mortality is the most terrible of all things to deal with. There's no way to describe the tragedy that strikes people who lose a child and the question of an autopsy can be uncomfortable in such cases."

Hanna paused.

"We have some of this on record on our computers," she continued, "and the rest is in the archive stored in this building. They keep fairly detailed records. The hospitals' largest collection of organs is on Barónsstígur. You realise that little medical teaching takes place here on campus. It's done in the hospitals. That's where the knowledge comes from."

"The pathologist didn't want to show me the organ bank," Erlendur said. "He wanted me to talk to you first. Does the university have any say in the matter?"

"Come on," Hanna said, without answering his question. "Let's see what's in the computers."

She stood up and Erlendur followed her. She used a key to unlock a spacious room and entered a password in a security device on the wall by the door. She went over to a desk and switched on a computer while Erlendur took a look around. There were no windows in the room and rows of filing cabinets stood against the walls. Hanna asked for Audur's name and date of death and entered it in the computer.

"It's not here," she said thoughtfully, glaring at

the monitor. "Computer records only go back to 1984. We're digitising all the data from the time the medical faculty was established, but we haven't got any further than that with our records yet."

"So it's the filing cabinets then," Erlendur said.

"I really don't have the time for all this," Hanna said, looking at the clock. "I'm supposed to be in the lecture theatre again."

She went over to Erlendur and took a quick look around, walked between the cabinets and read their labels. She pulled out a drawer here and there and browsed through the documents, but quickly closed them again. Erlendur had no idea what the files contained.

"Have you got medical records in here?" he asked.

Hanna groaned. "Don't tell me you're here for the data privacy committee," she said and slammed yet another drawer shut.

"Only asked," Erlendur said.

Hanna took out a report and read from it.

"Here's something about bio-samples," she said. "1968. There are several names here. Nothing you're interested in." She put the report back in the cabinet, shoved the drawer closed and pulled out another one. "Here are some more," she said. "Wait a minute. Here's the girl's name, Audur, and her mother's name. Here it is."

Hanna read quickly through the report.

"One organ removed," she said, as if to herself. "Taken at Keflavík hospital. Permission of next of kin … nothing there. There's nothing here about the organ being destroyed."

Hanna closed the file. "It's not around any more."

"May I see that?" Erlendur asked, not attempting to conceal his eagerness.

"You won't learn anything from it," Hanna said, put the file back in the drawer and closed it. "I've told you what you need to know."

"What does it say? What are you hiding?"

"Nothing," Hanna said, "and now I have to get back to my teaching."

"Then I'll get a warrant and come back later today and that report had better be where it belongs," Erlendur said and walked in the direction of the door.

"Do you promise that the information from here won't go any further?" she said when Erlendur had opened the door and was about to leave.

"I've told you that. This is private information, for me."

"Take a look at it then," Hanna said, reopened the cabinet and handed him the file.

Erlendur closed the door, took the file and immersed himself in it. Hanna took out a pack of cigarettes and lit one while she waited for Erlendur to finish reading. She ignored the NO SMOKING sign and soon the room was filled with smoke.

"Who's Eydal?"

"One of our most accomplished medical scientists."

"What was it here that you didn't want me to see? Can't I talk to this man?"

Hanna didn't reply.

"What's going on?" Erlendur said.

Hanna sighed. "I understand he keeps a few organs himself," she said eventually.

"The man collects organs?" Erlendur said.

"He keeps a few organs, a small collection."

"An organ collector?"

"That's all I know," Hanna said.

"It's conceivable that he's got the brain," Erlendur said. "It says here he was given a sample to study. Is this a problem for you?"

"He's one of our leading scientists," she repeated, through clenched teeth.

"He keeps the brain of a 4-year-old girl on his mantelpiece!" Erlendur shouted.

"I don't expect you to understand scientific work," she said.

"What is there to understand about this?"

"I should never have let you in here," Hanna shouted.

"I've heard that one before," Erlendur said.

32

Elínborg found the woman from Húsavík.

She had two remaining names on her list so she left Sigurdur Óli behind in Nordurmýri with the forensic team. The first woman's reaction was a familiar one, great but somehow predetermined surprise, she'd heard the story elsewhere, even several times. She said that to tell the truth she'd been expecting the police. The second woman, the last one on Elínborg's list, refused to talk to her. Refused to let her in. Closed the door saying she didn't know what Elínborg was talking about and couldn't help her.

But the woman was somehow hesitant. It was as if she needed to summon up all the strength she could muster to say what she wanted and Elínborg felt the role was rehearsed. She behaved as if she'd been expecting the police, but, unlike the others, she didn't want to know anything. Wanted to get rid of Elínborg immediately.

Elínborg could tell she'd found the woman they'd been looking for. She took another look at her documents. The woman's name was Katrín and she was a department manager at Reykjavík City

Library. Her husband was the manager of a large advertising agency. She was 60. Three children, all born from 1958 to 1962. She'd moved from Húsavík in '62 and had lived in Reykjavík ever since.

Elínborg rang the bell a second time.

"I think you ought to talk to me," she said when Katrín opened the door again.

The woman looked at her.

"There's nothing I can help you with," she said at once, in a surprisingly sharp tone of voice. "I know what the case is about. I've heard the rumours. But I don't know about any rape. Hopefully you'll make do with that. Don't disturb me again."

She tried to close the door on Elínborg.

"I may make do with that but a detective called Erlendur, who's investigating Holberg's murder, won't. The next time you open the door he'll be standing here and he won't leave. He won't let you slam the door in his face. He could have you brought down the station if things get difficult."

"Will you please leave me alone," Katrín said as the door shut against the frame.

I wish I could, Elínborg thought. She took out her mobile phone and called Erlendur, who was just leaving the university. Elínborg described the situation to him. He said he'd be there in ten minutes.

He couldn't see Elínborg anywhere outside Katrín's house when he arrived, but he recognised her car in the parking space. It was a large detached house in Vogar district, two storeys with a double garage. He rang the bell and to his astonishment Elínborg answered the door.

"I think I've found her," she said in a low voice and let Erlendur in. "She came out to me just now and apologised for her behaviour. She said she'd rather talk to us here than down the station. She'd heard stories about the rape and she was expecting us."

Elínborg went inside the house ahead of Erlendur and into the sitting room where Katrín was standing. She shook his hand and tried to smile, but didn't make a very good job of it. She was conservatively dressed, wearing a grey skirt and white blouse, with straight, thick hair down to her shoulders, combed to one side. She was tall, with thin legs and small shoulders, pretty with a mild but anxious expression.

Erlendur looked around in the sitting room. It was dominated by books shelved in closed, glass-fronted cupboards. A beautiful writing desk stood by one of the book cupboards, an old but well-preserved leather suite was in the middle of the room, a smoking table in one corner. Paintings on the walls. Little watercolours in beautiful frames, photographs of her family. He took a closer look at them. All the photographs were old. The three boys with their parents. The most recent ones had been taken when they were confirmed. They did not seem to have graduated from school or university, or got married.

"We're going to buy a smaller place," Katrín said

almost apologetically when she saw Erlendur looking around. "It's far too big for us, this huge house."

Erlendur nodded.

"Your husband, is he at home too?"

"Albert won't be home until late tonight. He's abroad. I was hoping we could talk about this before he gets back."

"Shouldn't we sit down?" Elínborg asked. Katrín apologised for her rudeness and invited them to sit down. She sat down on the sofa by herself, with Erlendur and Elínborg in the two leather armchairs facing her.

"What exactly is it you want of me?" Katrín asked, looking at them each in turn. "I don't really understand how I fit into the picture. The man's dead. That's nothing to do with me."

"Holberg was a rapist," Erlendur said. "He raped a woman in Keflavík and, as a result, she had a child. A daughter. When we starting checking more closely we were told he'd done this before, to a woman from Húsavík, a similar age to the second victim. Holberg may have raped again, later. We don't know. But we need to track down his victim from Húsavík. Holberg was murdered at his home and we have reason to presume that the explanation may be found in his sordid past."

Erlendur and Elínborg both noticed how his speech didn't seem to have any effect on Katrín. She wasn't shocked at hearing about Holberg's rapes or his daughter, and she asked neither about the woman from Keflavík nor the girl.

"You're not shocked to hear that?" he said.

"No," Katrín said, "what should I be shocked about?"

"What can you tell us about Holberg?" Erlendur asked after a pause.

"I recognised him at once from the photos in the papers," Katrín said, and it was as if the last trace of resistance vanished from her voice. Her words turned into a whisper. "Even though he'd changed a lot," she said.

"We had his photograph on file," Elínborg said by way of explanation. "The photo was from an HGV licence he had recently renewed. Lorry driver. Drove all over the country."

"He told me at the time he was a lawyer in Reykjavík."

"He was probably working for the Harbour and Lighthouse Authority at that time," Erlendur said.

"I'd just turned 20. Albert and I had two children when it happened. We started living together very young. He was at sea, Albert I mean. That didn't happen very often. He ran a little shop and was an agent for an insurance company."

"Does he know what happened?" Erlendur asked.

Katrín hesitated for a moment.

"No, I never told him. And I'd prefer it if you didn't tell him now."

They fell silent.

"Didn't you tell anyone what happened?" Erlendur asked.

"I didn't tell anyone." She fell silent again.

Erlendur and Elínborg waited.

"I blame myself for it. My God," she sighed. "I know that isn't right of me. I know it was none of my doing. It was nearly 40 years ago and I'm still accusing myself although I know I shouldn't. Forty years."

They waited.

"I don't know how much detail you want me to go into. What matters to you. As I said, Albert was at sea. I was out having fun with some friends and we met these men at the dance."

"These men?" Erlendur interjected.

"Holberg and someone else who was with him. I never found out what his name was. He showed me a little camera that he carried around with him. I spoke to him about photography a bit. They went back to my girlfriend's place with us and we went on drinking there. There was a group of four of us girlfriends who went out together. Two of us were married. After a while I said I wanted to go and he offered to walk me home."

"Holberg?" Elínborg said.

"Yes, Holberg. I said no and said goodbye to my friends and walked home alone. It wasn't far to walk. But when I opened the door – we lived in a little detached house in a new street they were building in Húsavík – suddenly he was standing behind me. He said something I didn't hear properly, then pushed me inside and closed the door. I was completely taken aback. Didn't know whether to be scared or surprised. The alcohol dulled my senses. Of course I didn't know that man in the slightest, I'd never seen him before that night."

"So why do you blame yourself?" Elínborg asked.

"I'd been fooling around at the dance a bit," Katrín said after a while. "I asked him to dance. I don't know why I did it. I'd had a bit to drink and I could never handle alcohol. I was having fun with my friends and let my hair down a bit. Irresponsible. Drunk."

"But you mustn't blame yourself . . ." Elínborg began.

"Nothing you say can change that in the slightest," Katrín said in a subdued tone and looked at Elínborg, "so don't go telling me who I can and can't blame. There's no point."

"He hung around us at the dance," she continued after a pause. "Certainly didn't make a bad impression. He was funny and he knew how to make us girls laugh. Played games with us and got us to play along. I remembered later that he had asked about Albert and found out I was at home alone. But he did it in such a way that I never suspected what lay behind it."

"In principle it's the same story as when Holberg attacked the woman in Keflavík," Erlendur said. "She let him walk her home, admittedly. Then he asked to use the phone and attacked her in the kitchen."

"Somehow he turned into a completely different person. Revolting. The things he said. He tore off the coat I was wearing, pushed me inside and called me awful names. He got very worked up. I tried to talk to him but it was useless and when I started to shout for help he jumped on me and silenced me. Then he dragged me into the bedroom . . ."

She mustered up all the courage she could and told them what Holberg did, systematically and without holding anything back. She hadn't forgotten anything about that evening. On the contrary, she remembered every tiniest detail. Her account was devoid of sentimentality. It was as if she were reading out cold facts from a page. She'd never talked about the incident in this way, with such precision, but she'd created such a distance from it that Erlendur felt she was describing something that had befallen another woman. Not her personally, but someone else. Somewhere else. At another time. In another life.

At one point in her account Erlendur grimaced and Elínborg cursed under her breath.

Katrín stopped talking.

"Why didn't you press charges against that bastard?" Elínborg asked.

"He was like a monster. He threatened to finish me off if I told anyone and the police arrested him. And what was worse, he said if I made an issue of it he'd claim I'd asked him to meet me at home and wanted to sleep with him. He didn't use exactly those words, but I knew what he was getting at. He was incredibly strong, but he hardly left a mark on me. He made sure of that. I started thinking about that later. He hit me in the face a couple of times, but never hard."

"When did this happen?"

"It was 1961. Late. In the autumn."

"And wasn't there any aftermath? Didn't you ever see Holberg again or . . ."

"No. I never saw him after that. Not until I saw the photo of him in the paper."

"You moved away from Húsavík?"

"That was what we'd planned to do anyway really. Albert always had it in the back of his mind. I wasn't against it so much after that. The people in Húsavík are nice and it's a good place to live, but I've never been back there since."

"You had two children before, sons from the look of them," Erlendur said, nodding in the direction of the confirmation photographs, "and then you had the third son . . . when?"

"Two years later," Katrín said.

Erlendur looked at her and could see that, for some reason, for the first time in their conversation, she was lying.

33

"Why did you stop there?" Elínborg said when they left the house and went into the street.

She'd had trouble concealing her surprise when Erlendur suddenly thanked Katrín for being so cooperative. He said he knew how difficult it was for her to talk about these things and he'd make sure that nothing they had talked about would go any further. Elínborg gaped. They were only just starting to talk.

"She'd started lying," Erlendur said. "It's too much of an ordeal for her. We'll meet her later. Her phone needs tapping and we should have a car outside the house to check on her movements and any visitors. We need to find out what her sons do, get recent photos of them if we can, but without drawing attention to ourselves, and we need to locate people who knew Katrín in Húsavík and could even remember that evening, although that might be a bit of a long shot. I asked Sigurdur Óli to contact the Harbour and Lighthouse Authority to see if they can tell us when Holberg worked for them in Húsavík. Maybe he's done that by now. Get a copy of Katrín and Albert's marriage certificate to find out the year they were married."

Erlendur had got into his car.

"And Elínborg, you can come along the next time we talk to her."

"Is anyone capable of doing what she described?" Elínborg asked, her mind still on Katrín's story.

"With Holberg it seems anything's possible," Erlendur replied.

He drove down into Nordurmýri. Sigurdur Óli was still there. He'd contacted the phone company about the calls made to Holberg the weekend he was murdered. Two were from the Iceland Transport yard where he worked and another three were from public telephones: two from a phone box on Laekjargata and one from a payphone at Hlemmur Bus Station.

"Anything else?"

"Yes, the porn on his computer. Forensics have looked at quite a lot of it and it's appalling. Downright sick. All the worst stuff you can find on the Internet, including animals and children. That guy was a total pervert. I think they gave up looking at it."

"Maybe there's no need to subject them to it any more," said Erlendur.

"It does give us a small picture of what a filthy, disgusting creep he was," Sigurdur Óli said

"Do you mean he deserved to be smashed over the head and killed?" Erlendur said.

"What do you think?"

"Have you asked the Harbour and Lighthouse Authority about Holberg?"

"No."

"Get a move on then."

"Is he waving to us?" Sigurdur Óli asked. They were standing in front of Holberg's house. One of the forensic team had come out of the basement and was standing there in his white overalls waving to them to come over. He seemed quite excited. They got out of the car, went down into the basement and the forensic technician gestured to them to come over to one of the screens. He was holding a remote control which he told them operated the camera that had been inserted into one of the holes in the corner of the sitting room.

They watched the screen, but they couldn't see anything on it that they could at all identify. The image was speckled, poorly lit, blurred and dull. They could see gravel and the underside of the flooring, but otherwise nothing unusual. Some time passed until the technician couldn't hold back any longer.

"It's this thing here," he said, pointing to the top centre of the screen. "Right up underneath the flooring."

"What?" said Erlendur, who couldn't see a thing.

"Can't you see it?" the forensics technician said.

"What?" Sigurdur Óli said.

"The ring."

"The ring?" Erlendur said.

"That's clearly a ring we've found under the floor. Can't you see it?"

They squinted at the screen until they thought they could make out an object that could well be a ring. It was unclear, as if something was blocking the view. They couldn't see anything else.

"It's as if there's something in the way," Sigurdur Óli said.

"It could be insulating plastic like they use in building," the technician said. More people had gathered around the screen to watch what was happening. "Look at this thing here," he continued, "This line by the ring. It could easily be a finger. There's something lying out in the corner that I think we ought to take a closer look at."

"Break up the floor," Erlendur ordered. "Let's see what it is."

The forensic team went to work at once. They marked out the spot on the sitting-room floor and began breaking it up with the pneumatic drill. A fine concrete dust swirled around the basement and Erlendur and Sigurdur Óli put gauze masks over their mouths. They stood behind the technicians, watching the hole widening in the floor. The base plate was seven or eight inches thick and it took the drill some time to get through it.

Once they'd broken through, the hole quickly widened. The men swept the concrete fragments away as fast as they were chipped loose and they could soon see the plastic that had been revealed by the camera. Erlendur looked at Sigurdur Óli, who nodded at him.

The plastic came increasingly into view. Erlendur thought it was thick building insulation plastic. It was impossible to see through. He'd forgotten the noise in the basement, the revolting stench and the dust swirling up. Sigurdur Óli had taken his mask off to see better. He bent down and called over the forensic team which was breaking up the floor.

"Is this how they open the Pharaohs' tombs in Egypt?" he asked and the tension eased a little.

"Except I'm afraid there's no Pharaoh under here," Erlendur said.

"Could it actually be that we've found Grétar under Holberg's floor?" Sigurdur Óli said in eager anticipation. "After twenty-fucking-five years! Bloody brilliant!"

"His mother was right," Erlendur said.

"Grétar's mother?"

"'It was like he'd been stolen,' she said."

"Wrapped up in plastic and stashed away under the floor."

"Marion Briem," Erlendur muttered to himself and shook his head.

The forensic team bored away with their electric drills, the floor split open under the pressure and the hole widened until the entire plastic package could be seen. It was the length of an average man. The forensic team discussed how they ought to go about opening it. They decided to remove it from the floor cavity in one piece and not touch it until they'd taken it to the morgue on Barónsstígur where it could be handled without the loss of any potential evidence.

They fetched a stretcher they had taken into the basement the night before and put it next to the hole in the floor. Two of them tried to lift the plastic package, but it turned out to be too heavy, so another two went down to help them. Soon it began to budge and they worked it free from its surroundings, lifted it out and placed it on the stretcher.

Erlendur went up to the package, bent over it and tried to see through the plastic. He thought he could make out a face, shrivelled and rotten, teeth and part of a nose. He straightened up again.

"He doesn't look so bad, considering," he said.

"What's that?" Sigurdur Óli asked, leaning down into the hole.

"What?" Erlendur said.

"Are those rolls of film?" Sigurdur Óli said.

Erlendur went up closer, knelt down and saw rolls of photographic film half buried in the gravel. Yards of film spread all around. He was hoping that some of it had been used.

34

Katrín didn't leave the house for the rest of the day. No-one visited her and she didn't use the telephone. In the evening a man driving an estate car pulled up outside the house and went in carrying a medium-sized suitcase. This was presumably Albert, her husband. He was due back from a business trip to Germany that afternoon.

Two policemen in an unmarked car were watching the house. The phone was tapped. The whereabouts of the two older sons had been ascertained, but nothing was known about where the youngest one was. He was divorced and lived in a flat in the Gerdi district but there was nobody home. A watch was mounted outside it. The police were gathering information about the son and his description was sent to police stations all over the country. As yet there were not considered to be grounds for releasing an announcement about him to the media.

Erlendur pulled up in front of the morgue on Barónsstígur. The body of the man who was thought to be Grétar had been taken there. The pathologist, the same one who had examined Holberg and Audur, had removed the plastic from the body. It turned out to be the body of a male with his head snapped back, his mouth open as if screaming in anguish and his arms by his sides. The skin was parched and shrivelled and pallid, with large patches of rot here and there on the naked body. The head appeared to have been badly damaged, and the hair was long and colourless, hanging down the sides of the face.

"He removed his innards," the pathologist said.

"What?"

"The person who buried him. A sensible move if you want to keep a body. Because of the smell. He gradually dried up inside the plastic. Well preserved in that sense."

"Can you establish the cause of death?"

"There was a plastic bag over his head which suggests he may have been suffocated, but I'll have to take a better look at him. You'll find out more later. It all takes time. Do you know who he is? He's a bit of a runt, the poor bugger."

"I have my suspicions," Erlendur said.

"Did you talk to the professor?"

"A lovely woman."

"Isn't she just?"

Sigurdur Óli was waiting for Erlendur at the office but when he arrived he said he was going straight to forensics. They had managed to develop and enlarge several exposures from the film that had been found in Holberg's flat. Erlendur told him about the conversation he and Elínborg had had with Katrín.

Ragnar, the head of forensics, was waiting for them in his office with several rolls of film on his desk and some enlarged photographs. He handed them the photographs and they huddled over them.

"We could only manage these three," Ragnar said, "and I can't actually tell what they show. There were seven rolls of Kodak with 24 exposures each. Three were completely black and we can't tell whether they'd been used, but from one of them we managed to enlarge the little we can see here. Is this anything you recognise?"

Erlendur and Sigurdur Óli squinted at the photographs. They were all black-and-white. Two of them were half black as if the aperture hadn't opened properly; the pictures were out of focus and so unclear that they couldn't make them out. The third and final print was intact and reasonably sharp and showed a man taking his own photograph in front of a mirror. The camera was small and flat, with a flash cube on the top with four bulbs, and the flash lit up the man in the mirror. He was wearing jeans and a shirt and a waist-length summer jacket.

"Do you remember flash cubes?" Erlendur said with a hint of nostalgia in his voice. "What a revolution."

"I remember them well," said Ragnar, who was the same age as Erlendur. Sigurdur Óli looked at them in turn and shook his head.

"Is that what you'd call a self-portrait?" Erlendur said.

"It's difficult to see his face with the camera in the

way," Sigurdur Óli said, "but isn't it probable it's Grétar himself?"

"Do you recognise the surroundings, what little of them is visible?" Ragnar asked.

In the reflection they could make out part of the room behind the photographer. Erlendur could see the back of a chair and even a coffee table, the carpet on the floor and part of something that could have been a floor-length curtain, but everything else was difficult to discern. The face of the man in the mirror was brightly lit but to the sides the light faded to total darkness.

They pored over the photograph for a long time. After much effort Erlendur began to distinguish something in the darkness to the left of the photographer, which he thought might be a human form, even a profile, eyebrows and a nose. This was only a hunch, but there was something uneven in the light, tiny shadows, that kindled his imagination.

"Could we enlarge this area?" he asked Ragnar, who stared hard at the same part but couldn't see a thing. Sigurdur Óli took the photograph and held it up in front of his face, but he couldn't make out what Erlendur thought he could see either

"It will only take a second," Ragnar said. They followed him from the office and over to the forensic team.

"Are there any fingerprints on the film?" Sigurdur Óli asked.

"Yes," Ragnar said, "two sets, the same ones as

on the photo from the cemetery. Grétar's and Holberg's."

The photograph was scanned and came up on a big computer screen. The area was enlarged. What had been only an unevenness in the light became countless dots that filled the screen. They couldn't discern anything from the photo and even Erlendur lost sight of what he thought he'd seen. The technician worked on the keyboard for a while, entered some commands and the image was reduced and compressed. He continued, the dots arranged themselves together until gradually the outline of a face began to emerge. It was still unclear, but Erlendur thought he recognised Holberg there.

"Isn't that the bastard?" Sigurdur Óli said.

"There's more here," the technician said and went on sharpening up the photograph. Waves soon appeared which reminded Erlendur of a woman's hair, and another more blurred profile. Erlendur stared at the image until he thought he could make out Holberg sitting talking to a woman. A strange hallucination seized him at the moment he saw this. He wanted to shout out to the woman to get out of the flat, but it was too late. Decades too late.

A phone rang in the room, but no-one made a move. Erlendur thought the one on the desk was ringing.

"It's yours," Sigurdur Óli said to Erlendur.

It took Erlendur a while, but eventually he managed to find his mobile phone and fished it out of his coat pocket.

It was Elínborg.

"What are you playing around at?" she said when finally he answered.

"Get to the point, will you," Erlendur said.

"The point? What are you so stressed about?"

"I knew you couldn't just say what you're going to say."

"It's about Katrín's boys," Elínborg said. "Or men, actually, they're all grown men now."

"What about them?"

"All of them nice guys, probably, except one of them works at a rather interesting place. I thought you ought to hear about it straightaway but if you're so tense and busy and can't bear the thought of a little chat, I'll just phone Sigurdur Óli instead."

"Elínborg."

"Yes?"

"Good Lord, woman," Erlendur shouted and looked at Sigurdur Óli, "are you going to tell me what you're going to tell me?"

"The son works at the Genetic Research Centre."

"What?"

"He works at the Genetic Research Centre."

"Which son?"

"The youngest one. He's working on their new database. Works with family trees and illnesses, Icelandic families and hereditary diseases, genetic diseases. The man's an expert on genetic diseases."

35

Erlendur got home late in the evening. He planned to visit Katrín early the next morning and talk to her about his theory. He hoped that her son would soon be found. A prolonged search posed the risk of the story being sensationalised by the media, and he wanted to avoid that.

Eva Lind wasn't at home. She had tidied up in the kitchen after Erlendur's tantrum. He put one of the two meals he'd bought at the late-night shop in the microwave, then pressed Start. Erlendur recalled when Eva Lind had come to him a few nights before, when he'd been standing by the microwave, and she told him she was pregnant. He felt as though a whole year had gone by since she had sat there facing him, scrounging money and dodging his questions, but it was only a few nights. He was still having bad dreams. He had never had many dreams and only ever remembered snatches of them when he woke up, but a feeling of discomfort lingered in him when he was awake and he couldn't shake it off. It didn't help that the pain in his chest was constantly making itself felt, a burning pain that he couldn't rub away.

He thought about Eva Lind and the baby and about Kolbrún and Audur and about Elín and Katrín and her sons, about Holberg and Grétar and Ellidi in the prison and about the girl from Gardabaer and her father, and about himself and his own children, his son Sindri Snaer, whom he seldom saw, and Eva, who had made the effort to find him and with whom he argued bitterly when he disliked what she did. She was right. Who was he to go around handing out scoldings?

He thought about mothers and daughters and fathers and sons and mothers and sons and fathers and daughters and children that were born and no-one wanted and children who died in that little community, Iceland, where everyone seemed related or connected in some way.

If Holberg was the father of Katrín's youngest son, had he in fact been killed by his own son? Did the young man know Holberg was his father? How had he found out? Had Katrín told him? When? Why? Had he known all the time? Did he know about the rape? Had Katrín told him Holberg had raped her and she had fallen pregnant by him? What kind of a feeling is that? What kind of a feeling is it to discover you're not the person you thought you were? Not who you are? That your father isn't your father, you're not his son, you're the son of someone else you didn't know existed. Someone violent: a rapist.

What's that like? Erlendur thought. How can you come to terms with that? Do you go and find your father and murder him? And then write: "I am him"?

And if Katrín didn't tell her son about Holberg, how did he find out the truth? Erlendur turned the question over in his mind. The more he thought about the matter and considered the options, the more his thoughts turned to the message tree in Gardabaer. There was only one other way the son could have found out the truth and Erlendur intended to check that the following day.

And what was it that Grétar saw? Why did he have to die? Was he blackmailing Holberg? Did he know about Holberg's rapes and plan to turn him in? Did he take photographs of Holberg? Who was the woman sitting with Holberg in the photograph? When was it taken? Grétar went missing in the summer of the national festival, so it had to have been taken before then. Erlendur wondered whether there weren't more victims of Holberg who had never said a thing.

He heard a key turn in the lock and he stood up. Eva Lind was back.

"I went to Gardabaer with the girl," she said when she saw Erlendur coming out of the kitchen, and closed the door behind her. "She said she was going to charge that sod for all the years he abused her. Her mother had a nervous breakdown. Then we left."

"To see the husband?"

"Yeah, back to their cosy little pad," Eva Lind said, kicking off her shoes by the door. "He went mad, but calmed down when he heard the explanation."

"How did he take it?"

"He's a great guy. When I left he was on his way to Gardabaer to talk to the old sod."

"Really."

"Do you think there's any point in charging that bastard?" Eva Lind asked.

"They're difficult cases. The men deny everything and somehow they get away with it. Maybe it depends on the mother, what she says. Maybe she ought to go to the rape crisis centre. How are you doing, anyway?"

"Just great," Eva Lind said.

"Have you thought about a sonar or whatever they call it?" Erlendur asked. "I could go with you."

"The time will come for that," Eva Lind said.

"Will it?"

"Yeah."

"Good," Erlendur said.

"What have you been up to anyway?" Eva Lind asked, putting the other meal into the microwave.

"I don't think about anything except children these days," Erlendur said. "And a message tree, which is a kind of family tree: it can contain all kinds of messages to us if we only know what we're supposed to be looking for. And I'm thinking about obsessions with collecting things. How does that song about the carthorse go?"

Eva Lind looked at her father. He knew she knew a lot about music.

"Do you mean 'Life is Like a Carthorse'?" she said.

"'Its head is stuffed with hay'," Erlendur said.

"'Its heart is frozen solid'."

"'And its brain has gone astray'," Erlendur finished the verse. He put on his hat and said he wouldn't be gone for long.

36

Hanna had warned the doctor so he wasn't surprised to see Erlendur that evening. He lived in an elegant house in the old part of Hafnarfjördur and welcomed Erlendur at the door, the very picture of gentility and courteousness, a short man, bald as a billiard ball and portly beneath his thick dressing gown. A bon viveur, Erlendur thought, with a perpetual and slightly feminine redness in his cheeks. He was of an indeterminate age, could be around 60. Greeted Erlendur with a hand as dry as paper and invited him into the lounge.

Erlendur sat on a large wine-red leather sofa and declined the offer of a drink. The doctor sat facing him and waited for him to begin. Erlendur looked around the lounge, which was spacious and lavishly adorned with paintings and objets d'art, and wondered whether the doctor lived alone. He asked him.

"Always lived alone," the doctor said. "I'm extremely happy with that and always have been. It's said that men who reach my age regret not having had a family and children. My colleagues go around waving pictures of their grandchildren at conferences all around the world, but I've never had any interest in starting a family. Never had any interest in children."

He was convivial, talkative and chummy as if Erlendur was a bosom pal, as if implicitly recognising him on equal terms. Erlendur was not impressed.

"But you're interested in organs in jars," he said.

The doctor refused to let Erlendur throw him off balance.

"Hanna told me you were angry," he said. "I don't know why you should be angry. I'm not doing anything illegal. Yes, I do have a little collection of organs. Most of them are preserved in formalin in glass jars. I keep them in the house here. They were due to be destroyed, but I took them and kept them a little longer. I also keep another type of bio-sample, tissue samples.

"Why, you're probably wondering," he continued, but Erlendur shook his head.

"How many organs have you stolen? was actually the question I was going to ask," he said, "but we can get to that later."

"I haven't stolen any organs," the doctor said, slowly stroking his bald head. "I can't understand this antagonism. Do you mind if I have a drop of sherry?" he asked and stood up. Erlendur waited while he went over to the drinks cabinet and poured himself a glass. He offered one to Erlendur, who declined, and sipped at the sherry with his thick lips. It was clear from his round face how he relished the taste.

"People don't normally wonder about this," he

said then, "and there's no reason to either. Everything dead is useless in our world, and so is a dead human body. No need to get sentimental about it. The soul's gone. Only the dross left and dross is nothing. You have to look at it from a medical perspective. The body's nothing, you understand?"

"It clearly is something to you. You collect body parts."

"In other countries, university hospitals buy organs for teaching purposes," the doctor continued. "But that hasn't been the custom in Iceland. Here we ask for permission to perform an autopsy on a case-by-case basis and sometimes we request to remove an organ even though it might not necessarily have anything to do with the death. People agree or refuse, the way things go. It's mainly older people whose bodies are involved. Nobody steals organs."

"But it wasn't always like that," Erlendur said.

"I don't know how things were in the old days. Of course, they didn't keep such a close watch on what went on then. I simply don't know. I don't know why you're shocked at me. Do you remember that news report from France? The car factory that used real human bodies in their crash tests, children too. You ought to be shocked at them instead. Organs are bought and sold all over the world. People are even killed for their organs. My collection can hardly be called criminal."

"But why?" Erlendur said. "What do you do with them?"

"Research, of course," the doctor said, sipping his

sherry. "Examine them through a microscope. What won't a collector do? Stamp collectors look at postmarks. Book collectors look at years of publication. Astronomers have the whole world in front of their eyes and look at things of mind-boggling proportions. I'm continually looking at my microscopic world."

"So your hobby's research, you have facilities for studying the samples or organs that you own?"

"Yes."

"Here in the house?"

"Yes. If the samples are well preserved they can always be studied. When you get new medical information or want to look at something in particular they're perfectly usable for research purposes. Perfectly."

The doctor stopped talking.

"You're asking about Audur," he said then.

"Do you know of her?" Erlendur said in surprise.

"You know if she hadn't had an autopsy and had her brain removed you might never have found out what killed her. You know that. She's been lying in the ground too long. It wouldn't have been possible to study the brain effectively after 30 years in the soil. So, what you are so disgusted at has actually helped you. Presumably you realise that."

The doctor thought for a moment.

"Have you heard about Louis XVII? He was the son of Louis XVI and Marie Antoinette, imprisoned during the French Revolution, executed at the age of 10. It was on the news a year ago or more. French scientists had found out he died in prison and did not escape as some people claimed. Do you know how they found that out?"

"I don't remember the story," Erlendur said.

"His heart was removed and kept in formalin. When they could do DNA and other tests they found out that the alleged relatives based their kinship with the French royal family on lies. They weren't related to the prince. Do you know when Louis died in childhood?"

"No."

"More than two hundred years ago. In 1795. Formalin is a unique fluid."

Erlendur became thoughtful.

"What do you know about Audur?"

"Various things."

"How did the sample come into your hands?"

"Via a third party. I don't think I'd care to go into that."

"From Jar City?"

"Yes."

"Did they give you Jar City?"

"Part of it. There's no need to talk to me as though I'm a criminal."

"Did you ever establish the cause of death?"

The doctor looked at Erlendur and took another sip of his sherry.

"Actually, I did," he said. "I've always been more inclined towards research than medical practice. With this obsession of mine for collecting things,

I've been able to combine the two, although only on a small scale of course."

"The coroner's report from Keflavík only mentions a brain tumour, without any further explanation."

"I saw that. The report is incomplete, it was never more than preliminary. As I say, I've looked into this more closely and I think I have the answer to some of your questions."

Erlendur leaned forward in his chair. "And?"

"A genetic disease. It occurs in several families in Iceland. It was an extremely complex case and even after examining it in depth I wasn't sure for a long time. Eventually I thought the tumour was most probably linked to a genetic disease, neurofibromatosis. I don't expect you've heard of it before. In some cases there aren't any symptoms. In some cases people can die without the illness ever surfacing. There are symptom-free carriers. It's much more common for the symptoms to emerge at an early stage, though, mainly in the form of marks on the skin and of tumours."

The doctor sipped his sherry again.

"The Keflavík people didn't describe anything of that sort in their report, but I'm not sure they knew what they were looking for either."

"They told the relatives about the skin."

"Did they, really? Diagnosis isn't always certain."

"Is this disease passed on from father to daughter?"

"It can be. But genetic transmission isn't confined

to that. Both sexes can carry and contract the disease. It's said that one strain of it came out in the Elephant Man. Did you see the film?"

"No," Erlendur said.

"Certain people contract extreme bone growth which causes deformity, as in that particular case. In fact there are other people who claim that neurofibromatosis has nothing to do with the Elephant Man. But that's a different story."

"Why did you start looking for it?" Erlendur interrupted the doctor.

"Brain diseases are my specialist field," he said. "This girl is one of my most interesting cases. I read all the reports about her. They weren't very precise. The doctor who looked after her was a poor GP, he was drinking at the time, so I'm told. But be that as it may, he wrote about acute tubercular infection of the head in one place, which was the term that was sometimes used when the disease appeared. That was my starting point. The coroner's report from Keflavík wasn't very precise either, as we talked about before. They found the tumour and left it at that."

The doctor stood up and went over to a large bookcase in the lounge. He took out a journal and handed it to Erlendur.

"I'm not sure you'll understand all this, but I wrote a short scientific article about my research in a highly respected American medical journal."

"Have you written a scientific article about Audur?" Erlendur asked.

"Audur has helped us on our way towards understanding the disease. She's been very important both to me and to medical science. I hope I'm not disappointing you."

"The girl's father could be a genetic carrier," Erlendur said, still trying to grasp what the doctor had told him. "And he passed the disease on to his daughter. If he'd had a son, wouldn't he also have inherited the disease?"

"It wouldn't necessarily have to come out in him," the doctor said, "but he could be a genetic carrier, like his father."

"So?"

"Yes. If he had a child, the child could also have the disease."

Erlendur thought about what the doctor had said.

"But you really ought to talk to the scientists at the Genetic Research Centre," the doctor said. "They've got the answers to the genetic questions."

"What?"

"Talk to the Genetic Research Centre. That's our new Jar City. They've got the answers. What's wrong? Why are you so shocked? Do you know anyone there?"

"No," Erlendur said, "but I soon will."

"Do you want to see Audur?" the doctor asked.

At first Erlendur didn't take the doctor's hint.

"Do you mean . . . ?"

"I've got a small laboratory down here. You're welcome to take a look."

Erlendur hesitated.

"All right," he said.

They stood up and Erlendur followed the doctor down the narrow stairs. The doctor switched on a light and a pristine laboratory appeared, with microscopes, computers, test tubes and equipment for purposes that Erlendur couldn't even begin to imagine. He remembered a remark that he happened to read somewhere about collectors. Collectors make a world for themselves. They make a little world all around them, select certain icons from reality and turn them into the chief characters in that artificial world. Holberg was a collector too. His obsession with collecting things was connected with pornography. It was from that he made his private world, just as the doctor did from organs.

"She's here," the doctor said.

He went over to a large, old, wooden cabinet, the only article of furniture in the room and out of place in the sterilised environment, he opened it and took down a thick glass jar with a lid. He put it carefully on the table and Erlendur could see in the strong fluorescent light a little child's brain floating in formalin.

When he left the doctor, Erlendur took with him a leather case containing Audur's earthly remains. He thought about Jar City as he drove home through the empty streets, hoping that no part of him would ever be kept in a laboratory. It was still raining when he pulled up outside the block of flats where he lived. He switched off the engine, lit a cigarette and stared out into the night.

Erlendur looked at the black bag on the front seat. He was going to put Audur back where she belonged.

37

At around 11.00 that same night, the policemen on duty in front of Katrín's house watched her husband leave, slam the door behind him, storm into his car and drive off. He seemed to be in a tearing rush and they noticed he was carrying the same suitcase as when he arrived home earlier that day. The policemen saw no further movement during the night and there was no sign of Katrín. A police patrol car was called to the neighbourhood and followed Albert to Hotel Esja where he checked in for the night.

Erlendur turned up outside Katrín's house at eight o'clock the following morning. Elínborg was with him. It was still raining. The sun hadn't come out for days. They rang the bell three times before they heard a rustling inside and the door opened. Katrín appeared in the doorway. Elínborg noticed she was wearing the same clothes as on the day before and she had clearly been crying. Her face was drawn and her eyes were red and swollen.

"Sorry," Katrín said as if in a daze, "I must have fallen asleep in the chair. What's the time?"

"May we come in?" Erlendur said.

"I never told Albert what happened," she said

and went inside, without inviting them in. Erlendur and Elínborg exchanged glances and followed her.

"He walked out on me last night," Katrín said. "What's the time anyway? I think I must have fallen asleep in the chair. Albert was so angry. I've never seen him that angry."

"Can you contact some of your family?" Elínborg asked. "Someone who can come and stay with you? Your sons?"

"No, Albert will come back and everything will be all right. I don't want to disturb the boys. It'll be all right. Albert will come back."

"Why was he so angry?" Erlendur asked. Katrín had sat down on the sofa in the sitting room, Erlendur and Elínborg sat down opposite her just as before.

"He was furious, Albert was. And he's generally so calm. Albert's a good man, such a good man, and he's always been so good to me. It's a good marriage. We've always been happy."

"Maybe you want us to come back later," Elínborg said. Erlendur glared at her.

"No," Katrín said, "it's all right. It'll be all right. Albert will come back. He just needs to get over it. My God, how difficult this is. I should have told him straightaway, he said. He couldn't understand how I could keep quiet about it all that time. He shouted at me."

Katrín looked at them.

"He's never shouted at me before."

"Can I get you some help? Shall I call your

doctor?" Elínborg said and stood up. Erlendur looked at her in bewilderment.

"No, it's all right," Katrín said. "That's not necessary. I'm just a bit sleepy-headed. It'll be all right. Sit down, dear. Everything will be all right."

"What was it you told your husband?" Erlendur asked. "Did you tell him about the rape?"

"I'd wanted to all these years, but I never had the guts to. I've never told anyone about that incident. I tried to forget it, pretend it had never happened. It's often been difficult, but I've managed, somehow. Then you came and I found myself telling you everything. Somehow I felt better. It was like you'd relieved me of a great burden. I knew I could finally talk openly and that was the only right thing to do. Even after all this time."

Katrín stopped talking.

"Did he get angry with you because you hadn't told him about the rape?" Erlendur asked.

"Yes."

"Didn't he understand your point of view?" Elínborg asked.

"He said I should have told him about it straight-away. That's understandable, of course. He said he'd always been honest with me and he didn't deserve this."

"But I don't quite understand," Erlendur said. "Albert sounds like a better person than that. I'd have thought he'd try to comfort you instead and stand by you, not storm out through the door."

286

"I know," Katrín said. "Maybe I didn't tell him about it in the right way."

"The right way," Elínborg said, not even trying to conceal her disbelief. "How can you tell anyone about that sort of thing in the right way?"

Katrín shook her head.

"I don't know. I swear, I don't know."

"Did you tell him the whole truth?" Erlendur asked.

"I told him what I told you."

"And nothing else?"

"No," Katrín said.

"Only about the rape?"

"Only," Katrín repeated. "Only! As if that's not enough. As if it's not enough for him to hear that I'd been raped and never told him about it. Isn't that enough?"

They all fell silent.

"Didn't you tell him about your youngest son?" Erlendur asked eventually.

Katrín suddenly looked daggers at him.

"What about our youngest son?" she said, spitting out the words.

"You named him Einar," said Erlendur, who had looked through the details Elínborg had collected about the family the day before.

"What about Einar?"

Erlendur looked at her.

"What about Einar?" she repeated.

"He's your son," Erlendur said. "But he's not his father's son."

"What are you talking about? Not his father's son? Of course he's his father's son! Who isn't his father's son?"

"Sorry, I'm not being precise enough. He isn't the son of the father he thought was his," Erlendur said calmly. "He's the son of the man who raped you. Holberg's son. Did you tell your husband that? Was that why he left as he did?"

Katrín stayed silent.

"Did you tell him the whole truth?"

Katrín looked at Erlendur. He sensed she was preparing to resist. A few moments passed and then he saw how her lips gave in. Her shoulders sank, she closed her eyes, she half collapsed in the chair and burst into tears. Elínborg glared at Erlendur but he just watched Katrín in the chair and gave her time to collect herself.

"Did you tell him about Einar?" he asked again when he thought she had managed to pull herself together.

"He didn't believe it," she said.

"That Einar wasn't his son?" Erlendur said.

"They're particularly close, Einar and Albert, they always have been. Ever since he was born. Albert loves his other two sons as well, of course, but especially Einar. Right from the start. He's the youngest child and Albert's pampered him."

Katrín paused.

"Maybe that's why I never said anything. I knew Albert wouldn't be able to stand it. The years went by and I pretended there was nothing amiss. Never said a thing. And it worked. Holberg had left a wound and why not let it heal in peace? Why should he be able to destroy our future together? To ignore it was my way of dealing with the horror."

"Did you know at once that Einar was Holberg's son?" Elínborg asked.

"He could well have been Albert's son."

Katrín fell silent again.

"But you saw it in his face," Erlendur said.

Katrín looked at him.

"How do you know all this?"

"He looks like Holberg, doesn't he?" Erlendur said. "Holberg as a young man. A woman saw him in Keflavík and thought it was Holberg himself."

"There's a certain resemblance between them."

"If you never told your son anything and your husband didn't know about Einar, why this big showdown now between you and Albert? What started it?"

"What woman in Keflavík?" Katrín said. "What woman who lives in Keflavík knows Holberg? Did he live with a woman there?"

"No," Erlendur said, wondering whether he ought to tell her about Kolbrún and Audur. She'd hear about them sooner or later and he couldn't see any valid reason for Katrín not to learn the truth now. He'd already told her about the rape in Keflavík, but now he named Holberg's victim and told her about Audur, who died young after a serious and difficult illness. He told her how they'd found the photograph of the gravestone in Holberg's desk and how it had led them to Keflavík and to Elín, and he told of the treatment Kolbrún had been given when she tried to press charges.

Katrín took in every word of the account. Tears welled up in her eyes when Erlendur told her about Audur's death. He also told her about Grétar, the man with the camera, whom she'd seen with Holberg, and how he vanished without trace, but had been found underneath the concrete floor of Holberg's basement flat.

"Is that all the fuss in Nordurmýri that's been in the news?" Katrín said.

Erlendur nodded.

"I didn't know Holberg raped any other women. I thought I was the only one."

"We know only about you two," Erlendur said. "There could be others. We can't be sure we will ever know."

"So Audur was Einar's half-sister," Katrín said, deep in thought. "The poor child."

"Are you sure you didn't know about this?" Erlendur asked.

"Of course I'm sure," she said. "I didn't have the faintest idea about it."

"Einar knows about her," Erlendur said. "He tracked down Elín in Keflavík."

Katrín didn't answer. He decided to try a different question.

"If your son didn't know anything and you never

told your husband about the rape, how has Einar suddenly found out the truth now?"

"I don't know," Katrín said. "Tell me, how did the poor girl die?"

"You know your son is suspected of Holberg's murder," Erlendur said, not answering her. He tried to phrase what he had to say as carefully as he could. He thought Katrín was astonishingly calm, as if it didn't surprise her that her son was suspected of murder.

"My son's no murderer," she said softly. "He could never kill anyone."

"There's a strong probability that he hit Holberg over the head. Maybe he didn't intend to murder him. He probably did it in a fit of rage. He left a message for us. It said: I am him. Do you understand what that means?"

Katrín said nothing.

"Did he know Holberg was his father? Did he know what Holberg did to you? Did he know about Audur and Elín? How?"

Katrín stared into her lap.

"Where's your son now?" Elínborg asked.

"I don't know," Katrín said quietly. "I haven't heard from him for several days."

She looked at Erlendur.

"Suddenly he found out about Holberg. He knew something wasn't right. He found it out at work. He said we couldn't hide any secrets these days. He said it was all in the database."

38

Erlendur looked at Katrín.

"Is that how he got the information about his real father?" he asked.

"He discovered that he couldn't be Albert's son," Katrín said in a low voice.

"How?" Erlendur asked. "What was he looking for? Why was he looking himself up in the database? Was it a coincidence?"

"No," Katrín said. "It wasn't a coincidence."

Elínborg had had enough. She wanted to stop the questioning and give Katrín a break. She stood up saying she needed to fetch a glass of water and gestured to Erlendur to come with her. He followed her into the kitchen. Elínborg told him she thought the woman had been through enough for the time being and that they should leave her alone and tell her to consult a lawyer before she said anything else. They ought to save further questioning until later in the day, talk to her family and ask someone to stay with her and help her. Erlendur pointed out that Katrín hadn't been arrested, wasn't suspected of anything, that this wasn't a formal interrogation, just collecting information, and that Katrín was very cooperative at the moment. They ought to continue.

Elínborg shook her head.

"Strike while the iron's hot," Erlendur said.

"What a thing to say!" Elínborg hissed.

Katrín appeared at the kitchen door and asked if they should continue. She was ready to tell them the truth and not conceal anything this time.

"I want to get it over with," she said.

Elínborg asked whether she wanted to contact a lawyer, but Katrín said no. She said she didn't know any lawyers and had never had occasion to consult one. Didn't know how to go about it.

Elínborg looked accusingly at Erlendur. He asked Katrín to continue. When they had all sat down Katrín resumed her story. She wrung her hands and sadly began her story.

*

Albert was going abroad that morning. They got up very early. She made coffee for them both. They talked yet again about selling the house and buying somewhere smaller. They'd often talked about this, but had never got round to it. Maybe it seemed like too big a step, as if underlining how old they were. They didn't feel old, but it seemed an increasingly pressing matter for them to buy a smaller place. Albert said he would talk to an estate agent when he came back, and then he left in his Cherokee.

She went back to bed. She didn't have to go to work for two hours, but she couldn't get back to sleep. She lay there tossing and turning until eight o'clock. Then she got up. She was in the kitchen when she heard Einar come in. He had a key to the house.

She could tell at once that he was upset but she didn't know why. He said he'd been up all night. Paced the sitting room and went into the kitchen but refused to sit down.

"I knew there was something that didn't fit," he said, and gave his mother an angry look. "I knew it all the time!"

She couldn't understand what he was angry about.

"I knew something didn't bloody fit," he repeated almost shouting.

"What are you talking about, love," she said, unaware of why he was angry. "What doesn't fit?"

"I cracked the code," he said. "I broke the rules to crack the code. I wanted to see how the disease is passed on through families – and it *is* passed on through families, I can tell you that. It's in several families, but it's not in our family. Not in Dad's family and not in yours. That's why it doesn't fit. Do you understand? Do you understand what I'm saying?"

*

Erlendur's mobile phone rang in his coat pocket and he asked Katrín to excuse him. He went into the kitchen to answer it. It was Sigurdur Óli.

"The old girl from Keflavík's looking for you," he said, without introducing himself.

"The old girl? Do you mean Elín?"

"Yes, Elín."

"Did you talk to her?"

"Yes," Sigurdur Óli said. "She said she needed to talk to you straightaway."

"Do you know what she wants?"

"She flatly refused to tell me. How are you doing?"

"Did you give her my mobile number?"

"No."

"If she calls again give her my number," Erlendur said and hung up. Katrín and Elínborg were waiting for him in the sitting room.

"Sorry," he said to Katrín. She continued her story.

*

Einar paced the sitting room. Katrín tried to calm him down and work out what had made her son so upset. She sat down and asked him to sit beside her, but he wouldn't listen. Walked back and forth in front of her. She knew he'd been having problems for a long time and that the separation didn't help. His wife had left him. She wanted a fresh start. She didn't want to be overwhelmed by his sorrow.

"Tell me what's wrong," she said.

"So much, Mum, just so much."

And then came the question she'd been waiting for all these years.

"Who's my dad?" her son asked and stopped in front of her. "Who's my real father?"

She looked at him.

"We haven't got any secrets any more, Mum," he said.

"What have you found out?" she asked. "What have you been up to?"

"I know who isn't my father," he said, "and that's Dad." He roared with laughter. "Did you hear that? Dad isn't my dad! And if he isn't my dad, who am I then? Where did I come from? My brothers. Suddenly they're just half-brothers. Why haven't you ever told me anything? Why have you lied to me all this time? Why? Why?"

She stared at him and her eyes filled with tears.

"Did you cheat on Dad?" he asked. "You can tell me. I won't tell anyone. Did you cheat on him? No-one need know except the two of us but I have to hear it from you. You have to tell me the truth. Where do I come from? How was I made?"

He stopped talking.

"Am I adopted? An orphan? What am I? Who am I? Mum?"

Katrín burst into tears with heavy sobs. He stared at her, just beginning to calm down, while she wept on the sofa. It took him some time to register how much his words had upset her. Eventually he sat down and put his arm around her. They sat for a while in silence until she started to tell him about the night in Húsavík when his father was at sea. She was out with her girlfriends and met some men, including Holberg, who burst into her house. He listened to her story without interruption.

She told him how Holberg had raped her and threatened her and she'd decided for herself to have the baby and never tell anyone what had happened. Not his father and not him. And that had been fine. They'd lived a happy life. She hadn't allowed Holberg to rob her of her happiness. He hadn't managed to kill her family.

She told him that, though he was the son of the man who raped her, that didn't prevent her from loving him as much as her other two sons and she knew Albert was particularly fond of him. So Einar had never suffered for what Holberg did. Never.

It took him a few minutes to digest what she'd said.

"Sorry," he said at last. "I didn't mean to get angry with you. I thought you'd been cheating and that's where I came from. I had no idea about the rape."

"Of course not," she said. "How could you have known? I've never told anyone until now."

"I should have seen that possibility too," he said. "There was another possibility, but I didn't consider it. Sorry. You must have felt terrible all these years."

"You shouldn't think about that," she said. "You shouldn't suffer for what that man did."

"I've already suffered for it, Mum," he said. "Endless torment. And not just me. Why didn't you have an abortion? What stopped you?"

"Oh Lord, God, don't say that, Einar. Never talk like that."

*

Katrín stopped.

"Didn't you ever consider an abortion?" Elínborg asked.

"All the time. Always. Until it was too late. I thought about it every day after I found out I was pregnant. Anyway, the child could well have been Albert's. That probably made all the difference. And then I got depressed after the birth. Postnatal depression, isn't it? I was sent for psychiatric treatment. After three months I was well enough again to look after the boy and I've loved him ever since."

Erlendur waited a moment before he continued his questioning.

"Why did your son start looking up genetic diseases in the Research Centre's database?" he asked eventually.

Katrín looked at him.

"How did that girl from Keflavík die?" she asked.

"Of a brain tumour," Erlendur said. "The disease is called neurofibromatosis."

Katrín's eyes filled with tears and she heaved a deep sigh.

"Didn't you know?" she said.

"Didn't I know what?"

"Our little love died three years ago," Katrín said. "For no reason. Absolutely no reason."

"Your little love?" Erlendur said.

"Our little sweetheart," she said. "Einar's daughter. She died. The poor, sweet child."

39

A deep silence fell across the house.

Katrín was sitting with her head bowed. Elínborg looked first at her and then at Erlendur, thunderstruck. Erlendur stared into space and thought about Eva Lind. What was she doing now? Was she at his flat? He felt the urge to talk to his daughter. Felt the urge to hug her, snuggle up to her and not let go until he'd told her how much she meant to him.

"I can't believe it," Elínborg said.

"Your son's a genetic carrier, isn't he?" Erlendur said.

"That was the phrase he used," Katrín said. "A genetic carrier. They both are. He and Holberg. He said he inherited it from the man who raped me."

"But neither of them got ill," Erlendur said.

"It seems to be the females who become ill," Katrín said. "The males carry the disease, but don't necessarily show any symptoms. But it comes in all kinds of forms, I can't explain it. My son understands it. He tried to explain it to me, but I didn't really know what he was talking about. He was heartbroken. And so was I of course."

"And he found all this out from that database they're making," Erlendur said.

Katrín nodded.

"He couldn't understand why his little girl got the disease so he started looking for it in my family and Albert's. He talked to relatives and just wouldn't give up. We thought it was his way of dealing with the shock. All that endless searching for the cause. Searching for answers where we didn't think there were any answers to be found. They split up some time ago, Lára and him. They couldn't live together any longer and decided on a temporary separation, but I can't see things ever improving."

Katrín stopped talking.

"And then he found the answer," Erlendur said.

"He became convinced that Albert wasn't his father. He said it couldn't be right according to the information he had from the database. That's why he came to me. He thought I'd been unfaithful and that was where he came from. Or that he was adopted."

"Did he find Holberg in the database?"

"I don't think so. Not until later. After I told him about Holberg. It was so absurd. So ridiculous! My son had made a list of his possible fathers and Holberg was on it. He could trace the disease back through certain families using the genetics and genealogy databases and he found out he couldn't be his father's son. He was a deviation. A different strain."

"How old was his daughter?"

"She was seven."

"It was a brain tumour that caused her death, wasn't it?" Erlendur said.

"Yes."

"She died of the same disease as Audur. Neurofibromatosis."

"Yes. Audur's mother must have felt terrible; first Holberg, and then her daughter dying."

Erlendur hesitated for a moment.

"Kolbrún, her mother, committed suicide three years after Audur died."

"My God," Katrín sighed.

"Where's your son now?" Erlendur asked.

"I don't know," Katrín replied. "I'm worried sick he'll do something terrible to himself. He feels so depressed, the boy. So terrible."

"Do you think he's been in contact with Holberg?"

"I don't know. I just know he's no murderer. That I know for certain."

"Did you think he looked like his father?" Erlendur asked and looked at the confirmation photographs.

Katrín didn't answer.

"Could you see a resemblance between them?" Erlendur asked.

"Come on, Erlendur," Elínborg snapped, unable to take any more of this. "Don't you think you've gone far enough, seriously?"

"Sorry," Erlendur said to Katrín. "I'm just being nosy. You've been extremely helpful to us and if it's any consolation I doubt that we'll ever find a more steadfast or stronger character than you, being able to suffer in silence for all those years."

"It's all right," Katrín said to Elínborg. "Children can take after anyone in the family. I could never see Holberg in my boy. He said it wasn't my fault. Einar told me that. I wasn't to blame for the way his daughter died."

Katrín paused.

"What will happen to Einar?" she asked. She wasn't putting up any resistance now. No lies. Only resignation.

"We have to find him," Erlendur said, "talk to him and hear what he has to say."

He and Elínborg stood up. Erlendur put on his hat. Katrín remained on the sofa.

"If you want I can talk to Albert," Erlendur said. "He stayed at Hotel Esja last night. We've been watching your house since yesterday in case your son happend to turn up. I can explain to Albert what's going on. He'll come to his senses."

"Thank you," Katrín said. "I'll phone him. I know he'll come back. We need to stand together for the sake of our boy."

She stared Erlendur in the eye.

"He is our boy," she said. "He always will be our boy."

40

Erlendur didn't expect Einar to be at home. They went to his flat on Stóragerdi straight from Katrín's house. It was noon and the traffic was heavy. On the way, Erlendur phoned Sigurdur Óli to describe the developments. They needed to ask the public about Einar's whereabouts. Find a photograph of him to put in the papers and on television along with a short announcement. They arranged to meet on Stóragerdi. When Erlendur arrived there he got out of the car and Elínborg drove off. Erlendur waited a while for Sigurdur Óli. The flat was in the basement of a three-storey house with the front door at street level. They rang the bell and hammered on the door but there was no answer. They tried the floors above and it turned out that Einar rented from the owner of one of the other flats, who had come home for lunch but was willing to go down with them and open his tenant's flat. He said he hadn't seen Einar for several days, possibly even a week; said he was a quiet man, had no complaints about him. He always paid the rent promptly. Couldn't imagine what the police wanted him for in the first place. In order to avoid speculation, Sigurdur Óli said his family hadn't heard from him and they were trying to find out where he might be. The owner of the flat asked whether they had a warrant to search the house. They didn't, but would get one later that day. They asked him to excuse them when he had opened the door and they went inside. All the curtains were closed so it was dark inside. It was a very small flat. A sitting room, bedroom, kitchen and bathroom. Carpets everywhere except in the bathroom and the kitchen, which had linoleum. A television in the sitting room. A sofa in front of the television. The air in the flat was muggy. Instead of opening the curtains Erlendur switched on the sitting-room light so that they could see better.

They stared at the walls in the flat and looked at each other. The walls were covered with words they knew so well from Holberg's flat, written with ballpoint pen, felt-tip and spray paint. Three words that had once been indecipherable to Erlendur but now became clear.

I am HIM

There were newspapers and magazines spread all around, Icelandic and foreign ones, and scientific textbooks were stacked here and there on the floor of the sitting room and the bedroom. Large photo albums were included in the stacks. In the kitchen were wrappers from takeaway food.

"Paternity," Sigurdur Óli said, putting on his rubber gloves. "Can we ever be sure about that in Iceland?"

Erlendur started thinking again about genetic

research. The Genetic Research Centre had recently begun collecting medical data about all the Icelanders, past and present, to process into a database containing health information about the whole nation. It was linked up to a genealogy database in which the family of every single Icelander was traced back to the Middle Ages; they called it establishing the Icelandic genetic pool. The main aim was to discover how hereditary illnesses were transmitted, study them genetically and find ways to cure them, and other diseases if possible. It was said that the homogenous nation and lack of miscegenation made Iceland a living laboratory for genetic research.

The Genetic Research Centre and the Ministry of Health, which issued the licence for the database, guaranteed that no outsider could break into the database and announced a complex encryption system for the data which was impossible to crack.

"Are you worried about your paternity?" Erlendur asked. He'd also put on rubber gloves and stepped carefully further into the sitting room. He picked up one of the photo albums and leafed through it. It was old.

"Everyone always said I never resembled my father or mother or anyone else in my family."

"I've always had that feeling too," Erlendur said.

"What do you mean?"

"That you were a bastard."

"Glad you've got your sense of humour back," Sigurdur Óli said. "You've been a little distant recently."

"What sense of humour?" Erlendur said.

He flicked through another of the albums. These were old black-and-white photographs. He thought he recognised Einar's mother in some of them. So the man would be Albert and the boys, their three sons. Einar was the youngest. There were photographs taken at Christmas and on summer holidays, many of them ordinary snapshots taken of the boys in the street or at the kitchen table, wearing patterned, knitted sweaters, which Erlendur remembered from the late '60s. The elder brothers had let their hair grow long.

Further on in the album the boys were older and with longer hair and they were wearing suits with wide lapels and black shoes with stacked heels. Katrín with her hair waved. The photos were in colour now. Albert beginning to turn grey. Erlendur looked for Einar and when he compared his features with those of his brothers and his parents he could see how different he looked. The other two boys had strong features from their parents, especially their father. Einar was the ugly duckling.

He put the old album down and picked a more recent one. The photographs seemed to have be taken by Einar himself, showing his own family. They didn't tell such a long story. It was as if Erlendur had dipped into the course of Einar's life when he was getting to know his wife. He wondered if they were honeymoon photos. They had travelled around Iceland, been to Hornstrandir, he thought. Thórsmörk. Herdubreidarlindir. Sometimes they were on bicycles. Sometimes driving a battered old car. Camping photos. Erlendur presumed they had been taken in the mid-'8os.

He flicked quickly through the album, put it down and picked up what looked to him like the most recent one. In it he saw a little girl in a hospital bed with tubes in her arms and an oxygen mask over her face. Her eyes were closed and she was surrounded by instruments. She seemed to be in intensive care. He hesitated for a moment before going on.

Erlendur was surprised by the sudden ringing of his mobile phone. He put the album down without closing it. It was Elín from Keflavík and she was very agitated.

"He was with me this morning," she said at once.

"Who?"

"Audur's brother. His name's Einar. I tried to get hold of you. He was with me this morning and told me the whole story, the poor man. He lost his daughter, just like Kolbrún. He knew what Audur died of. It's a disease in Holberg's family."

"Where is he now?" Erlendur asked.

"He was so terribly depressed," Elín said. "He might do something stupid."

"What do you mean, stupid?"

"He said it was over."

"What was over?"

"He didn't say, just said it was over."

"Do you know where he is now?"

"He said he was going back to Reykjavík."

"To Reykjavík? Where?"

"He didn't say," Elín answered.

"Did he give any indication of what he was going to do?"

"No," Elín said, "none at all. You must find him before he does something stupid. He feels so terrible, the poor man. It's awful. Absolutely awful. My God, I've never known anything like it."

"What?"

"He's so like his father. He's the spitting image of Holberg and he can't live with that. He just can't. After he heard what Holberg did to his mother. He says he's a prisoner inside his own body. He says Holberg's blood is running through his veins and he can't stand it."

"What's he talking about?"

"It's as if he hates himself," Elín said. "He says he isn't the person he used to be any more, but someone else, and he blames himself for what happened. No matter what I said, he wouldn't listen to me."

Erlendur looked down at the photo album, at the girl in the hospital bed.

"Why did he want to meet you?"

"He wanted to know about Audur. All about Audur. What kind of girl she was, how she died. He said I was his new family. Have you ever heard the like?"

"Where could he have gone?" Erlendur said, looking at his watch.

"For God's sake try to find him before it's too late."

"We'll do our best," Erlendur said and was about to say goodbye but sensed that Elín had something else to say. "What? Was there anything else?" he asked.

"He saw when you exhumed Audur," Elín said. "He found out where I was and followed us to the cemetery and saw you take the coffin out of the grave."

41

Erlendur had the search for Einar stepped up. Photographs of him were sent to police stations in and around Reykjavík and the main regional towns; announcements were sent to the media. He ordered that the man was to be let alone; if anyone sighted him they were to contact Erlendur immediately and not do anything else. He had a short telephone conversation with Katrín who said she didn't know where her son was. Her two elder sons were with her. She had told them the truth. They didn't know anything about their brother's whereabouts. Albert had stayed in his room at Hotel Esja all day. He made two phone calls, both to his office.

"What a bloody tragedy," Erlendur mumbled on his way back to his office. They hadn't found any clue in Einar's flat as to where he might be staying.

The day passed and they shared out the duties. Elínborg and Sigurdur Óli talked to Einar's ex-wife while Erlendur went to the Genetic Research Centre. The company's large new premises were on the West Country Road outside Reykjavík. It was a five-storey building with strict security at the entrance. Two security guards met Erlendur in the impressive lobby. He'd announced that he was coming and the director of the company had felt compelled to talk to him for a few minutes. The director was one of the company owners, an Icelandic molecular geneticist, educated in Britain and America, who had championed the idea of Iceland as a base for genetic research targeted at pharmaceutical production. Using the database, all the medical records in the country could be centralised and health information processed which could help to identify genetic disorders.

The director was waiting for Erlendur in her office, a woman aged about 50 by the name of Karítas, slim and delicate with short, jet-black hair and a friendly smile. She was smaller than Erlendur had imagined from seeing her on television, but cordial. She couldn't understand what the CID wanted from the company. She offered Erlendur a seat. While he looked at the walls adorned with contemporary Icelandic art he told her bluntly there were grounds for suspecting that someone had broken into the database and retrieved potentially damaging information from it. He didn't know exactly what he was talking about himself but she seemed to understand perfectly. And she didn't beat about the bush, to Erlendur's great relief. He had been expecting opposition. A conspiracy of silence.

"The matter's so sensitive because of data privacy," she said as soon as Erlendur finished speaking, "and that's why I have to ask you to keep this completely between the two of us. We've known for some time about unauthorised accessing of the database. We've made an in-house inquiry into the matter. Our suspicions are directed at one particular biologist but we've been unable to speak to him because he seems to have disappeared off the face of the planet."

"Einar?"

"Yes, that's him. We're still designing the database, so to speak, but naturally we don't want word to get out that the encryption can be cracked and people can waltz through it as they please. You understand that. Although in fact it's not a question of encryption."

"Why didn't you inform the police about the matter?"

"As I say, we wanted to sort it out ourselves. It's embarrassing for us. People trust that the information in the database isn't passed around or used for dubious purposes or simply stolen. The community is extremely sensitive about this as you perhaps know and we wanted to avoid mass hysteria."

"Mass hysteria?"

"Sometimes it's like the whole country is against us."

"Did he crack the code? Why isn't this a question of encryption?"

"You really do make it sound like a cloak-and-dagger affair. No, he didn't crack any code. Not really. He went about it differently."

"What did he do?"

"He set up a research project that no-one had

authorised. He forged signatures, including mine. He pretended the company was researching the genetic transmission of an oncogenic disease found in several families in Iceland. He tricked the data privacy committee – a kind of monitoring agency for the database. He tricked the scientific ethics committee. He tricked us all here."

She stopped talking for a moment and looked at her watch. She stood up and went over to her desk and called her secretary to postpone a meeting for ten minutes then sat back down with Erlendur.

"That's been the dynamics up to now," she said.

"Dynamics?" Erlendur said.

Karítas looked at him thoughtfully. The mobile phone in Erlendur's pocket started ringing. He excused himself and answered. It was Sigurdur Óli.

"Forensics have been through Einar's flat on Stóragerdi," he said. "I called them and they haven't really found anything except that Einar got himself a fire-arms licence two years ago or so."

"A fire-arms licence?" Erlendur repeated.

"It's on our register. But that's not all. He owns a shotgun and we found the sawn-off barrel under his bed."

"The barrel?"

"He'd sawn off the barrel. They do that sometimes. Makes it easier to shoot themselves."

"Do you think he could be dangerous?"

"When we find him," Sigurdur Óli said, "we need to approach him carefully. We can't predict what he'll do with a gun."

"He can hardly intend to kill anyone with it," said Erlendur, who had stood up and turned his back on Karítas for some kind of privacy.

"Why not?"

"He would have already used it," Erlendur said in a low voice. "On Holberg. Don't you think?"

"I honestly don't know."

"See you," Erlendur said, switched off the phone and repeated his apologies before he sat down again.

"That's been the process up to now," Karítas resumed where she'd left off. "We apply to these authorities for permission to conduct a research project, like in Einar's case, the study of the genetic transmission of a specific disease. We're given an encrypted list of names of people who suffer from the disease or are conceivable carriers and compare it to the encrypted genealogy database. Then we can produce a kind of encrypted family tree."

"Like a message tree," Erlendur said.

"What?"

"No, do go on."

"The data privacy committee decodes the list with the names of the people we want to study, what we call a sample group, both patients and relatives, and it produces a list of participants with their ID numbers. Do you follow?"

"And that's how Einar obtained the names and ID numbers of anyone who had the disease in their family."

She nodded.

"Does this all go through the data privacy committee?"

"I don't know how deeply you want to go into this. We're working with doctors and various establishments. They submit the names of patients to the privacy committee, which encrypts the names and ID numbers and sends them here to the Genetic Research Centre. We have a dedicated genealogical tracer program which arranges patients into cluster groups on the basis of their relationship to one another. Using this program we can select the patients who provide the best statistical information for searching for specific genetic disorders. Then we ask individuals from this group to take part in the study. Genealogy is valuable for seeing whether a genetic disease is involved, selecting a good sample, and it's a powerful tool in the search for genetic disorders."

"All that Einar needed to do was to pretend to create a sample and have the names decoded, all with the help of the data privacy committee."

"He lied and tricked everyone and he got away with it."

"I can understand how this could be embarrassing for you."

"Einar is among our top management here and one of our most capable scientists. A fine man. Why did he do it?" the director asked.

"He lost his daughter," Erlendur said. "Didn't you know about that?"

"No," she said, staring at him.

"How long's he been working here?"

"Two years."

"It was some time before then."

"How did he lose his daughter?"

"She had a genetically transmitted neural disease. He was the carrier but didn't know about the disease in his family."

"A question of paternity?"

Erlendur didn't answer her. Felt he'd said enough.

"That's one of the problems with this kind of genealogy database. Diseases tend to jump out of the family tree at random and then pop up again where you least expected them."

Erlendur stood up. "And you keep all these secrets. Old family secrets. Tragedies, sorrows and death, all carefully classified in computers. Family stories and stories of individuals. Stories about me and you. You keep the whole secret and can call it up whenever you want. A Jar City for the whole nation."

"I don't know what you're talking about," Karítas said. "A Jar City?"

"No, of course not," Erlendur said and took his leave.

42

When Erlendur got back to his flat that evening there was still no word about Einar. His family had gathered at his parents' house. Albert had checked out of his hotel in the afternoon and returned home after an emotional telephone conversation with Katrín. Their elder sons were there with their wives and Einar's ex-wife soon joined them. Elínborg and Sigurdur Óli had spoken to her earlier that day but she said she couldn't imagine where Einar was staying. He hadn't been in touch with her for about half a year.

Eva Lind arrived home soon after Erlendur and he told her all about the investigation. Fingerprints found at Holberg's flat matched Einar's own prints from his home on Stóragerdi.

He had finally gone to meet his father and had apparently murdered him. Erlendur also told Eva Lind about Grétar, how the only palpable theory about his disappearance and death was that Grétar had been blackmailing Holberg in some way, probably with photographs. Exactly what they showed was uncertain but based on the evidence they had Erlendur thought that it wasn't unlikely that Grétar had photographed what Holberg got up to, even rapes no-one knew about and would probably never surface after all this time. The photograph of Audur's gravestone suggested that Grétar knew what had happened and might even have testified, and that he'd been gathering information about Holberg, possibly to blackmail him.

The two of them talked together into the night while the rain beat down on the windows and the autumn winds howled. She asked him why he was rubbing his chest, almost instinctively. Erlendur told her about the pains he'd been feeling. He blamed his old mattress but Eva Lind ordered him to see a doctor. He wasn't keen on the idea.

"What do you mean, you're not going to the doctor?" she said and Erlendur immediately regretted having admitted to his pain.

"It's nothing," he said.

"How many have you smoked today?"

"What is all this?"

"Hang on, you've got chest pains, you smoke like a chimney, never go anywhere except by car, you live on deep-fried junk food and refuse to get yourself looked at! And then you hurl abuse at me about my lifestyle until I end up crying like a little baby. Do you think that's normal? Are you crazy?"

Eva Lind was standing up, glaring down, like the god of thunder, at her father who flinched from looking up at her and stared sheepishly at the floor.

"I'll have it looked at," he said at last.

"Have it looked at! You bet you'll have it looked

at!" Eva Lind shouted. "And you should have done long ago. Wimp."

"First thing tomorrow morning," he said, looking at his daughter.

"Just as well," she said.

Erlendur was going to bed when the phone rang. It was Sigurdur Óli to tell him that the police had received a report of a break-in at the morgue on Barónsstígur.

"The morgue on Barónsstígur," Sigurdur Óli repeated when he received no response from Erlendur.

"Oh Christ," Erlendur groaned. "And?"

"I don't know," Sigurdur Óli said. "The report just came in. They called me and I said I'd contact you. They don't know anything about the motive. Is there anything except dead bodies down there?"

"I'll meet you there," Erlendur said. "Get the pathologist down there too," he added and put the phone down.

Eva Lind was asleep in the sitting room when he put on his coat and hat and looked at the clock. It was past midnight. He closed the door carefully behind him so as not to wake his daughter, then hurried down the stairs and into his car.

When he reached the morgue three police cars with flashing lights were parked outside. He recognised Sigurdur Óli's car and just as Erlendur was entering the building he saw the pathologist turn the corner, his tyres screeching on the wet tarmac. The pathologist had a ferocious look on his face. Erlendur hurried down the long corridor lined with policemen and Sigurdur Óli came out of the operating theatre.

"Nothing seems to be missing," Sigurdur Óli said when he saw Erlendur storming down the corridor.

"Tell me what happened," Erlendur said and went into the operating theatre with him. The operating tables were empty, all the cupboards were closed and there was no evidence of a break-in there.

"There were footprints all over the floor in here but they've mostly dried up now," Sigurdur Óli said. "The building's connected to an alarm system that calls the security company's headquarters and they contacted us about 15 minutes ago. It looks as though the burglar smashed a window at the back and put his hand through to undo the lock. Not very complicated. As soon as he entered the building the alarm went off. He wouldn't have had much time to do anything."

"Definitely enough time," Erlendur said. The pathologist had joined them and was visibly disturbed.

"Who the hell breaks into a morgue?" he said.

"Where are Holberg and Audur?" Erlendur asked.

The pathologist looked at Erlendur.

"Is this anything to do with Holberg's murder?" he asked.

"It could be," Erlendur said. "Quick, quick, quick."

"They keep the bodies in this side room here," the pathologist said and showed them to a door which he opened.

"Are these doors always unlocked?" Sigurdur Óli asked.

"Who steals bodies?" the pathologist snapped, but he stopped in his tracks when he looked inside the room.

"What now?" Erlendur asked.

"The girl's gone," the pathologist said as if he couldn't believe his eyes. He hurried through the storage room, opened another door inside it and switched on the light.

"What?" Erlendur asked.

"Her coffin's gone too," the pathologist said. He looked at Sigurdur Óli and Erlendur in turn. "We'd got a new coffin for her. Who does that sort of thing? Who would ever think of such a perversion?"

"His name's Einar," Erlendur said, "and it's not a perversion."

He turned round. Sigurdur Óli followed fast behind and they hurried out of the morgue.

43

There wasn't much traffic on the Keflavík road that night and Erlendur drove as fast as his little ten-year-old Japanese car could manage. The rain pounded on the windscreen too hard for the wipers to clear and Erlendur thought back to the first time he went to see Elín a few days before. It was like it would never stop raining.

He had ordered Sigurdur Óli to put the Keflavík police on alert and make sure that a back-up force from Reykjavík was available. Also to contact Einar's mother and warn her about the recent turn of events. He wanted to drive directly to the cemetery himself in the hope that Einar would be there with Audur's body. He could only imagine that Einar intended to return his sister to her grave.

When Erlendur pulled up by Hvalsnes cemetery gate he could see Einar's car there with the driver's door and one of the rear doors open. Erlendur switched off the engine, stepped out into the rain and looked at Einar's car. He strained to listen but could only hear the rain dropping vertically to the ground. There was no wind and he looked up into the black sky. In the distance he could see a light above the entrance to the church and when he looked across the cemetery he saw a gleam where Audur's grave was. He thought he could make out something moving at the graveside.

And the miniature white coffin.

He set off cautiously and crept up to the man he took to be Einar. The light came from a powerful lantern that the man had brought with him and put down on the ground by the coffin. Erlendur stepped slowly into the light. He looked up from what he was doing and stared into Erlendur's eyes. Erlendur had seen photographs of Holberg as a young man and there was no question about the resemblance. His forehead was low and a little rounded, his eyebrows thick, eyes close together, prominent cheekbones on a thin face and slightly protruding teeth. His nose was narrow and so were his lips, but his chin was large and his neck long. They looked each other in the eye for an instant.

"Who are you?" Einar asked.

"I'm Erlendur. Holberg's my case."

"Are you surprised how much I look like him?" Einar said.

"There is a certain resemblance," Erlendur said.

"You know he raped my mother," Einar said.

"That's not your fault," Erlendur said.

"He was my father."

"That's not your fault either."

"You shouldn't have done this," Einar said, pointing to the coffin.

"I felt I had to," Erlendur said. "I found out that she died from the same disease as your daughter."

"I'm going to put her back where she belongs," Einar said.

"That's all right," Erlendur said, inching his way over to the coffin. "You'll surely want to put this in the grave too." Erlendur held out the black leather case that he'd kept in his car ever since he left the collector.

"What's that?" Einar asked.

"The disease," Erlendur said.

"I don't understand . . ."

"It's Audur's bio-sample. I think we ought to return it to her."

Einar looked at the bag and at Erlendur in turn, unsure of what to do. Erlendur moved even closer until he was beside the coffin, which separated them, and he put the bag down on it and calmly backed away again to where he had been standing before.

"I want to be cremated," Einar suddenly said.

"You've got your whole life to arrange that," Erlendur said.

"Oh yes, a whole life," Einar said, raising his voice. "What's that? What's a life when it's seven years? Can you tell me that ? What kind of life is that?"

"I can't answer that," Erlendur said. "Do you have the gun on you?"

"I talked to Elín," Einar said, ignoring his question. "You probably know. We talked about

Audur. My sister. I knew about her but I didn't know she was my sister until later. I saw you taking her out of the grave. I could understand Elín when she tried to attack you."

"How did you know about Audur?"

"From the database. I found all the people who died of this particular strain of the disease. I didn't know then that I was Holberg's son and Audur was my sister. I found that out later. How I was conceived. When I asked my mother."

He looked at Erlendur.

"After I discovered I was a carrier."

"How did you link Holberg and Audur?"

"Through the disease. The strain of it. The brain tumour is that rare."

Einar fell silent for a moment and then began giving, methodically and without any digressions or sentimentality, an exact account of his doings, as if he'd been preparing to do so. He never raised his voice but always spoke in the same low tone which sometimes dropped to a whisper. The rain fell to the ground and onto the coffin and the hollow echo from it could be heard in the still of the night. He described how his daughter fell ill out of the blue when she was four years old. The disease proved difficult to diagnose and months went by until the doctors concluded it was a rare neural disease. It was thought to be genetically transmitted and was confined to certain families but the peculiar thing was that it didn't occur on either his mother's or his father's side of the family. It was a kind of deviation or variant strain, which the doctors had difficulty explaining, unless some kind of mutation had taken place.

They said the disease was in the child's brain and could kill her in the space of a couple of years. What followed was a period that Einar said he couldn't begin to describe to Erlendur.

"Have you got any children?" he asked.

"Two," Erlendur said. "A boy and a girl."

"We just had her," he said, "and we split up when she died. Somehow there was nothing to keep us together except the sorrow and memories and the struggles at the hospital. When that was over it was like our lives were over too. There was nothing left."

Einar stopped talking and closed his eyes as if he was about to fall asleep. The rain dripped down his face.

"I was one of the first employees at the new company," he said then. "When the database was set up I seemed to come back to life. I couldn't accept the doctors' answers. I had to find explanations. I regained my interest in finding out how the disease had been transmitted to my daughter, if that was possible. The health database is linked to a genealogy database and the two can be processed together and if you know what you're looking for and have the key to the encryption you can see where the disease lies and you can trace it back along the family tree. You can even see the deviations. Deviations like me. And Audur."

"I talked to Karítas at the Genetic Research

Centre," Erlendur said, wondering how he could get through to Einar. "She described to me the trick you played. This is all so new for us. People don't understand exactly what can be done with all the information that's been collected. What it contains and what you can read into it."

"I was beginning to suspect something. My daughter's doctors had a theory it was genetically transmitted. At first I thought I was simply adopted and it would certainly have been better that way. If they'd adopted me. Then I started suspecting my mother. I tricked her into giving me a blood sample. My father too. I couldn't find anything in them. Neither of them. But I found it in me."

"You don't have any symptoms?"

"Very few," Einar said, "I've lost most of my hearing in one ear. There's a tumour by the aural nerve. Benign. And I've got marks on my skin."

"*Café au lait*?"

"You've done your homework. I could have contracted the disease through a genetic change. A mutation. But I thought the other explanation was more plausible. In the end I went to the database and got the names of several carriers my mother could have had a relationship with. Holberg was one of them. She told me the whole story straight-away when I challenged her with my suspicions. How she'd kept quiet about the rape and that I'd never suffered for my origins. On the contrary. I'm the youngest son," he said by way of explanation. "The little baby boy."

"I know," Erlendur said.

"What a thing to hear!" Einar shouted out into the still of the night. "I wasn't my father's son; my real father raped my mother; I was the son of a rapist; he'd given me corrupt genes that hardly touched me but killed my daughter; I had a half-sister who died of the same disease. I still haven't taken it all in. Still haven't managed to grasp it. When my mother told me about Holberg the rage swelled up in me and I just snapped. He was a repulsive character."

"You started by phoning him."

"I wanted to hear his voice. Don't all bastards want to meet their father?" Einar said, a smile playing across his lips. "Even if it is just the once."

44

The rain had been gradually letting up and now it stopped. The lantern cast a yellow glow onto the ground and the rain, which ran in little streams down the path by the graves. They stood motionless, facing one another, with the coffin between them, looking each other in the eye.

"He must have been shocked to see you," Erlendur said eventually. He knew the police were on their way to the cemetery and he wanted to make the most of this time he had with Einar before the fuss began. He also knew Einar was almost certainly armed. There was no sign of the shotgun but he couldn't rule out that Einar had it with him. Einar had one hand inside his coat.

"You should have seen his face," Einar said. "It was like he'd seen a ghost from the past, and that ghost was his own self."

*

Holberg stood in the doorway looking at the man who rang the bell. He had never seen him before but still he recognised the face immediately.

"Hello, Dad," Einar said sarcastically. He couldn't hide his rage.

"Who are you?" Holberg said, astonished.

"I'm your son," Einar said.

"What is all this . . . are you the one who's been phoning me? I want to ask you to leave me in peace. I don't know you in the slightest. You're not in your right mind."

They were similar in height and appearance but what Einar found most surprising was how elderly and feeble Holberg looked. When he spoke it was with a wheeze from deep within his lungs after decades of smoking. His face was drawn, sharp-featured, with dark rings under the eyes. His dirty, grey hair stuck down firmly against his head. His skin withered, his fingertips yellow, a slight stoop, his eyes colourless and dull.

Holberg was about to close the door but Einar was stronger and pushed his way into the flat. He sensed the smell immediately. Like the smell of horses, but worse.

"What are you keeping in here?" Einar said.

"Will you get out this minute." Holberg's voice was squeaky when he shouted at Einar and he backed away into the sitting room.

"I've got every right to be here," Einar said, looking around at the bookcase and the computer in the corner. "I'm your son. The prodigal son. Can I ask you one thing, Dad? Did you rape more women besides my mother?"

"I'll call the police!" The wheezing became more noticeable as he got worked up.

"Someone should have done that long ago," Einar said.

Holberg hesitated.

"What do you want from me?" he said.

"You haven't got a clue about what's happened and it's none of your business. You couldn't care less about it. I'm right, aren't I?"

"That face," Holberg said but didn't finish the sentence. He looked at Einar with his colourless eyes and watched him for a long while until it dawned on him what Einar had been saying, that he was his son. Einar noticed him hesitate, saw how he puzzled over what he'd said.

"I've never raped anyone in my life," Holberg said eventually. "It's all a bloody lie. They said I had a daughter in Keflavík and her mother accused me of rape but she could never prove it. I was never convicted."

"Do you know what happened to that daughter of yours?"

"I think the girl died young. I never had any contact with her or the mother. Surely you understand that. She accused me of rape, dammit!"

"Maybe you're aware of child mortality in your family?" Einar asked.

"What are you talking about?"

"Have any children died in your family?"

"What's all this about?"

"I know of several cases this century. One of them was your sister."

Holberg stared at Einar.

"What do you know about my family? How . . . ?"

"Your brother, 20 years older than you, died 15 years ago. Lost his young daughter in 1941. You were 11. There were just you two brothers and you were born so far apart."

Holberg said nothing and Einar continued.

"The disease should have died with you. You should have been the last carrier. You're the last in line. Unmarried. Childless. No family. But you were a rapist. A hopeless fucking rapist!"

Einar stopped talking and stared at Holberg with hateful eyes.

"And now I'm the last carrier."

"What are you talking about?"

"Audur got the disease from you. My daughter got it from me. It's as simple as that. I've looked at this in the database. There hadn't been any new cases of the disease in this family since Audur died, apart from my daughter. We're the last ones."

Einar moved a step closer, picked up a heavy glass ashtray and rolled it in his hands.

"And now it's over."

*

"I didn't go there to kill him. He must have thought he was in big danger. I don't know why I picked up the ashtray. Maybe I was going to throw it at him.

Maybe I wanted to attack him. He moved first. Attacked me and grabbed me by the throat but I hit him over the head and he fell to the floor. I did it without thinking. I was angry and could just as easily have attacked him. I'd wondered how our meeting would end, but I never foresaw that. Never. He hit his head on the table when he fell and then he hit the floor and started bleeding. I knew he was dead when I bent down to him. I looked around, saw a piece of paper and a pencil and wrote that I was him. It was the only thing I could think of after I saw him at the door. That I was him. That I was that man. And that man was my father."

Einar looked down at the open grave.

"There's water in it," he said.

"We'll fix that," Erlendur said. "If you've got the gun on you, let me have it." Erlendur inched closer to him but Einar didn't seem to care.

"Children are philosophers. My daughter asked me once at the hospital, 'Why have we got eyes?' I said it was so we could see."

Einar paused. "She corrected me," he said as if to himself. He looked at Erlendur. "She said it was so we could cry."

Then he seemed to make a decision.

"Who are you if you're not yourself?" he said.

"Take it easy," Erlendur said.

"Who are you then?"

"Everything will be all right."

"I didn't plan for it to turn out this way but it's too late now."

Erlendur couldn't figure out what he meant.

"It's over."

Erlendur looked at him in the lamplight.

"It ends here," Einar said.

Erlendur saw Einar take the gun out from under his coat and point it at him as he moved closer. Erlendur stopped. In a flash, Einar turned the barrel round and pointed it at his heart. He did it in a split second. Erlendur made a move for him, shouting as he did so. A thundering shot rang out. Erlendur was deafened for a second. He threw himself at Einar and they both fell to the ground.

45

Sometimes he felt as if his life had deserted him and only his empty body remained, staring with vacant eyes out into the darkness.

Erlendur stood on the edge of the grave and looked down at Einar lying beside it. He picked up the lantern, shone it down and saw that Einar was dead. After putting the lamp down he started to lower the coffin into the ground. He opened it first, put the jar inside and closed it again. He had to struggle to lower the coffin by himself but he managed it in the end. He found a shovel that had been left behind on a pile of dirt. After making the sign of the cross over the coffin he started shovelling dirt over it and it pained him every time the heavy soil slammed onto the white lid with a dark, hollow thud.

Erlendur took the white pegging that lay broken beside the grave, tried to put it back in its place and drew on every ounce of his strength to raise the headstone. He was finishing the job when he heard the first cars and people calling out as they arrived at the cemetery. He heard Sigurdur Óli and Elínborg shouting at him in turn. He heard the voices of people who were lit up by the headlights, their shadows gigantic in the dark night. He saw more and more torch beams approaching him.

He saw Katrín and soon afterwards he noticed Elín. Katrín gave him a questioning look and when she realised what had happened she threw herself on top of Einar, crying, and hugged him. He didn't try to stop her. He saw Elín kneel down beside her.

He heard Sigurdur Óli ask if he was all right and saw Elínborg pick up the shotgun that had dropped to the ground. He saw other policemen arriving and the flash bulbs of cameras in the distance like little bolts of lightning.

He looked up. It had started raining again but he thought the rain was somehow milder.

Einar was buried by his daughter's side in Grafarvogur cemetery. It was a private funeral. Erlendur contacted Katrín. He told her about the meeting between Einar and Holberg. Erlendur talked about self-defence but Katrín knew he was trying to soothe her pain.

It kept on raining but the autumn winds died down. Soon it would be winter and frost and darkness. Erlendur welcomed that.

At his daughter's insistence Erlendur finally went to the doctor. The doctor said the pain in his chest was caused by a bruised costal cartilage which was probably the fault of sleeping on a bad mattress and a general lack of exercise.

*

One day, over a piping bowl of meat stew, Erlendur asked Eva Lind whether he could choose the name if she gave birth to a girl. She said she'd expected him to make some suggestions.

"What do you want to call her?" she asked.

Erlendur looked at her.

"Audur," he said. "I thought it would be nice to call her Audur."

ARNALDUR INDIRIÐASON

Silence of the Grave

'A fascinating mystery . . . Inðridason is a writer worth
seeking out'
Daily Telegraph

Building work in an expanding Reykjavík uncovers a
shallow grave. Years before, this part of the city was all
open hills, and Erlendur and his team hope this is a
typical Icelandic missing person scenario; perhaps someone once lost in the snow, who has lain peacefully buried
for decades. Things are never that simple.

Whilst Erlendur struggles to hold together the crumbling
fragments of his own family, his case unearths many
other tales of family pain. The hills have more than one
tragic story to tell: tales of failed relationships and
heartbreak; of anger, domestic violence and fear; of
family loyalty and family shame. Few people are still alive
who can tell the story, but even secrets taken to the grave
cannot remain hidden forever.

Winner of the CWA Gold Dagger and the Glass Key
Award for Best Noridic Crime Novel

'Here is a new voice that demands to be listened to'
Reginald Hill

VINTAGE BOOKS
London

BY ARNALDUR INDRIÐASON
ALSO AVAILABLE FROM VINTAGE

☐ **Silence of the Grave**   009 946954 5   £6.99

FREE POST AND PACKING
Overseas customers allow £2.00 per paperback

BY PHONE: 01624 677237

BY POST: Random House Books
C/o Bookpost, PO Box 29, Douglas
Isle of Man, IM99 1BQ

BY FAX: 01624 670923

BY EMAIL: bookshop@enterprise.net

Cheques (payable to Bookpost) and credit cards accepted

Prices and availability subject to change without notice.
Allow 28 days for delivery.
When placing your order, please mention if you do not wish to receive
any additional information.

www.randomhouse.co.uk/vintage